The din in the hall stilled. The masked figure stepped ponderously off the dais, sat down at the baize-covered table and indicated with a gloved hand that I should join him. I staggered across. I don't know why. Perhaps it was pure mischief in me. Or was it something else? Perhaps the thought of dice had stirred memories of that terrible evening in the Golden Turk when the Luciferi had trapped me. Anyway, the very devil was in me. The masked figure clapped his hands, a cup of dice was produced. My opponent (of course it was the Great Killer) emptied his purse on the table, so did I, and the game began. I played as if my very life depended upon it. The rest of the hall left their places and gathered around us. I saw Benjamin's anxious eyes but ignored his warning look. I played to win and I did. I won the first purse of gold, then a second, then a third. The joy and gaiety seeped from that hall as the masked player's irritation became obvious. A courtier leaned over and whispered in my ear.

'For God's sake, man, lose!'

But not old Shallot! I threw the dice and almost my every throw beat his until Wolsey, standing behind the king's chair, gave a sign for the trumpeters to blow and the game ended. My opponent drew off his mask and I gazed into the red, sweaty face of the king . . .

The Poisoned Chalice

Being the second journal of Sir Roger Shallot
concerning certain wicked conspiracies
and horrible murders perpetrated
in the reign of King Henry VIII

Paul Doherty

HEADLINE

First published in 1992
by HEADLINE BOOK PUBLISHING

First published in paperback in 1993
by HEADLINE BOOK PUBLISHING

5

ISBN 978 0 7472 3965 9

Printed and bound in Great Britain by
CPI Group (UK) Ltd, Croydon, CR0 4YY

HEADLINE PUBLISHING GROUP
A division of Hodder Headline
338 Euston Road
London NW1 3BH

www.headline.co.uk
www.hodderheadline.com

To my eldest son, Hugh Francis, and the laughs Shallot has given us.

Historical Personages Mentioned in this Text

Richard III – The last Yorkist king, called the Usurper or Pretender. He was defeated by Henry Tudor at Market Bosworth in August 1485. He was the wearer of the White Rose, his personal emblem being *Le Blanc Sanglier* – the White Boar.

Henry Tudor – The Welshman. The Great Miser, the victor of Bosworth, founder of the Tudor dynasty and father of Henry VIII and Margaret of Scotland. He died in 1509.

Arthur – Henry Tudor's first born. He died young and the crown went to his brother Henry.

Henry VIII – Bluff King Hal, the Great Killer, the Great Beast, Fat Harry. A king who had six wives and a string of mistresses. He is the Mouldwarp or the Dark One, as prophesied by Merlin.

Catherine of Aragon – A Spanish princess, Henry VIII's first wife and mother of Mary Tudor.

Anne Boleyn – Daughter of Sir Thomas Boleyn. Second wife of Henry VIII and mother of Elizabeth Tudor.

Bessie Blount – One of the more dazzling of Henry VIII's mistresses.

Mary Tudor – Daughter of Catherine of Aragon and Henry VIII, nicknamed Bloody Mary because of her persecution of Protestants.

Elizabeth I – Queen of England, daughter of Henry VIII

and Anne Boleyn, nicknamed the Virgin Queen though Shallot claims to have had a son by her.

Catherine Howard – Henry VIII's fifth wife. Executed for her extra-marital affairs.

Francis I – King of France, brilliant, dazzling and sex mad.

Will Shakespeare – English playwright.

Chris Marlowe – English playwright and spy, killed in a tavern brawl.

Thomas Wolsey – Son of an Ipswich butcher, he went to Oxford and embarked upon a brilliant career. He became Cardinal, Archbishop and First Minister of Henry VIII.

Suleiman the Magnificent – Turkish Emperor.

Mary, Queen of Scots – Granddaughter of Margaret Tudor and mother of James I of England and Scotland.

Thomas More – Humanist, scholar. Minister of Henry VIII, later executed for opposing Henry's divorce from Catherine of Aragon.

Edward VI – Son of Henry VIII and Jane Seymour, a sickly boy who died young.

Catherine de Medici – Italian Princess. Married Henry II, King Francis I's son. She dominated France after her husband's death: a subtle intriguer, nicknamed Madame Serpent.

Claude – The ugly, dumpy, pleasant wife of Francis I.

Charles VIII – Ruler of France in the 1490s. Husband of Anne of Brittany whose province he annexed. An ugly little man, he is supposed to have died accidentally after hitting his head on a cupboard.

Louis XII – Charles VIII's successor, thought to have died from exhaustion after marrying Henry VIII's sister, the Princess Mary.

Michael Nostradamus – Seer and necromancer, often used by Catherine de Medici.

Prologue

If Murder is Satan's eldest son then Poison, Queen of the Night, is his favourite daughter. Why do I say this? Because I dreamt about her last night when my manor house had fallen silent and its mullioned windows gazed like sightless eyes over the dark, lush fields of my estate. I'd slipped out of bed, leaving Margot the launderess and her sister Phoebe gently snoring (they sleep on either side to keep me warm), and crept downstairs to my secret chamber, behind the high table in the Great Hall. Only I know which carved wooden panel to press to release the catch and allow me into the sanctuary of my past. Everything is there. Sometimes I just light the candles and squat, going through this coffer or that. Well, last night, I chose one 'specially. I unlocked the three clasps, took out the faded petals of a flower wrapped in oiled leather, as well as all the letters and documents from that fateful summer of 1520. I read them and cried as they took me back through time, down the long bloody passageways of the last seventy-five years.

I became maudlin, drinking more rich claret than my chaplain would like to imagine. I hummed a little tune, even as the ghosts gathered round me, silent and threatening. I didn't care. Old Shallot never gives a rat's arse.

I leaned against the cold brick wall, cradling the faded flower petals in my hands, and drifted into a demon-haunted nightmare.

I was in Paris again, standing in the dark fields around the Château de Maubisson. Above me, a strange moon, white as snow, waned behind purple clouds. Strangely, the sun also shone, though it turned a dusty red, blotted out by the dark wings of vultures. A terrible rushing wind tore at my hair and clothes as merciless demons appeared from all directions, faces twisted with rage, teeth bared between snarling lips, eyes shining like stars whilst flames burst out of their mouths. Behind them, in the blackest darkness, rode the Lord Satan (oh, yes, I've met the evil bugger a number of times) on his dark-winged steed. He swept towards me, like the wind raising a storm as soaring eagles raise dust. When he stopped before me, the steel-shod hooves of his war horse drew sparks from the ground. I looked up but his terrible face was hidden in the shadow of a helmet.

Suddenly a devil appeared beside me, with red hands and feet and a head as bald as a pig. This tormentor lifted a gold-ringed trumpet and brayed a terrible blast. I just stood wondering what would happen. (Even in my dreams, I follow one of the basic tenets of old Shallot's philosophy: In danger always run and, if you can't run, do nothing!) I looked towards the château entrance and saw Queen Poison, dreadful as an army in battle array, sweep towards me across the lowered drawbridge, arms extended as if she wished to clasp me to her deceitful bosom. I stared into her white beautiful face, the carmined lips pursed into a kiss, and crumpled to my knees before this most dread Queen of the Abyss.

I woke stiff as a poker. My back ached, my bum was sore and my mouth caked with the rich tang of the wine. I staggered back to a cold bed but Margot and Phoebe had fled. They always do that, the saucy wenches, they like to tease and make me beg for them to come back. I was too exhausted. I slept the sleep of the just till the chapel bells roused me late this afternoon. Now I feel refreshed, I've downed a venison pie, a tankard of ale and two cups of claret, and have returned to the centre of my maze to dictate my memoirs. I will tell you what happened in that dreadful summer of 1520, for that's what the dream was about.

I am comfortable in my maze which is laid out like the one at Hampton Court was by the Great Killer's chief minister, Cardinal Thomas Wolsey. My chair with its high back and strong iron wheels is positioned correctly to catch the sun. I have a jug of wine, two silver goblets and a jewel-encrusted plate of doucettes. My clerk is also ready. My little Mephistopheles, my darling chaplain. The little turd!

He always takes his time: he must get his ink horn out, his parchment smooth, his quill sharpened, and make sure his little arse is comfortable on the softest cushions my manor can provide. He says he is ready to take down my memoirs. The little hypocrite! I can see the smirk on his fat, greasy face. He thinks I am a liar. A liar! I, Sir Roger Shallot, Lord of Burpham Manor in Guildford, Surrey, Commissioner of Array, Justice of the Peace, the holder of many awards and decorations, Member of the Privy Council (believe me, that's well named), Member of Parliament (I'll tell you a funny story about that soon).

3

Oh, yes, Sir Roger Shallot, now well past his ninetieth year, the darling and most loyal subject of the great Elizabeth, daughter of Anne Boleyn (she had the most beautiful tits) and, allegedly, the Great Killer himself, Henry VIII – the fat syphilitic bastard! I say 'allegedly' because I know different. Oh, I'll tell you the truth some day but that's another story.

Anyway, back to my chaplain. I grip my cane tightly and watch his smile disappear. Old Shallot is not a liar! True, sometimes my memory fails me, I get things slightly mixed up, but I am not a liar. Well, even if I am, at least I am not a hypocrite like him. Yes, he's a hypocrite and I can prove it. Two weeks ago in church the snivelling little bastard got up in the pulpit and told us not to be frightened of death. I sat in my pew and heard him prate on for at least an hour and a half. Now, usually I don't mind. I always take a bottle of claret and a meat pie to help me through the service and, when it's finished, I gaze around to catch the eye of some pretty maid. When I do, I wink and smile at her. She, of course, becomes agitated and it's so lovely to watch full ripe bosoms rise and fall!

On that particular Sunday my chaplain wouldn't shut up and I was getting hungry. On and on he droned about how we shouldn't fear death but welcome the joys of heaven, so I picked up my two horse pistols and gave the sod both barrels. You can still see the holes on either side of the pulpit. Well, I laughed myself silly. The chaplain went white as snow and fainted straight out of the pulpit. I didn't intend to kill him. I just wanted to see if he practised what he preached. Instead I concluded he was about as frightened of death as I am so why, in the good Lord's name, did he get up and bore us stiff telling us different?

He didn't know I always carry pistols under my cloak, and he may well ask why. For the same reason I dictate my memoirs in the centre of a maze. You see, old Shallot has many enemies and memories die hard. The secret order of the Templars still has a price on my life. The Luciferi of France (I'll come to those bastards later) would like to see my head on a pole. The Council of Ten in Venice have sent three assassins against me just because I borrowed some of their gold and forgot to repay it. The silly idiots came nowhere near me. The great Irish wolf hounds who roam my estate tore them to pieces. Marvellous animals! They lounge round my chair now, staring at the chaplain and licking their lips.

Of course, other assassins might come. Do you know, I once played a game of human chess against the Ottoman Emperor, Suleiman the Magnificent? Instead of pieces we played with human beings on a great white and black piazza. When we lost a 'piece', the 'gardeners', the Ottoman's mute executioners, immediately strangled the poor victim. Now I won that game, losing just two 'pieces', but only after I left with the comeliest 'piece' of all, a wench from the imperial harem, did Suleiman discover that I had cheated and publicly marked me down for death. Perhaps his 'gardeners' will come but I am not frightened. I have my maze, I have my secret chamber, my own silent guards, my wolf hounds and my beloved pistols. Moreover, I have seen it all. The knife, the sword, the rope, the garrotte – they don't chill my heart.

Poison, however, is a different matter. That's why I make my chaplain taste what I eat and drink. Everything,

5

that is, except my best claret. I mean, the Bible does say we shouldn't throw our pearls before swine! Poison . . . That takes me back to my nightmare. Now I have met poisoners, dark, subtle souls who can strike at any time and in a million ways. You name a poisoner and I'll tell you all about him or her. By the way, have you noticed that? How the best poisoners are women? I mean, look at Agrippina, wife to the Emperor Claudius. If you have read your books you will discover that the Romans used to have tasters too and loved food so much they'd make themselves sick after each course by sticking a feather down their throats. Do you know what Agrippina did? She didn't poison the food. No, cunning bitch, she poisoned the feather and got rid of her husband.

She reminds me of Catherine de Medici, Queen of France, 'Madame Serpent' as I used to call her. I never accepted anything from Catherine, for what she didn't know about poisons wasn't worth knowing. I was talking about her last week when our Queen came to visit me – Elizabeth, with her white painted face, black teeth and red wig. The great Virgin Queen – don't you believe it! Well, she brought me sad news. How our love-child, Robin, had been captured at sea by the Spanish and taken to Madrid. I told her not to worry. If Robin was truly our child, the bloody Spanish wouldn't hold him long and, if they do, then he is not worthy of our blood. I made her laugh and she reminded me of how Robin had been conceived. You want to know? Fine, I'll tell you. I was once a Member of Parliament and one day in the chamber at Westminster, a Puritan, a lozenge of sanctified humility, got up from his arse and roared at me because I called him a blackened turd.

'Shallot,' he bellowed, 'you'll either die by hanging or die of the pox!'

'That, sir,' I coldly replied, 'depends on whether I embrace your principles or your wife.'

Well, the chamber was in an uproar. I refused to apologise to the Speaker so the Serjeant-at-arms hustled me to the Tower. Elizabeth (because I had been defending her) came to visit me. She insisted on seeing me alone, and you know Shallot! A cup of wine and a pretty girl in an empty room and anything could happen. On that occasion it certainly did! In her younger days Elizabeth was a passionate girl. She had a cloying sensuousness and, like her mother, Anne Boleyn, she could ride anything. (I see my chaplain snigger so a quick rap across the knuckles reminds him to keep his mouth shut and his thoughts clean about his betters.)

Ah, poison, the subtle murderer of my dreams. Well, I have now marshalled my thoughts, summoning memories from that summer over seventy years ago. Oh, Lord, it seems only yesterday when I and my master, Benjamin Daunbey, nephew to the great Cardinal Wolsey, were sent to the Château de Maubisson outside Paris to resolve certain mysteries. Ah, I have mentioned his name! Benjamin, with his long, dark face, kindly eyes and lawyer's stoop. When I think of him I always smile. He was one of the few really good men I have ever met. If you have read my earlier memoirs you will know how this occurred. We went to school together, I saved him from a beating and he rescued me from a hanging, twice; once in Ipswich and then again at Montfaucon, that great forest of gibbets which stands near the Porte St Denis in Paris.

Now, Benjamin's uncle, the great Wolsey, and his black

familiar, the enigmatic Doctor Agrippa, used us both on countless errands in the sinister twilight world of treason, murder and lechery of the courts of Europe. Lackaday, they have all gone now! They're just shadows, ghosts who dance under the shade of the spreading yew trees which border the far end of the lawn in front of my manor house.

Ghosts they may be but they bring back memories of broken hearts, foul deeds, sinister minds, and souls stained with the blackness of hell. I'll tell you this as I sit in the centre of my maze and listen to the clear song of the thrush: the murderous soul I met at Maubisson was one of the most chilling I have ever encountered.

Chapter 1

In the spring of 1520 Benjamin Daunbey and I were the proud occupants of a large manor house on the outskirts of Ipswich. Really, it was more of a pleasaunce than a manor with its white lathed plaster, ornamental chimney pots, squat black beams, with panelled rooms with carved furniture, and a cellar well stocked with a variety of wines. On our estate were granges, barns, a mill, carp ponds, lush fields and fertile meadows. We were the grateful beneficiaries of the largesse of Benjamin's uncle, the great Wolsey, who lavished rewards on us for resolving, only a few months earlier, the sinister White Rose murders.

Now success had not changed Benjamin. He still dressed drably. Indeed, I well remember him as he was then, long and lanky, his sombre, solemn face framed by jet black hair. At the time I was of the same colouring (there's a portrait of me hanging at Burpham). I was dark, my black hair cropped close, a slight cast in one eye, and a cheeky expression which many said would send me to the gallows. In a way they were right but, thankfully, I was never hanged though I was close to it on many occasions. What amuses me is that many of those who claimed I would hang, died violent deaths themselves in some pot-holed alleyway, bleak battlefield or gory execution yard. I was a bigger rogue then than I am now but Benjamin was as different as chalk from cheese. He had that irritating manner of believing all was well and trusting everyone completely.

In theory Benjamin was Lord of the Manor and I, a true man of the world, his steward, his trusted servant and bosom friend. I was wise beyond my nineteen years and kept a sharp weather eye on all the human kites and ravens attracted by Benjamin's generosity. You know the sort: wandering musicians, ballad mongers, sharp-eyed priests. (I see my chaplain's shoulders twitch with annoyance.)

This unsavoury pack of rogues streamed across the meadows to our Manor House like rats towards an unguarded hen coop. Old Shallot did what he could. I bought the biggest mastiffs I could find and sent the beggars screaming for the trees, at least for a while. At the time I had little knowledge of dogs. One day I took the beasts hunting and they raised a big fat buck. I never saw the buck again, nor the mastiffs. God knows what happened to them. They scampered off, barking like the devil. Those four-footed mercenaries must have met someone else who took better care of them because they never returned.

Nevertheless my problems with my master's open-handed generosity persisted. At last I had a serious discussion with Benjamin in our great oak-panelled hall, the walls above the panelling painted a light green and decorated with cunningly devised shields bearing the arms of Wolsey, Daunbey and, finally, Shallot. Of course, I made the latter up though I am still very proud of them; a mailed fist, middle finger extended, and underneath the Latin motto '*In dubito curre*' which, roughly translated, means 'In doubt, run'. I bear the same arms now but the middle finger of the mailed fist is no longer extended since the Queen's herald, Rouge-Croix, discovered that in certain parts of France such a gesture could be taken as offensive or obscene. Nevertheless, at the time I was proud of my skill. I had developed a deft hand at writing bills and counterfeiting other people's signatures, my master's included. No, I wasn't a thief! I just had to look after our property. And that provoked the confrontation with Benjamin.

'Master,' I wailed, 'we cannot keep feeding every rogue in the neighbourhood. I am tired of naughty nuns, fornicating friars, mouldy monks, ruthless rogues and virile villains!'

He leaned back in his chair in front of the hearth and laughed till the tears ran down his face.

'You have a way with words, Roger.' He straightened his face and sat up. 'But I still insist that we help those less fortunate. So, what do you propose?'

'Children,' I answered without thinking. (That's another of my faults, I am too kind-hearted and often speak without thinking.) 'Start a school,' I stammered. 'For the children of the village. Help those who need such learning.'

'Marvellous!' Benjamin replied. 'But how can I assist you, Roger?'

I looked away, embarrassed. 'You have helped me enough, master.'

'You're bored aren't you, Roger? You miss London?'

Good Lord, it was wonderful how my master could read my mind! Now, we very rarely went up to the great city and, when we did, Benjamin kept a close eye and a tight rein on me. You see, he knew me to be like a dog on a leash, straining to break free and head hell for leather into

11

the nearest mischief. Of course, we had been to London to visit Benjamin's former betrothed, Johanna, a sweet girl whom he adored. Johanna had fallen for Cavendish, one of the great lords of the land, who'd broken her heart and destroyed her wits. Now the girl lived in the care of the nuns at Syon on the Thames, a mere shadow of her former self. (Oh, by the way, Benjamin killed the nobleman concerned in a duel with swords in Leicester Fields. Mind you, it wasn't the last time he fell in love. Oh, no! But that's another story.)

'You should go, Roger,' Benjamin continued. 'But stay here at least until Easter. I'll need your help to clear one of the chambers and set up a school room. You will help?'

I needed no second bidding and, in the last two weeks of Lent, when Benjamin fasted on water and salted fish and abstained from wine (I did the same during the day but, at night, I always crept out to one of the nearby taverns; I have great difficulty fasting for I get this terrible thirst!), I worked like a Trojan, clearing, cleaning, painting and refurbishing, until the old solar on the ground floor of our manor house gleamed as fresh and as opulent as one of the great Halls of Cambridge. (Oh, yes, Benjamin and I had also been to university but, due to minor misunderstandings, had both been asked to leave before we received our degrees. Well, who cares?)

On Easter Sunday, just after morning Mass, Benjamin, as Lord of the Manor, announced the opening of his school to his incredulous parishioners. My master expected little response. Sometimes he could be the most idealistic of fools! The villagers, however, took him at his word, only too willing to dump their scruffy-arsed offspring on him between the hours of ten and five. Benjamin didn't mind.

He took to schoolmastering like a duck to water. Horn books, quills, pens, ink horns, an abacus and rolls of parchment were bought. The hall was invaded by legions of snotty-nosed, tousle-haired, black-faced imps. I feared the little bastards would destroy the place but Benjamin was always good with children. He had a way of listening to them as if their every word was a pearl of wisdom. Sometimes I joined him in the school room.

You see, usually I worked on the accounts and managed the estate. We raised sheep, corn and crops for the local market and sold hunting rights to our neighbours. The work proved no real challenge for me. Benjamin always thought the smooth running of our affairs was due to his just treatment of others. Don't you believe it! The best gamekeepers are former poachers and no one took old Shallot for a ride.

Anyway, I'd go down to the schoolroom. The place seemed awash with dirty, little ankle-biters; some sat on benches, others squatted on the floor listening like round-eyed owls as Benjamin revealed the secrets of Mathematics, the divine truths of the Gospels and, for the most able, the courtly hand, as well as the basics of Greek, Latin, Geometry and Geography. Do you know, I envied him? Take Shallot's word for it, most people couldn't give a rat's arse about anyone else but Benjamin was different.

However, I soon tired of his attempts to help our neighbours. On the Monday after Low Sunday, I saddled my horse, loaded a sumpter pony, tied a money belt round my waist, grasped sword and dagger and made my farewells.

Hell's teeth, I remember it well! A beautiful spring morning. The sun made the mullioned glass of the manor house windows shimmer like pools of light. The air was thick and sweet with the smell of fresh-cut grass and the wild flowers which Benjamin had allowed to flourish in front of the hall. My master, his eyes heavy with sleep, came out to bid me farewell. He stood holding the bridle of my horse and stared innocently up at me like one of the children from his own school room.

'You will take care, Roger? You'll come home if aught happens?'

I clasped his hand. 'I'll take care, master,' I lied. 'I have a letter for our banker, Master Waller in the Mercery. If I run out of silver there's more there.'

'What,' Benjamin asked, his eyes narrowing, 'are you going to do?'

'Make my fortune, master.'

He smiled. 'Then make your fortune, Roger, and if Great-uncle sends for me, I shall come for you in London. Where will you lodge?'

I chewed my lip and stared into the faint mist being burnt off by the early morning sun. The last thing I wanted was Great-uncle interfering! I was tempted to lie but, thank God, I decided to break a lifelong habit and tell the truth.

'Near St Paul's,' I replied. 'There's a printer's under the Red Sign and next to it a tavern, the Golden Turk. You know it? I will lodge there.'

I clasped my master's hand and, spurring my horse, rode bravely down the tree-lined path, the hooves of the pack pony behind me digging up flurries of white dust. I felt like a knight-errant riding out for adventure. Little did I know I was a fool slipping into danger and the black shadow of Benjamin's great-uncle would soon trap me.

My journey was uneventful enough. When I was young,

14

England seemed green and fresh, in the morning-time of its life. No armies marched the land, no great lords unfurled the banners of rebellion. The Great Killer saw to that. Even then no one dared cross him and he had yet to show the dark side of his soul and prove Merlin's prophecy that he was 'The Mouldwarp who would drown his kingdom in a sea of blood'.

The abbeys and priories I passed slumbered gently in the lee of fresh green hills, unaware of the destruction about to crawl from the hellish pit of Henry's lusts. The villages, hamlets and the red-tile-roofed manors boasted their peace and prosperity for Henry was still living on the treasure bequeathed to him by his father. He had not yet unleashed his army of tax gatherers, commissioners, purveyors and assessors. The bridges were mended, the ruts in the roads filled in, the spring corn sown, and fat-tailed sheep browsed in the fields.

Oh, there were signs of the furies to come. At crossroads the gibbets provided plump carrion for the hungry crows and ravens; landless men turned out of their fields as the great lords changed to tending sheep rather than raising crops. Some were sturdy beggars, thieves and rogues but now and again you passed the honest yeomen, the skeletal, white-faced, puny children and worried, dark-eyed wives who tramped the roads looking for work. Shallot did what he could. I have a list of vices as long as your arm but I am not mean. I scattered pennies and rode on like a young lord through Aldgate and into London.

Now, I have always loved that city, its stench, the colour, bustle and noise, the way the blood beats ever faster through your veins. I had worked there many years before as a footman in one of old Mother Nightbird's molly

15

houses, from where she sold plump, perfumed flesh to the great lords and merchants of the city. Now things were different. At nineteen Shallot was virtuous, a prosperous man soon to be a merchant prince who would show both Master Benjamin and the great Wolsey that he could rise without their help. I rode through Cheapside, greedily drinking in the sights and sounds. I noted with envy the gold-embossed timber mansions of the merchants, the stalls in front of them piled high with goods of every kind: rich cloth of gold, rolls of murrey, silks and satins, leather bottles, Spanish riding boots, gold cord and testers, blankets of pure wool, and tapestries heavy with silver needlework and gold filigree.

The air dinned with the cries of the apprentices, the roar of the crowd, the curses of carpenters, whilst in every corner hawkers and tinkers shouted their wares. Young nobles from the court, their horses' harness shining in the sunlight, rode through with hawks, falcons and peregrines perched on their wrists, cruel faces hidden by small leather hoods, jesses tinkling like the bells of a tiny church.

I found the Golden Turk where it nestled in a small alleyway, just beneath the great mass of St Paul's. A fine, well-kept establishment, three storeys high, made all the more welcoming by horn-glazed windows, the beams smartly painted and the white plaster glowing like freshly laid snow. The landlord knew me, for Benjamin and I often lodged there when we came up to town. I did think of going down to Syon House but remembered Benjamin's instructions never to approach Johanna without him being present for she dwelt in a twilight world where every man, except Benjamin, was her seducer.

So I made myself at home at the Golden Turk; the

two-faced landlord greeted me civilly enough, providing a chamber on the second floor with a pallet bed and a few sticks of furniture. He also promised to change the sheets and rushes at least once every six weeks, provide stabling for my horse as well as a meal at morning and night for myself. On my first day there I acted like a young lord, lying on my bed, my boots on, sipping from a cup of canary and wondering what steps I should take next.

However, business is business and pleasure is pleasure. I went down to the tap room and ordered a meal though I was hungrier for the dark-eyed slattern I had glimpsed on my last visit with Benjamin.

She was a veritable Venus with her dark eyes and black, curling hair which tumbled down to her shoulders. And what shoulders! White as marble, with the juiciest and roundest pair of tits I had ever clapped eyes on. (There goes my chaplain again, squirming on his stool. I notice he does that whenever I talk about my 'amours', my little love trysts. The colour of his face always reddens just as it does when fat Margot, the launderess, who keeps me supplied with cups of sack, bends and dips to provide me with a generous view of the most famous cleavage in all of Surrey.)

Anyway, on that spring day so many years ago, I lounged around, teasing and humouring the girl. Now you know the way of the flesh! A glance, a smile, a love cup shared, silver exchanged, then heigh-ho to the bed-chamber. Lack-aday, lackaday, what a time we had! We bounced round on that pallet bed, so much laughing and shouting that the landlord came up. He banged on our door, saying he was running an honest house, not some bawdy shop in Southwark. When the bed collapsed under us and the girl's

17

shrieks could be heard in the taproom below; the landlord came up again shouting abuse through the door, but I ignored him. He knew what the girl was when he hired her, the bald-faced hypocrite!

The next morning I decided to begin my business. I rose, broke my fast and slipped the landlord some pieces of silver which made his vinegarish face look more congenial and subservient. The maid – I think her name was Anna – looked a little more tired and heavy-eyed after her exertions of the previous evening. I, however, strutted out like a barnyard cock, booted and cloaked, a broad-brimmed hat on my head with a black and white plume hanging from it. I thought I was a Hector and Paris combined. Good Lord, the folly of youth! I decided to go to St Paul's, walk past Duke Humphrey's tomb and along the Mediterranean, the main aisle where most men did business; there, the dirty round pillars were festooned with notices, men and women begging for work or prospective employers offering terms. At one end the professional scriveners sat at their desks, quills and parchment at the ready, to draw up wills, indentures, bills of sale, a letter to a friend or a *billet doux* to a lover. At the other end lawyers, in ermine-edged cloaks, touted for business, serjeants-at-law consulted clients, and outside in the porch, booksellers and pamphleteers did a roaring trade.

Now I avoided all of these. I was looking for a business venture worthy of my silver, some trade across the Narrow Seas or perhaps commerce with the Baltic. You see, in my youth trade was close. The Cabots had sailed for Newfoundland but that was as far as it went. The seas down the west coast of Africa and the routes to the Hispanic colonies across the Atlantic were not yet open for English ships. We had no sea dogs, no Frobishers or Grenvilles who would fight their way past Spanish galleons. And, of course, there was no Drake. (I knew Sir Francis. Have I told you the story? I was playing bowls with him when the Great Armada was spotted off Lizard Point and the beacons along the south coast flared into life. I am sure you must have heard the tale? When the messenger arrived to inform Drake of the possible invasion, the old sea dog announced he would finish his game of bowls, then he would finish off the Spanish. The red-bearded pirate was telling a lie! I had wagered a purse that I would beat him at bowls and Drake never could resist gold. Moreover, it was I who wet my finger to test the wind and pointed out that, even if he wanted to leave the game, it would be no use. The wind had to change before his fighting ships could sail against the Spanish. My chaplain says I am a liar. What the bloody hell does he know? I drank with all our great sailors. Of course, the greatest is Raleigh. He is still at sea with the silver I gave him to discover fresh treasure. He says he can find his way up the Orinoco and discover the Seven Cities of Gold where the streets are paved with precious metals, and dusky, full-bosomed maidens scatter gems and pennies. I only hope the old sea dog is telling the truth!)

Lackaday, I digress! In Fat Harry's time business was not so adventurous. Merchants came to St Paul's and walked up and down, thumbs pushed into their belts, looking for gold and bullion to invest in their ventures: wool to Flanders, wine from Gascony, wood to Italy, silks and costly fabrics from Venice and the mills of Florence. I ignored such men with their closed faces and pinched noses. Their pompous promises and grandiloquent phrases

19

failed to convince me so I quickly took the air in the graveyard where all the wolfs-heads, villains and counter-feit men hid from the law. You see, St Paul's used to be a sanctuary, a refuge against the sheriff's men and, as long as you stayed there, you were safe. I wondered if some of my old cronies from my days with old Mother Nightbird were still lurking there. I stalked amongst the booths and ramshackle dwellings built against the wall. Lord, I have never seen such a collection of rogues, palliards and foists! Indeed, the whole canting crew. I kept one hand on my sword hilt and the other on my wallet as I mentally phrased the letter I intended to send to Cardinal Wolsey demanding the graveyard be cleared of such a collection of villains.

At length I grew tired and went back to the joys of the tavern, both the board and the bed. The only curious thing was that I found in my room a handbill from a Frenchman trying to solicit backers to export parchment to France and import wine into England. I read it with interest, then forgot it. The next day I returned to St Paul's and, this time, was successful.

It must have been noon, the time for the Angelus, and the bells of the cathedral clanging fit to break when I first caught sight of the fellow. He was dressed soberly in a dark brown jerkin with leggings of the same colour pushed into black soft leather boots. His grey cloak was of pure wool pushed back over his shoulders, yet it was his face which attracted me. His features reminded me of Benja-min; kindly, honest and open. Now you know Shallot's golden rule: It takes one rogue to know another, and a real rogue to recognise an honest man. This man was very honest. He had a number of handbills which he was distributing to everyone who passed so I took one nonchalantly and his kind, brown eyes smiled. He must have been about fifty summers old, his copper-coloured face was lined, his swept back hair silver-grey, but the moustache and the neatly clipped beard still showed traces of a golden youth.

I sauntered into a pie shop and carefully scrutinised the handbill which declared its distributor to be a foreigner: Jean Pierre Ralemberg, from Dijon, with a dwelling and warehouse in an alley off Bread Street. Basically, the man was a parchment-seller trying to raise good hard silver or gold to finance the export of parchment to Nantes and the import of wine. Now, I don't want to give you a boring lesson about the markets of the day, suffice to say that in 1520 hard cash was rare, most of it being tied up in fields, lands and houses, so it was natural for people like Ralemberg to tout for business.

It was an intriguing prospect and I was all the more curious why I had found one of his handbills in my chamber at the Golden Turk. On the one hand I suspected a trap, but on the other the man was patently honest. I sat in the pie shop kicking my heels and pondering the problem. The landlord of the Golden Turk didn't know about the handbill, so who had put it there? Was it some anonymous well-wisher or was I being manipulated?

I slowly munched diced meat pie stuffed with herbs. The Frenchman looked honest and I was shrewd enough to recognise a prosperous trade venture. English parchment was needed all over Europe, whilst in England French wines would always be sold. You see, neither commodity could go stale. Indeed, the longer you kept them, the better they became. I walked back to St Paul's and found Ralemberg leaning despondently against a pillar, tapping

21

the handbills against the side of his leg. I strode up and doffed my hat.

'Monsieur Ralemberg, I am Roger Shallot. I have read your announcement. You look hungry. Perhaps we could dine and talk?'

The Frenchman's eyes were guarded. 'You are young,' he murmured.

'What difference does that make to my silver?'

He made a face. 'No, the truth is you look like a rogue.'

'That's because I am one,' I answered. 'However, my word is good, though my silver is better.'

Ralemberg grinned. 'An honest rogue! We shall eat, and we shall talk. You will buy the food but I will provide the wine.'

Well, it was heigh-ho for the nearest cookshop and, if I remember correctly, a quail pie, the crust golden and crisp, the meat fresh and smothered in a rich sauce, and a jug of new Bordeaux. I never forget good meals. I mean, if you have starved like I have in the wilds of Muscovy or the deserts of North Africa, you always remember what you have eaten. I can swear to every pie I have swallowed, to every cup of sack I have gulped, to the few good women I have met and, thankfully, to every bad woman I have slept with. Ah, well, back to that cookshop.

At first, Ralemberg told me about himself. I suspected there was a mystery behind his banal description of a parchment-seller born and raised at Nantes in Brittany; a stationer who knew how to work the new presses from Gutenberg and, for reasons he kept to himself, had moved both his family and business to England. I didn't tell him about the handbill I had found; indeed, I quickly dismissed that as a mere coincidence. Moreover, the wine loosened

22

Ralemberg's tongue and the more he spoke the more convinced I became that his trading venture would be the basis of my own success. He had, so he related, the service of a trusted captain and a three-masted, seaworthy cog, sailing out of London. Ralemberg intended to export parchment to Brittany and, for the homeward journey, his ship would bring wine to the London market.

'I couldn't sell it myself,' he declared. 'And nor could you. We are not members of the Vintners' Guild. But we could sell it to the wine merchants themselves and still make a handsome profit.'

I leaned back against the high, wooden bench, assessing Ralemberg as a true businessman who knew the workings of the London market. In turn he came quickly to the point: his venture needed capital and what monies he had were tied up in his house. He chattered about bills of sale, the purchase of canvas and parchment, the cost of carters and the money needed for ship and crew.

'What about warehouses?' I asked.

'I have a house off Bread Street,' he replied, 'with vacant rooms and a dry, stone-vaulted cellar. All I need,' he repeated, 'is the money to move this business.'

So it was his turn to ask questions and, of course, I only told him what I wanted to. No! Not lies, the truth – albeit cut and tailored to suit my own purposes. Ralemberg studied me attentively throughout and I glimpsed the disbelief in his eyes. A true rogue recognises an honest man so, I suppose, a truly honest man can recognise a rogue. My grandiose descriptions faltered so I undid my money belt and emptied one of the pouches on the table.

'That's my surety,' I said. 'You can take it as a pledge of my good faith.'

(This is one of my favourite roles, putting my money where others put hot air and spit.)

Ralemberg pushed the coins back at me.

'I want to be honest!' I burst out.

'Don't we all, Master Shallot? If I took your silver, I would only be a thief. But, come, let me show you the warehouse you asked about.'

We rose and he took me a short distance to Bread Street. His house was a three-storeyed affair. The horn windows were dusty and holed, the paintwork on the beams cracked and the front door swung crookedly on its hinges. Ralemberg just shrugged and grinned apologetically. Inside, however, it smelt sweet and clean. (The French are always more precise in such matters than the English.) We went down a passageway to a small panelled hall. I remember it being dark-beamed with windows high in the wall and wax candles already lit. Rugs covered the floor and a lap dog played before a small log fire. On one side of the fireplace a grey-haired woman was absorbed in some needlework whilst on the other side, with her back to us, a young girl crouched over a book, loudly reciting a French poem in a voice shot through with gaiety and laughter.

An old servant, bald as a badger, yellow-faced and wizened, bustled towards us with all the speed of a snail; he mumbled apologies in French but Ralemberg just tapped him gently on the shoulder and told him not to worry. Of course, our entrance disturbed the domestic tableau around the fireplace. Both women rose with cries of joy. Madame Ralemberg was truly French, dark olive features, expressive eyes and neatly coiffed hair. She looked merry, though her eyes were guarded. She studied me suspiciously and this strengthened my belief that Ralemberg had his

24

own secrets. The other woman, Ralemberg's daughter . . . well, how can you describe a poem in the flesh? She must have been sixteen or seventeen summers old, tall and slender, and her eyes were as blue as a clear summer sky. She had the face of an angel, high cheek bones and perfectly formed nose and mouth. If she had been at court the young dandies would have written odes and sonnets to her eyebrows, her finger nails and her sweet rose mouth. Good Lord, she was beautiful!

She was dressed simply enough in a brown gown with a lacy ruff round the neck but she would have outshone any queen. Her voice was low and musical and her command of English only enhanced by a slight French accent. She said something to me, a simple introduction, but all I could do was stare open-mouthed at her. Suddenly she giggled and I realised I was still holding her fingers. You see, it was those eyes, so blue in a face so dark, one of God's most beautiful mixtures. I have met such women since, young girls from the west of Ireland, but Agnes Ralemberg was the queen.

Believe me, if the eyes are the windows of the soul, then Agnes's soul was as beautiful as she looked. She was totally guileless, honest, with a mordant sense of humour and sardonic wit. She knew me to be a rogue as soon as she clapped eyes on me and, whilst her father ushered me to a seat, she watched girlishly out of the corner of her eye. She was laughing at me but I didn't care.

Ralemberg talked and I listened. As far as I was concerned he could have my every piece of silver if he just allowed me to gaze at his daughter. Good Lord, I feel tears pricking my eyes now. Old Shallot, who would be under a woman's skirts, given half a chance, sat tongue-tied before

25

this chit of a young girl. Do you know, I was frightened of her – or was I shy? (My chaplain is smirking. He had better be careful! Agnes was one of the great loves of my life. Indeed, the first and only one. Perhaps I loved those who came after because they were faint imitations of her.) Ah well, Ralemberg chattered gaily, then took me on a tour of the house. I walked like some sleepwalker as he showed me empty rooms and a steep, stone-vaulted cellar.

Afterwards, when I would have preferred to stay and stare at Agnes, he took me down to King's Wharf near the Vintry and into a small ale house which stank of carp and salt. He introduced me to burly, red-faced Bertrand de Macon, the master of a fat-bellied cog and prospective third partner in our business venture. We sat and drank, discussing sea routes, harbour charges, the hiring of a crew, the wine markets and the stowing of cargo. To be sure, I was rather bemused but the honesty of both men was apparent. De Macon was a born sailor who had braved the storms of Biscay. He agreed to do the first voyage there and back before receiving payment, as long as Ralemberg agreed to underwrite the voyage, using his house as collateral. I would buy the parchment and arrange its transport down to the wharves and we concluded that, if we sold the wine brought back on the first voyage, we would make a profit.

We all shook hands and drank to seal our agreement before returning to St Paul's and the desks of the scriveners where a tripartite indenture was drawn up. We agreed on two voyages from the Thames to Nantes and then we would review the situation. The duties of each of us were carefully delineated. However, before I signed, Ralemberg took me outside. I thought he wished to impart further information

26

but, with the speed of a striking cat, he suddenly pulled his dagger, nicking my neck with its point.

'Master Shallot,' he whispered. 'My daughter Agnes – your intentions must be honourable.'

Do you know, I wasn't one bit afraid? It was one of the few times in my life when I actually spoke the truth. I held up my right hand.

'Monsieur,' I declared, 'you have my word as your business partner that my intentions towards your daughter are perfectly honourable.'

Ralemberg smiled, sheathed his dagger and clapped me on the shoulder. We went back inside and signed the indentures, the scrivener cutting the parchment into three and keeping a duplicate copy. Letters were then drawn up to be enrolled at the Court of Chancery so we would have the necessary licence to trade. Well, what more can I say? I skipped back to the tavern as merry as a schoolboy intent on his holiday.

Now, the day had grown dark but I was a burly rogue, carrying sword and dagger, yet my assailants just seemed to step out of the shadows. They didn't attack me: my arms were pinioned and I was turned round, my face pressed into the dank wall of the alleyway. Perhaps it was the wine I had drunk but I only gave a short yell before my hair was grabbed and my head jerked violently back.

'Monsieur!' a voice hissed. 'Do not struggle! There are four of us. We mean you no harm but Monsieur Ralemberg is not the man he appears. It would be best if you looked for another business partner.'

'What do you mean?' I stuttered, my usual cowardice now taking hold. 'Ralemberg . . . who is he?'

'Monsieur,' the voice repeated slowly, 'you should not

be worried about Monsieur Ralemberg but rather us.'

One of my hands was seized and, strange upon strange, a small wax candle thrust into my palm.

'Next time you meet Monsieur Ralemberg, just tell him his old friends the Luciferi are with him!'

Suddenly a voice bellowed from the top of the alleyway.

'You, sirs! What are you doing?'

My face was banged against the wall and my assailants disappeared. I crouched, holding my bruised temple and cursing the arrow of pain which coursed through my face. My rescuers were three bully boys, swords and daggers stuck through their waists. You know the type, with their tight hose, protruding codpieces, puffed doublets and short cloaks. They didn't chase my assailants but helped me to my feet, solicitously enquiring after my health. It was dark, I couldn't make out their features, but I was terrified that I had jumped from the pot into the flames. Even then I should have known something was wrong. Why should three bully boys help a stranger in a darkened alleyway off Cheapside? However, they caused me no ill and I staggered back to the Golden Turk and the tender care of the slattern, a bowl of rich broth and countless frothing tankards of ale.

28

Chapter 2

The next morning I awoke anxious over what had happened. I stared wonderingly at the small, wax candle which I had thrown on to the floor of my chamber. I forgot about my rescuers, I was more concerned by the Luciferi.

I knew enough Latin to know this name meant the Light-Bearers, Satan's name before he was thrown out of heaven. But who were these Light-Bearers? I wondered. A rival company? Personal enemies of Ralemberg? I felt my stomach lurch and my heart beat a little faster. My hands felt clammy, the usual signs of old Shallot beginning to wonder whether it is time to cut and run. My elation of the previous day began to evaporate until I remembered Agnes, the indentures I had signed, and the basic honesty of Ralemberg and de Macon. I washed, dressed, strapped on my sword belt and strutted out, quietly vowing that a group of cut-throats and alley-sneakers could not frighten this new Merchant Prince. Oh, Lord, the foolishness of youth!

I went straight to Ralemberg's house, hungry to see the ever-smiling Agnes. My poor heart soared like a bird when she agreed to accompany me and her father to a parchment-seller in Lothbury. We kept off the beaten

29

track, away from those traders who fixed high prices, for Shallot knew where to go. This shop or that, then across London Bridge under the rotting, decapitated heads of traitors to a small parchment-seller's in Southwark. The gods smile on those they intend to destroy, and within three days the parchment we bought up was carted down to de Macon's cog and hoisted aboard. The captain was as happy as a pig in the mire.

'Better this,' he bellowed, 'than begging for trade from Westminster to the Wool Quay!'

He explained how, due to the cessation of hostilities between England and France, the hiring of vessels was now cheap and easy and, for what he had to sell, it was a buyer's market.

Two days later he sailed and I, forgetful of all dangers, was now in my seventh heaven. (One of my few virtues. When I am happy, I can't give a rat's arse about anything else!) Ralemberg was likeable. He reminded me of Benjamin with his dry wit, sardonic observations and palpable honesty. We roamed the streets together looking for possible future providers of parchment and, taking advantage of the good weather, rode north to Oxford to the parchment-sellers along Holywell and Broad Street as well as the little shops on the Turl near Exeter College.

Of course, there was always Agnes, and I lived for the nights when I joined the Ralembergs for their simple meal. The Frenchman treated me like a son; his wife was a little more distant and cool so I complimented her and brought her small gifts, wooing her as if she was the maid. As for my beloved, what shall I say? One memory will always remain. Seventy-five years later, whenever I feel the sun on my face, it springs as fresh in my mind as if

30

it occurred yesterday. There was a small garden at the back of Ralemberg's house where the roses grew wild, their stems trailing over the small banks of herbs. The garden was cut off from its neighbour by a high red brick wall. Ralemberg would sit with his wife in a flower-covered bower sharing a loving cup whilst Agnes and I would walk among the roses. At first she was shy but then she chattered about Nantes, how she missed the dark woods and green fields of Brittany. She gave me the names of all her friends and said how proud she was of the life her father had given her. Sometimes I would hold her lightly by the finger-tips and try to steer the conversation to matters of the heart, but she would blush and her beautiful eyes look down. She would shake her head and deftly speak of other matters, though never about her father's past.

Now, I knew some French. You may remember I spent some time in Paris – not the most pleasant of times – freezing in the snow, chased by wolves and being half-hanged at Montfaucon. Hence I had a working knowledge of the language and sometimes, at table, could follow the conversation, though when the Ralembergs lapsed into patois this became impossible. During these conversations their manner would be grave, their faces serious. One word they kept repeating was the Latin 'Luciferi' and I remembered my assailants in the alley. Nevertheless, I still believed this was a reference to a rival company and, as my attackers never returned, the memory of their dark threats receded. Or did it? Sometimes I felt I was being followed or watched whilst seated in a tavern or moving amongst the stalls in Cheapside. I had this feeling of menace, of quiet watchfulness.

Oh, yes, I felt tempted to question the Ralembergs. Once I did ask Agnes about the Luciferi but the girl just paled and shook her head.

'You must never mention that word again,' she whispered.

I was happy enough to let the matter drop. The weeks passed, a full month in all. De Macon's ship went to Brittany and back, the voyage helped by fair winds and calm seas. The ship returned with a hold full of wines and a handsome profit. Ralemberg insisted on meeting de Macon first, saying he wished to discuss some secret matter, so I joined them later in a small tavern on the corner of Vintry and La Reole. We toasted our success, de Macon informing us that the market was a prosperous one. Ralemberg said he already had a buyer for the wine, a vintner living in Trinity. We then laid plans for the next voyage.

I had now used most of my silver and, despite our profits, had to draw heavily, even borrow some more from the goldsmith, Waller, in his musty old shop in Mercery. At first, the tight old sod wasn't going to lend me a penny. (Have you noticed that about bankers? If you have money the bastards want to lend you it; if you haven't and want to borrow, they tell you to go to hell.) Anyway, this old miser drew up an indenture and the monies were made available. We bought cartloads of parchment from Charterhouse, Oxford and even sent orders to places as far north as Norwich and Cambridge.

On the day before de Macon sailed on his second voyage, the Ralembergs invited me to a formal supper. I was delighted. My wooing of Agnes was proceeding apace. I had bought her small gifts, I had kissed her hand whilst on May Day I'd helped deck the house with green boughs and later took her to dance around a Maypole set up near Cattle Street. However, when I went to the house that night I found the Ralembergs upset. Even the jovial de Macon was pale-faced and withdrawn. Agnes looked timid and I could hear the old servant weeping in the scullery. My hosts shuffled their feet and the meal was unusually silent but, when darkness had fallen and the candles on the table threw huge, black shadows against the wall, Ralemberg filled my glass to the brim, went back to his own chair and nodded at his wife.

'Master Shallot,' he began, 'we have our secrets and you have yours.' He waved a hand. 'I shall tell you why we left France.'

He stared down at the white damask tablecloth; I sipped my wine and studied the faces of the others. If anything, their fear had increased.

'What's the matter?' I asked testily.

'I am the matter,' Ralemberg answered. 'I was born in Brittany. That was an independent province until Duke Francis died, leaving his daughter Anne as his only heir. She was seized, married off to Charles VIII of France, and Brittany was absorbed into a greater France.' Ralemberg smiled wanly. 'Now Brittany had been given assurances by the present King of England's father that the Tudors would fight to protect Brittany's independence.' He shrugged. 'It just goes to show, princes are liars.'

(Well, that came as no surprise to me. Old Henry VII, father to the Great Killer, was a born miser and inveterate liar who wouldn't know the truth if it jumped up and bit him on the nose. Oh, by the way, Charles VIII of France was no better. He was a pygmy, an ugly little bastard, forever jumping on the ladies of the court as if he was a dog on heat. He fancied himself as a new Alexander and said he wanted to learn more about the Renaissance in the neighbouring country, so he invaded Italy. Charles sacked city after city. He also found syphilis, the first time that disease appeared in Europe. His soldiers caught it outside Naples and, when their balls began to drop off, he retreated. You must have heard how Charles died? Supposedly, he wandered into a darkened room and banged his head on a cupboard. I know different. He was murdered. I have met the assassin who was on top of the cupboard!)

'Brittany became part of France,' Ralemberg continued. 'I didn't care either way. I went to university at the Sorbonne in Paris, entered the royal service, and joined the French crown's legion of secret agents called the Luciferi, the Light-Bearers. These men move in the shadows. They do not act in the full light of day but deal in subtle trickery, clever fetches, secret assassinations, and every filthy trick of the devil. I became a high-ranking officer under the chief archangel, Vauban.'

He chewed his lip. 'The archangel is the title given to the leader of the Luciferi. He is appointed personally by the French king. I admit I was party to their tricks for a while but in Brittany the Luciferi began to remove, through assassination or spurious trials, any who opposed the French crown. One of these was my own brother who led the resistance in the countryside around Nantes.' He looked down at his splayed fingers. 'I suppose,' he murmured, 'that brought me to my senses. I began to see the Luciferi as evil. I fled from them and joined the rebels in Brittany.' He looked at the sea captain. 'De Macon was also one of us. When the resistance broke, I fled with what possessions I had.'

Ralemberg looked sharply at me. 'What's the matter, Roger? I thought you'd say this is England, the Luciferi have no power here?'

'I have met the Luciferi,' I replied, and heard Madame Ralemberg moan as I briefly described my assailants in the alleyway and the appearance of my mysterious protectors.

'Why didn't you tell us?' Ralemberg snapped.

'I thought they were another company, personal enemies. Threats,' I continued bravely, 'do not deter me. But you are right, Monsieur, this is England and the Luciferi have no real power.'

'The Luciferi are everywhere,' de Macon replied. 'Why do you think Monsieur Ralemberg needed your silver and gold? You were not the only one attracted by his business ventures. The Luciferi frightened the rest off.'

'Strange,' I mused.

'What is?'

'Well, Monsieur, before I met you in St Paul's, I found one of your handbills in my chamber at the Golden Turk. Would the Luciferi have put it there?'

'Yes, that is strange,' Ralemberg murmured. 'And you say that some others protected you?'

I nodded. He smiled thinly.

'You must have powerful protectors, Master Shallot.'

'What do you mean?'

'Well, the Luciferi threatened you but they were apparently warned off by someone more powerful.'

I went cold. I had this dreadful feeling that my journey to London and my meeting with this Frenchman had

35

all been carefully managed by Cardinal Wolsey and his blackguard, Doctor Agrippa. Was that why Benjamin had let me go? Was that the reason I found the handbill in my chamber? I thought back. Everything had gone so smoothly. Here was I writing to Benjamin, boasting about being a merchant prince, and it had all been contrived. Now, I'd mentioned Benjamin to the Ralembergs but told them nothing about his near kinsman, the great cardinal.

'Monsieur,' I snapped, 'were you told about me before we met?'

Ralemberg shook his head. 'No,' he answered. 'All I do know is that others who approached me were warned off. At first, I thought it was just the Luciferi but, on one occasion, I am sure it was due to intervention from the English court.'

'Why?' I asked.

'Why what?'

'Why is the English court interested in you?'

Ralemberg smiled and gently removed the crumbs from the table with the tips of his fingers. His companions sat frozen like statues, watching me intently. I am sure de Macon had his hand on his dagger hilt and I realised for all they knew I could be a member of the Luciferi. That's why de Macon was present, in case their gamble went wrong.

'I accepted you, Roger,' Ralemberg said, 'because I liked you. I also suspected that you had powerful patrons, someone high in your king's court.' He licked his lips. 'I was given sanctuary in England in return for information about the Luciferi.' He shrugged. 'You know, the usual details: names, places, agents, ciphers and letters. I told them all I knew except the one thing the great cardinal wanted.'

'Which is?'

'The Luciferi have a spy, a very high-ranking spy, at the English court who provides the French with information about Henry's plans against France, even before such plans are implemented. Cardinal Wolsey thought I knew his name.'

'And do you?'

'No, only that the Luciferi call him Raphael, but Wolsey already knew that.'

'You say "him"?'

'Yes.' Ralemberg smiled bleakly. 'Yes, you're right, Roger, it could be a woman. All I know is the name Raphael.'

'But Wolsey,' I persisted, 'and the Luciferi, think you know the identity of Raphael?'

He nodded.

'So why don't the Luciferi just kill you?'

'My dear Roger, in London there are spies in the service of the Papacy, the Doge of Venice, the Emperor of the Romans, Ferdinand of Aragon . . . and the same is true of every capital in Europe. They are like parasites. They are tolerated here because France tolerates English agents in Paris, but there are certain limitations on their actions – blatant assassination is one of them. Moreover, as soon as the English think I know the name of their traitor, I will be kept safe.'

I leaned back in my chair and studied Agnes's white face. I smiled to hide my own unease. Were Wolsey and Doctor Agrippa somehow managing me? I wondered. Did they think I would loosen Ralemberg's tongue or stir his memory?

'So why do you tell me all this now?' I accused.

'This afternoon,' de Macon spoke up, 'the Luciferi made their presence felt.'

Ralemberg pulled a small package from inside his doublet. He unrolled the piece of linen. In the centre lay a small, pure white beeswax candle stamped with the fleur de lys of France. I picked it up and studied it curiously. It was identical to the one thrust into my hand in the alleyway. It looked so simple, so pure, yet it had held terrors for the Ralembergs and would be the beginning of fresh horrors for me.

'You should be careful,' de Macon murmured.

Of course, Shallot made light of it. I joked and teased them all until some of the heaviness lifted. I didn't give a damn about the Luciferi. Benjamin's uncle would protect us! I was more concerned with persuading Agnes to go for a walk in the tree-lined garden, and foolishly dismissed the Ralembergs' unease.

The next day de Macon sailed. I wrote a short letter to Benjamin, proclaiming myself a merchant but asking if his uncle had written to him recently. I made the letter sound as if all was well, and I suppose it was. (I must pause. I can hear the little chaplain sniggering at me, the loathsome turd! He murmurs that my success is a fable like that of Dick Whittington who became Lord Mayor of London fifty years previously. Why should the little sod laugh? Can't old Shallot have a run of luck? Oh, no, the little bastard's more interested in seeing his patron, his generous master, hunted, beaten and starving in some rotting gaol or facing terrors which would reduce many a man to an inmate of Bedlam. Well, the little sod needn't worry, he can have his fill of all that before this murderous tale is finished.)

Four days after the Ralembergs told me about the Luciferi, I was in the Golden Turk carousing by myself. My partner had told me there were private matters he wished to attend to. I shrugged and left him alone. Now, isn't it strange how terrors begin? A band of gamesters joined me, with a cupful of dice and purses jingling merrily. Sturdy rogues intent on fleecing me, as I was them. The wine flowed freely, my pile of silver grew. The blood in my veins ran high and my usually sharp wits dulled. Young men who read this, take Shallot's advice! First, never drink and gamble; secondly, never drink and gamble with strangers; thirdly, if you do fall into temptation, as I sometimes did, make sure you know where the wine comes from. Anyway, I became as drunk as a vicar. The noise grew, flashes of fire burst before my eyes. I danced, I sang. I threw my largesse round the emptying tap room. I was full of joy at the prospect of meeting Agnes the next day. At last I fell back on to my stool and into the blackness of a drunken stupor. But, oh, what a wakening! I felt as if I was at the end of a long tunnel where someone was kicking my legs. I opened my eyes, groaned at the sunlight and peered around.

'The bastard's awake.'

A grizzled, bearded face pushed itself into mine. I looked away. I was in a garden, my clothes wet with dew. My head thumped with pain, my mouth tasted foul and stale. I was ringed by men, some in armour, and recognised the blue and mustard livery of the City of London. I struggled to rise but my arms were pinioned. I was dragged to my feet. My wrists were tied behind my back, an iron brace fixed around my neck and the long chain which hung from it secured round my ankles.

'For sweet pity's sake!' I murmured.

The soldier whose ugly face I had glimpsed on wakening punched me in the mouth. I turned and retched. I peered round once again. I was in the Ralembergs' garden where something black and white was floating in the small carp pond. I stared closer. It was the corpse of Agnes's dog. Thick blood from its slashed throat appeared to buoy it up. Over in the bower where Ralemberg and his wife used to sit were four corpses, each covered by a dirty, canvas sheet. I glimpsed the feet peeping out from beneath.

'Sweet mercy!' I cried. 'What's happened?'

The soldier seized me by the hair and pushed me across the garden. On his command the sheets were dragged back. How can I describe it? Ralemberg and his wife sprawled there, their throats gashed from ear to ear. The blood had splashed out, drenching their clothes. Agnes was different. Her neck was broken, carefully and expertly. She lay there as if asleep, those beautiful eyes half-open. Beside her the pathetic corpse of the servant, the garotte cord still round his scrawny neck. I howled like a dog, struggling against my captors, until someone gave me a crack across the head and I slipped into unconsciousness.

I awoke in the Little Ease, a smelly, rat-filled dungeon, watered by the sewers of the Fleet river and the slops of the prison bearing the same name.

I must have been half-mad. I whimpered like a child, crouching in the cold, slimy darkness, until the grille above was pulled back and a bailiff with a face like a gargoyle's lashed me with a whip, before lowering a stoup of brackish water and a fly-infested dish of rancid meat. At last I calmed in the face of the sheer horror of the tragedy. Agnes was gone. The Ralembergs were dead and, judging from the dark blood stains on the front of my doublet, I was cast as the murderer. Those men in the Golden Turk had made me drunk deliberately. They had drugged my wine before moving me to that horror-filled garden.

I was frightened. I crouched, shivering with cold, until I was dragged up and thrown into a huge cage on a gaudily painted cart and driven down through the Shambles and Westchepe to the magistrates at the Guildhall. There the bailiffs pushed and shoved me through a porticoed entrance, down a long, dark, musty passageway into the main well of the court, fastening me to the bar; beyond it sat the three magistrates before a square table ringed by clerks. I wanted to vomit or faint. Only the terror of what had happened, and what might yet occur, kept me conscious.

A clerk read the charges out.

'That he did foully murder and commit the most dreadful homicides . . .' Etc, etc.

Shallot's wits resurfaced. I felt the shadow of the noose and the true danger of my situation emerged. All my goods at the Golden Turk would be gone by now. That villain of a landlord was not the one to look a gift horse in the mouth. I had no money, I had no surety. De Macon was at sea, it would take weeks to send a petition to Wolsey, and my master was immersed in his good works at Ipswich. So who would speak for old Shallot? No one but dear Shallot himself so I pleaded not guilty and made my defence: I was Ralemberg's colleague, I had no grievance against him. I admired his family and loved his daughter. There were others, I pointed out, who might wish Ralemberg's death and I was their pathetic dupe. The chief magistrate, with the face of an old fox and the hard eyes of a weasel, heard me out. His two companions, however, sniggered as I referred to the great cardinal, affairs of state, and finally to the Luciferi.

Oh, yes, even then I dully understood that the Luciferi were the bastards who had perpetrated such a dreadful crime. They had decided to move just in case Ralemberg told me anything. They had executed him and his family, and made sure Shallot paid the price. Where, I wondered, were my bloody protectors?

Nevertheless, I had a glimmer of hope. The chief magistrate watched me intently as the prosecutor, a blundering serjeant-at-law, failed to prove I had any grievance against the Ralembergs and could not proffer any motive for the crime. Under questioning, the prosecutor did confess that a search of the house had revealed Ralemberg's and de Macon's indentures with me, as well as my own pathetic love letters to Mistress Agnes. His case came to hinge on one point. Had I left the Golden Turk to commit murder, or was I telling the truth about being drugged and placed in Ralemberg's garden after the dreadful crimes had been committed? The chief magistrate kept referring to this point and my opponent could not answer it. Yet I, too, had no proof of my innocence.

I was removed to the dungeon beneath the Guildhall whilst pursuivants were sent to the Golden Turk to investigate. Searches were also ordered throughout the port of London about de Macon's ship.

I was hustled away to a cold, stone-flagged cell beneath the Guildhall which I shared with two of the biggest rats I have ever clapped eyes on. Long, black, fat-bellied and red-eyed, the bastards watched me hungrily as if I was their next meal. I screamed and rattled my chains; they turned sluggishly away as if to say that one way or another they would eventually dine on my flesh. Later in the afternoon the sheriff's men came back and dragged me up before the justices. Weasel Eyes looked as if he hadn't moved but the other two hypocrites must have dined well for they were slouched, half-asleep, in their high-backed chairs. The court was quiet except for the scratching of the clerks' quills as they sat around their green baize-topped table.

'Master Shallot.' The chief justice's eyes seemed to smile. 'We have made enquiries at the Golden Turk.' The smile on his long face faded. 'The landlord cannot remember seeing you the night you were carousing there.'

'The lying bastard!' I screamed.

One of the escorts slapped me across the mouth.

'Master Shallot,' the justice intoned, 'moderate your language!'

'Or else what?' I yelled. 'You'll hang me? You are going to bloody well hang me anyway, for murders I never committed!'

I received a savage jab between the ribs. 'What about de Macon's ship?' I moaned.

'More bad news I am afraid, Master Shallot. De Macon will never confirm your story. His ship was seized and sunk by French privateers.'

Well, that was it. Shallot was going to hang. The

magistrate put on a black cap, a three-cornered piece of silk. The clerk of the court, his sanctimonious face relishing the sonorous words of condemnation, stood behind him.

'Roger Shallot,' the magistrate thundered, 'we find you guilty of these terrible murders and so you must pay the full penalty of the law. You are to be taken whence you came and, at a time appointed by this court, hanged by the neck till dead!'

I thought of everything; praying, begging, laughing, entreating, trying to escape, all the things old Shallot tries to do when he's in a tight corner.

'Wait!' a girl's voice shouted from the back of the court. I turned and saw my saviour, the wench with black curly hair from the tavern. Beside her, the half-witted ostler she was dragging by the hand struggled with the guards.

'What is the matter?' the magistrate roared.

'Proof!' I yelled. 'Sir, you must hear her!'

I give the old bastard his due, he was a fair man. I think he knew there was something wrong. Anyway, he ordered the girl forward. She took the oath and swore she had seen me drunk. The ostler, whose accent was almost unintelligible, muttered that on the night the murders had been committed, I had been hustled dead drunk out of the tavern and into the hands of strangers waiting in the yard. The magistrate, staring at the ceiling, asked why the landlord had not remembered this. The girl shrugged and mumbled about him being too busy. Who cared? I was free! Penniless, beaten, starving, wretched, but I was free! The guards threw me out. The wench was waiting for me in the street. She pressed up against me.

'I came back, Master Shallot. You are a rogue but you'd never kill anyone!'

'Did you see anybody?' I asked.

She smiled and shook her head. 'I was busy upstairs with one of my customers.'

'You committed perjury on my behalf?'

'Yes.'

'Why?'

'You make me laugh.'

'My possessions?' I asked.

'They are all gone. The landlord took them.'

'I'll kill the bastard!'

'No, you won't,' she whispered. 'He's dead already. He was found with his throat cut in one of the outhouses.'

'Do you know anything about it?'

'Men who spoke French have been seen near the tavern. You'd best not come back,' she added. 'Here, take this.' She slipped me a cloth containing strips of dried meat. Then she stood on tiptoe, kissed me and was gone.

I never saw her again. Months later I searched London but never found her. She was one of the kindest persons I ever met. She had the gentlest soul, and the finest pair of buttocks I have ever held. Let old Shallot tell you this: when you're in real trouble the women will help; most men are cowards. Oh, they like to show off in their peacock plumery, but it's all shadow and no substance with them.

Well, there I was in London, penniless; like the man in the gospel, I was too proud to go home so I begged and fought with the rest of the dispossessed in the dirty alleyways and streets of Whitechapel, Alsatia, and even across London Bridge amongst the stews of Southwark.

I went back to Ralemberg's house but it was all sealed up like a tomb so I left it alone.

But don't get me wrong. I mourned, I really did, and still do. If you go down to my secret chamber and look in one of the coffers you will find a crushed flower, a faded rose, more black than yellow now, but if I smell it and close my eyes (like I did last night), then I am back again in Ralemberg's garden and my blood runs free and the air is filled with the sweet fragrance of flowers. I wait for Agnes and, if I really pretend, she will come and stand with me. Oh, then I am young again and, for one of the few occasions in my life, deeply in love. I open my eyes and think of my riches. Before God, I'd give them all up just to see her again, just to touch her! Good Christ, will no one cry for poor Shallot?

Oh, I did swear vengeance but, believe me, revenge is a dish best served cold and somehow, deep in my innards, I knew that one day I would settle with the Luciferi. For the moment, however, old Shallot had to survive. I could have returned to Ipswich but I didn't want to go back like a beggar. On my third day of freedom I managed to steal some coins and sent a note to my master in Ipswich. I had a clerk in St Paul's write it out, then stood by Aldgate and bribed a royal messenger, carrying the white wand and wearing the royal gold-and-blue surcoat, who was travelling to King's Lynn, to leave the message with Master Daunbey. I suppose I should have just gone and begged for help but Shallot has his pride. God knows where, but I've got it. A day later I had a stroke of good fortune. I managed to steal some clothes from a butcher fastened in the stocks. Then misfortune once again struck.

I was near St Anthony's Hospital, between Bishopsgate and Bread Street, intent on lifting a purse, when my arm was suddenly seized: it was the goldsmith, Waller, demanding his money. Now, I was dirty and unshaven but he recognised me. Once again I landed back in prison, the debtor's hold in the Fleet; a dirty, ramshackle place with narrow corridors, windows as thin as a miser's lips, stinking with the refuse of the city. I was still there the morning my master came and rescued me.

The first I knew about it was a massive gaoler dragging me from the Common side up to the turnkey's lodge. Master Benjamin was waiting, sitting on a stool. He took one look at me, smiled and slipped some coins to the turnkey for food and wine. I sat there for an hour stuffing my stomach and telling him exactly what had happened. Benjamin listened – and that's what I liked about my master, he never judged, he never condemned.

'I received your letter,' he said. 'I came up to visit Johanna in Syon and made enquiries. All our gold?'

'Gone, master.'

Benjamin smiled. 'Never mind. I have horses ready. Uncle wishes to see us at Hampton Court.'

Then I did get frightened. Whenever 'Uncle', the great Lord Wolsey, intervened in our affairs, it always meant trouble. I wasn't frightened of Wolsey. He was just a butcher's son from Ipswich who had risen to be Lord Chancellor and leading churchman of England. Indeed, I always had a sneaking admiration for him and I think he liked me for, as you know, it takes one rogue to recognise another. In time I became Wolsey's friend, the only man to stand by him when he fell from power and lay in bed gasping out his life and cursing the king who had turned against him. Nor was I frightened of Wolsey's familiar, Doctor Agrippa, the black magician with his cherubic face and that strange perfumed smell which always accompanied him.

No, what really frightened old Shallot and turned my innards to water was the thought of the beast Wolsey served, Henry VIII by the grace of God, King of England, Ireland and France. A fat, bombastic, pig-eyed, treacherous son of a turd who destroyed the best of men because he wanted to get between Anne Boleyn's legs and, when he did, couldn't do much about it. The Great Slayer really frightened me. Some men kill because they have to but Henry genuinely thought he was God, with the power of life and death.

Let me give you an example. When he destroyed the monasteries and the north of the country rose in rebellion under Robert Aske (I'll tell you about that later, a real killing time!), the rebel leader sent envoys to Henry to treat over their grievances. Henry despatched his royal herald, Rouge Croix, in return. This poor bastard made the error of bowing before the rebel leader so, when he returned to London, Henry had him drawn, quartered, disembowelled and his balls cut off. Just because the poor sod made a mistake! Now you can see why old Shallot was frightened. No, I lie, not frightened – just terrified witless.

48

Chapter 3

My master and I left London. I changed and bathed at the tavern where my master was staying in Great Mary Axe Street near Bishopsgate. (Oh, by the way, I didn't forget Waller. I'd bought a special bottle of wine. I half-emptied it, filled the rest with horse piss and re-sealed it. Then I sent it to him. I hope the bastard enjoyed every drop!) Two days later we reached Kingston and, leaving our horses at the Robin Hood tavern, went by barge to Hampton Court.

The poet Cavendish described the new palace as a paradise on earth and so I thought when we first glimpsed its towers and golden cupolas above the trees. Wolsey had bought the manor of Hampton from the Knights Hospitallers, levelled it to the ground and, bringing in craftsmen from every part of Europe, built a palace breath-taking in its opulent beauty.

We were given lodgings in the gatehouse and were virtually kept prisoner as the king and the court, as well as the great cardinal, moved into residence. This palace swarmed with retainers either wearing the golden 'T.C.' of Thomas Cardinalis or the scarlet of Henricus Rex. Carts full of precious belongings were being unloaded in the courtyards; ostlers, grooms and farriers shouted and yelled. Chamberlains with white wands of office rapped out orders and, until the king and the lord cardinal were settled in their respective rooms, the common people were banished from the corridors and the galleries.

Wolsey never liked the common man. The Earl of Shrewsbury once told me that when he walked in the park, Wolsey would suffer no one to come within bowshot of him. Benjamin, his favourite nephew, was an exception and on the evening following our arrival Wolsey summoned us to his private apartments. We were led down black-and-white-tiled corridors, through a series of presence chambers, all huge and hung with tapestries which Wolsey had brought from abroad. Not just little square hangings. Some of these were five or six yards long and eight yards high, depicting scenes from the Bible or themes from Petrarch's love poetry.

We were ushered into a small chamber ostentatiously furnished. I noticed with amusement that the tapestries hanging there illustrated the seven deadly sins. Of course, I was fascinated by Lust, a young girl with long, golden hair, breasts like ripe melons, and long, white, slender legs. (I wager Wolsey kept an eye on that, too, being most interested in the sins of the flesh. He had a mistress, you know, a fat, dumpy, little thing, though Wolsey adored both her and the illegitimate children he had by her.) He was awaiting us, a small skull cap pushed to the back of his black, oily hair. He looked the powerful prince, his face dark and swarthy like an Italian's, thick, sensuous lips, a beaked nose and lustrous dark eyes. He was dressed in purple silk and satin trimmed with gold. On his feet were purple woollen buskins. Beside him, on a table, the flat tasselled hat of a cardinal.

Naturally, my master bowed and I had to follow suit,

reminding myself with a secret smile that Wolsey was only a commoner and no better than me. The floor was of polished cedar wood and I glanced round enviously at the stools covered with red satin and silver tassels: 'T.C.', Wolsey's personal monogram, was everywhere, sometimes a foot high in carved gold. The air smelt faintly of incense and, of course, that strange smell of faded flowers which emanated from the figure dressed in black who squatted beside Wolsey: Doctor Agrippa, supreme practitioner of the black arts though he looked like a mummer's version of Friar Tuck in some masque about Robin Hood.

Agrippa's face was round, cherubic, his features small and neat like those of a child, except for the hooded eyes and the look of sardonic amusement with which he watched everything about him. A strange man, I thought. Some people said Wolsey hired him as a defence against other wizards and warlocks. No one knew where he came from. I was wary of him though he was always pleasant to me. He once told me not to be afraid as my death was many years off and would come in a way I least expected.

(I see my chaplain sniggering at me so I'll voice my fear. I know that secret agents and societies still hunt me. I have given strict orders to my henchmen that if I die in suspicious circumstances, they are to hang my chaplain immediately. Ah, good, that's wiped the smile off the bugger's smug face!)

Anyway, back to Wolsey. He was eating sweetmeats from a silver dish and, whilst Benjamin and I knelt before him, he kept popping them into his mouth, watching us impassively. I glanced up under my eyebrows and caught Agrippa's eye. He grinned and winked, then studied the ring on his right hand, a stone of indeterminate colour.

51

Agrippa claimed he used it to make sure wine was free of poison, though I don't think it was possible for Agrippa to die. I believe he was the Wandering Jew, doomed to live forever.

Wolsey finished the plate of sweetmeats and told us to sit. Strangely enough, he first addressed me.

'Well, Shallot, you've met the Luciferi? You'd call them bastards, yes?'

'You could have protected me!' I replied bitterly.

'Oh, but we did. Don't you remember, in the alleyway?'

'What about my trial?'

'You would not have been hanged. A reprieve would have come through. That tavern wench was a stroke of good fortune – but then you go and get yourself lost!'

'It was all arranged, wasn't it?' I accused. 'You gave Ralemberg licence to trade. You put the handbill in my room. The Luciferi kept away other sponsors, and so did you – till I arrived.'

Wolsey smiled and pulled out a gold-edged handkerchief to wipe his nose. He was in good fettle, otherwise he would never have traded words with me.

'You could have saved the Ralembergs,' I added.

His face hardened. 'We tried to. Ralemberg was very useful. But the Luciferi sent their decoys.'

'And de Macon's ship?' I asked.

Wolsey shrugged. 'The fortunes of war, Master Shallot. If Ralemberg had been more open, such misfortunes would never have happened.' He saw my angry glance at Benjamin. 'My nephew had nothing to do with it, I assure you.'

'But now that road's closed,' Agrippa intervened.

'What road?' I queried.

'Oh, come, Roger. To the Luciferi, Vauban, the five archangels, Raphael!'

He must have seen from my face that I knew what he was talking about. Wolsey played with the gold pendant around his neck and smirked patronisingly at Agrippa as if he was a favourite son. A black cat, wearing a jewelled studded collar, crept from beneath a curtain, padded towards Agrippa and, lithe as a dancer, sprang into his lap. Agrippa stroked it carefully. (You know, he always wore black leather gloves. I saw his left hand ungloved once. The palm bore the inverted cross and the Eye of Osiris and on the back a blood red pentangle. Those of you who know about black magic will know what all that means, Agrippa was one of the high-ranking Dark Lords.) Anyway, enough of that. On that sunny evening at Hampton Court, Agrippa sat and chattered like some benevolent uncle.

'Let us come to the point,' he said briskly.

'Yes,' Benjamin agreed. He had been sitting quietly. 'Uncle, if you have a task for us, then let us begin it. Master Shallot and I have sworn to be your men in peace and war.' Benjamin quoted the last phrase from the agreement he had signed with Wolsey. 'Uncle, you must trust us more!'

Wolsey's hard eyes softened as he gazed back at Benjamin. For a few seconds that stony-visaged politician looked kindly and I realised that, apart from his mistress, Benjamin was one of the few people Wolsey really loved. The cardinal turned and stroked Agrippa's cat.

'My nephew is right,' he said softly. 'Let us describe the task.'

Agrippa rose, putting the cat gently down on the floor.

He stood beside the cardinal's chair, leaning against it with one hand on its gilded back.

'Our noble king,' he began, 'now wishes to contain the power of France. He can do that by alliance with the Emperor Charles V and the Hapsburgs who control the Low Countries and Spain. We intend to ring France and contain it like an army encircles a castle. Unfortunately, the French know in advance every move we make. We have spies in Paris, and the French Luciferi are in London. The difference is, the Luciferi have someone close to our hearts who betrays our every step and turn. Matters have now come to a head. The English embassy in France has a mansion in the Rue des Medeans, but in early spring they moved to a small castle outside Paris, the Château de Maubisson.

'At the château are a number of officials: Sir John Dacourt, our ambassador; his chief clerk, Walter Peckle; Doctor Thomas Throgmorton, physician; Michael Millet, personal assistant and clerk to Sir John Dacourt; and the man responsible for our agents . . . or rather, who was, Giles Falconer. We already knew there was a spy either in England or France selling secrets to the French. It was Falconer who discovered the spy's code-name: Raphael.'

'How?' Benjamin asked quietly.

'One of Falconer's agents was discovered in the Rue des Billets. He had been stabbed a number of times but, before he died, he used his own blood to etch on a piece of parchment the name Raphael. Now on Easter Monday last [almost six weeks ago I thought], Falconer retired to his chamber. Late that night both Millet and Throgmorton heard him going upstairs to the top of one of the towers of the château. Millet peeped out of his chamber, Falconer had a goblet in his hand, he was smiling but not drunk. Throgmorton heard him singing. On Tuesday morning, Falconer was found at the base of the tower, his neck broke, his head shattered.'

'He could have slipped,' Benjamin said.

'Impossible. The tower does have a crenellated wall but the gaps have iron bars across to prevent anyone falling. Moreover, the tower roof is sprinkled with fine sand to prevent anyone slipping. Throgmorton, who surveyed the area after Falconer's body had been discovered, found no trace of any such slip or, indeed, of anyone else being with Falconer on the top of the tower.'

'Could it have been suicide?' I asked.

'I doubt it. The rest of the embassy met Falconer at dinner that Monday. He was as happy as ever. Falconer was a bachelor but a man in love with life. He enjoyed his work and was one of the best agents we had.' Agrippa's eyes hardened. 'Indeed, he was a personal friend of mine.'

Another black magician? I wondered.

'No,' he snapped, 'Falconer was murdered.'

'The wine,' I asked. 'Was it poisoned?'

Agrippa smiled sweetly. 'We considered that but Sir John Dacourt, an honest old soldier, was with Falconer in his room when he broached the bottle. Dacourt had a cup of the same wine and suffered no ill effects.'

'Who could be the murderer?' I asked.

'Any of those four. Oh,' he added, 'we missed out one person: Richard Waldegrave, the chaplain.'

'You wish us to go to Paris?' Benjamin interrupted.

'Yes, we do, so perhaps it's time you met your companions.'

Wolsey picked up a silver bell but Agrippa raised his hand.

'Lord Cardinal, I believe your nephew has further questions?'

Benjamin gazed at the cardinal, then at his familiar.

'Doctor Agrippa,' he asked, 'when matters are decided regarding France, how are such conclusions reached and despatched abroad?'

'The Privy Council,' Agrippa replied, 'is divided into chanceries. There is a chancery for Italy, a chancery for the Papacy, a chancery for Germany, for Spain, and one for France. My Lord Cardinal chairs each of these but is assisted by a secretary and a number of clerks. These meet His Majesty in secret session, matters are discussed and, as you put it, conclusions are reached.'

'Then what happens?'

'Letters are sent in secret cipher to the English embassy, latterly in the Rue des Medeans, now at the Château de Maubisson. Such letters are sealed with the cardinal's own signet ring. This signet seal cannot be forged.'

'Why is that?'

'Because, my dear nephew,' Wolsey silkily intervened, 'only I know what the seal actually looks like. No one is present when those despatches are sealed, not even Doctor Agrippa.'

I stared at the cardinal. Do you know, I saw a flicker of fear in those cunning eyes and realised why his Satanic Eminence needed us so much. He was an archbishop, the king's chief minister, but he was also a cardinal of the Roman church. If such secret missives were sealed personally by him it might be only a matter of time before Wolsey's enemies at court and parliament began to point the

56

accusing finger in his direction.

'What happens then?' my master asked.

'The secrets are placed in a despatch bag and sealed with the chancery seal. Two messengers take them to Paris and deliver them personally to the ambassador.'

'Have the bag or despatches ever been interfered with?'

'Never. They are chained to one of the messenger's wrists.'

'Has anything ever happened to the messengers?'

Agrippa pursed his lips. 'Only once, just outside Paris. You know that in France there are secret societies, peasants with ideas of equality? They call themselves "Maillotins" or "Club-Wielders".'

(Oh, I knew about these. Last time I had been to Paris they had rescued me from the freezing streets and hungry wolf packs.)

'These Maillotins attacked the messengers and killed them but a party of royal guards, who by chance were in the vicinity, hunted the outlaws down. The bags were returned in accordance with diplomatic protocol, and were found to be unopened and untampered with.'

'Could the spy be in England?'

'We suspect he is in France at our embassy.'

'Why?'

'The French do not betray what they have learnt until the despatches reach our embassy.'

'What happens then?'

'The chief cipher clerk, Walter Peckle, decodes them and hands them to the ambassador.'

Benjamin tapped the toe of his boot on the soft carpet.

'These messengers?' he queried.

'They are professional couriers. There are two in

England and two in France. They often cross each other in their travels.'

'And two of them were killed?'

'Yes, but they have been replaced,' Agrippa answered.

'They are trustworthy men?'

'They cannot be faulted. You may question the two in England before you go. Now,' Agrippa picked up the bell, 'perhaps you should meet your travelling companions?'

The silver bell tinkled. A servant wearing the cardinal's livery slipped like a shadow into the room.

'Ah, yes.' Wolsey got up. 'Sir Robert Clinton?'

'He is in the presence chamber, Your Grace.'

'Bring him in!'

Clinton entered, a small man with silver hair brushed back from his forehead, a neatly clipped moustache and beard. He looked what he was, a veteran soldier, with sun-tanned face, clear eyes, dark doublet and hose, the only concession to fashion being the ornate, thick silver rings on each hand and a gold cross round his neck. Beside him stood his clerk, Ambrose Venner, a young man with thinning hair and the fat, cheerful face of an over-fed scholar. Agrippa introduced them, ushering them to seats, clicking his fingers for the servant to serve them wine and sweetmeats.

'Sir Robert,' Agrippa began, 'is chief secretary to the French chancery of the Privy Council. Sir Robert, Benjamin Daunbey and his servant, Roger Shallot.'

Clinton smiled and sketched a bow to both of us. He seemed a courtly gentleman with the inbred manners of a diplomat. Venner gave a gap-toothed grin.

'Sir Robert,' Agrippa continued, 'Master Benjamin and his manservant will be in your retinue. They will travel to

Maubisson to determine the true cause of Falconer's death and assist you in the hunting down of Raphael.'

'My Lord Cardinal, Doctor Agrippa.' Clinton's face was now severe. 'You already have my thoughts on this matter. Raphael may well be in England. I speak for all the servants of the embassy in Paris. They are loyal to His Majesty.'

'Yes, yes,' Wolsey testily interrupted. 'But we have established that the French only seem to know our secrets after the king's letters and memoranda are delivered to our embassy in Paris.'

'Yes, yes, Your Grace,' Clinton snapped back, revealing the tension between the two of them. 'And you also know my thoughts on that. His Majesty should stop such letters being sent.'

'Sir Robert,' Agrippa smoothly intervened, 'we have been down this path before. If our embassy in France cannot receive its instructions, His Majesty's affairs there will come to a halt.'

'How long has this been going on?' I asked.

Clinton looked at me in surprise, Wolsey in annoyance as if resenting my interruption.

'About eighteen to twenty months!' Agrippa snapped back.

Benjamin nudged me to keep quiet. I looked away and went cold with fright. Agrippa's black cat sat beneath one of the heavy, gold-encrusted arrasses, crouched like a panther, his amber eyes studying me as if I was a mouse. Not a blink, not a change of expression. I looked back at Agrippa. His eyes had turned the same colour and I caught a whiff of that strange perfume which sometimes emanated from him, sweet but sickly. He, too, was watching me and

I shivered. What deadly game, I wondered, was about to begin?

'Your Grace,' Clinton spoke up, 'your nephew and his companion will be most welcome in our retinue but I cannot promise you any success.'

'Like your last mission!' Wolsey snapped.

Clinton flinched. Wolsey stretched out a hand and patted him gently on the shoulder.

'Sir Robert,' he said softly, 'my words were harsh. I withdraw them. It was due to your efforts that we discovered the name of Raphael.'

'How's that?' Benjamin asked.

Clinton smiled and I noticed how white and even his teeth were. A careful, precise man, I thought at the time, one who looked after his health.

'Over two months ago,' Clinton explained, 'I and my wife, the Lady Francesca, visited Maubisson just before Lent to see what help could be given in tracking the spy down.' He shook his head. 'I think it was the week before Ash Wednesday. Falconer – well, Giles, for he and I were friends – devised a scheme whereby one of our agents would use one of Paris's most expensive whores to trap a leading member of the Luciferi. She passed on to our agent the name Raphael, though he paid for it with his life. He was attacked and killed whilst leaving Paris.' Clinton shrugged. 'I returned to England after Holy Week had begun. Six weeks later Falconer was discovered at the base of the tower.' He looked at Wolsey. 'My Lord Cardinal, have you told your nephew of the other matter?'

Wolsey stroked his chin as if feeling the gentle stubble now growing there. 'Ah, yes, the king's matter. Doctor Agrippa?'

The magician turned, stared at the cat and said something in a strange language. The cat immediately rose, padding like a shadow across the floor, and jumped into its master's lap. He played for a few seconds with the animal's jewelled collar then turned his eyes on me. I shivered for they were soulless, clear as ice.

'The matter of the king,' Agrippa announced, and I remembered a previous conversation with him on the wild heathlands of Leicester, how he had described Henry as the Great Dark Prince, the Mouldwarp. He was now using his powers to remind me of that as if the matter he was about to broach was more important than any spy. Undoubtedly, our journey to France was linked to the growing darkness in our king's twisted soul.

'Our noble king,' Agrippa continued, 'in his youth, went to Paris and visited the Château de Maubisson. He became friendly with a most learned old priest in the village, Abbé Gerard. Indeed, the abbé was his confessor. Henry gave him a book and now wants it back but the Abbé Gerard is dead, probably also murdered. On the Wednesday after Falconer was killed, the good priest was found floating in his own carp pond, no mark of violence on his body. His house had been searched and the book was missing.'

'What is this book?'

Agrippa grinned. 'A copy of Augustine's work *On Chastity*.'

'Do you think,' Benjamin asked, 'the Luciferi have this book? Why is it so important?'

'No, we think the Luciferi did not find it. The good abbé probably hid it.' Agrippa made a face. 'As for its importance? We do not wish to explain that.'

'And while we are gone?' my master asked. 'What about

the manor, my school in Ipswich?'

'All will be well. A steward will manage the manor and My Lord Cardinal has been only too pleased to appoint a schoolmaster so your noble establishment can continue. Now,' Agrippa stirred, 'Master Shallot, Sir Robert, I pray you excuse us. My Lord Cardinal wishes words alone with his nephew.'

Clinton smiled, rose and he and Venner slipped silently out of the room. I would have followed but Benjamin held my wrist fast.

'Master Shallot!' Agrippa repeated. 'I have asked you to leave!'

'Roger is my friend,' Benjamin answered. 'I trust him with my life.'

' "Master Shallot is my friend!" ' Wolsey mimicked spitefully. 'My good nephew, if you wish to protect Master Shallot, the less he knows the better.' He looked round. 'This is my palace but the king is here and God knows who listens in!'

Benjamin looked at me, his dark eyes troubled. I gently prised my wrist free.

'Master,' I said softly, 'it's best if I go.'

(Quite the diplomat, you think? Oh, no, old Shallot was getting frightened. If knowledge was to be imparted that might threaten me, then it was time to show a clean pair of heels and, perhaps, indulge in some honest lechery.)

My master did not demur and I slipped quietly out of the chamber. I tried to eavesdrop but the door was too thick. So I wandered round the corridors of Hampton Court. Now this was not as magnificent then as it is today. The Great Hall had yet to be built, as had the tennis court and tilt yard. Of course, if you go there now, you can look at the great clock built by those two witches Kratzer and Oursian. You see, when Wolsey fell from power and died in Leicester Abbey, crushing my hand and whispering, 'If I had served my God as well as I served my king, he would not leave me to die like this,' Agrippa transferred his allegiance to Henry and brought those two witches over to build a special clock. It's an astronomical device based on a twenty-four-hour pattern which tells the time of day, the position of the moon, the constellations of the zodiac. You must go and see it. It's a work of art!

Nevertheless, even in my green and salad days (Master Shakespeare has asked to borrow this phrase), Hampton Court was a diamond of a residence. Wainscoted walls. New hangings replaced every week by yeomen and grooms of the wardrobe. Silk coverings on the beds. Massive cupboards which covered an entire wall, all stuffed with silver and gold plate. Fresh water was brought in through leaden pipes built by Italian craftsmen, there were even privies, and underground streams cleaned the sewers. I wandered down to the kitchens where Wolsey's chefs were busy creating subtleties, strange confectionery creations: towers and castles of sugar ready to launch their assault on valiant teeth. The French master chef, dressed in his long bespattered apron, stood by his post chopping, slicing, stirring and mixing with a vigour which drenched him in sweat whilst he swore at his apprentices for this or that. Indeed, with the great roaring fires it looked like hell and the chef, Satan, attended by an army of demons labouring over turning spits and shining platters, interlarding the dripping, roasting lambs and piglets with their own globules of sweat.

I walked up this way and down that. Now I knew the king was in residence because his gold and leopard standards had been planted all around the entrance. By chance, I found myself in the royal apartments, a long, polished gallery where the freshly waxed wood winked in the sunlight and the walls shimmered with the exquisite tapestries hung there. I thought the king was hunting with his greyhounds or Flemish falconers. There were no guards about so I tip-toed along the gallery. My ear was caught by the sweet sounds of love-making: delicious 'Oohs' and 'Ahs', interspersed with the grunts and deep groans of a voice I recognised as the king's.

Well, as you know, I am as curious as the devil. I edged along the wall and peered quickly through a half-open door. The small chamber inside was brilliant with differing hues. I saw white wool carpets on the gleaming floor and also glimpsed clothing of the costliest taffeta, lace and cambric, but my eyes were drawn to the great silk-draped four-poster bed. All I could see were a pair of white legs wrapped round a creaking great torso and the royal arse going up and down like a pair of bellows whilst the 'Oohs' and 'Ahs' were chorused by Henry's groans of lustful delight. I wondered who the young girl was, acting the doe for Henry's buck, but I decided not to wait and see and promptly fled. Nevertheless, my excitement was aroused and, when Benjamin left the cardinal's chamber, he glared at my flushed face suspiciously.

'What have you been up to, Roger?'

'Nothing, master, just a little sightseeing. And what did dear Uncle wish to impart?'

Benjamin grinned and linked his arm through mine. 'Matters of state, Roger, matters of state.' He stopped, his face long and serious. 'A dance is about to begin,' he murmured as if speaking to himself. 'The musicians in the

gallery are about to put flute to lips and fingers to lyre.'
He breathed out heavily. 'A sinister dance, Roger.'

I shivered and wondered if it was time for old Shallot to
disappear or go ill with ague, but I remembered my promise. I was Benjamin's man and I was committed, whatever
happened. It sounds so brave, doesn't it? If I'd known
what was about to happen I would have fled like the wind.
(My chaplain squirms on his little bum. He liked my
description of royal love-making but that's nothing to what
we had to face: murder; secret assassins; blood-thirsty
rebels; the gleaming tusks of a wild boar; and that deadly
chase in the maze at the Tour de Nesle. And yet these are
as naught compared to the sheer wickedness of the Luciferi
and the treachery of the masters we served.)

We spent the next day lolling round Hampton Court.
Wolsey's clerks drew up the necessary letters of accredit-
ation, warrants and bills for the exchequer. Grooms and
ostlers furnished us with horses for our journey. That evening we attended a royal banquet in the magnificent setting
of Wolsey's hall. There were so many wax candles you
would think it was daylight and the flames dazzled the
gold and silver plate stacked high in the ornately carved
cupboards. The carpets on the floor were silk, the hangings
on the walls fresh from the looms of Flanders, and the air
was thick with the smell of red roses arranged in precious
vases round the room. The table on the dais where King
Henry would sit was overhung with a gorgeous cloth of
state.

We sat at one of the two tables just beneath the dais.
Benjamin, I remember, was on my left, some beautiful
damsel on my right. I would have liked to have got to know
her better but I drank too much. All the plate was of heavy

gold and the table cloths were silken, perfumed sheets hung heavy with gold embroidery. The meal was delicious, the wines the best from all over Europe. There were eighteen courses, the most exotic being the confectionery. Artists had been hired especially to prepare these culinary masterpieces in the lifelike forms of birds, beasts and cattle, jousting courtiers in full armour, soldiers battling with cross-bows, knights dancing with ladies; all were vividly depicted in the gilded confections which rose over a yard high from the groaning dining tables. Each one of us was given a chess board complete with chess men made entirely of sweetmeats. This was a parting gift but I dropped mine and the bloody dogs were on it in a flash, whilst Benjamin, kind as ever, gave his to the page who served us. Sweet-voiced children from the royal choir sang madrigals and, halfway through the meal, we were escorted by torchlight to watch a Latin comedy by Platus. One thing I must mention to you. During the meal a great spider crawled on to the table cloth and I went to kill it with the leg of chicken I was gnawing, but Benjamin stopped me.

'We must not,' he whispered, 'harm such insects. They are the cardinal's spiders.'

He then explained in a hushed voice how these bloody insects roamed all over the place. God knows why but the cardinal had taken a liking to them and decreed that no one should harm them. They were known (and still are) as the cardinal's spiders. I always wondered if they were his demons or familiars which could scuttle along the walls to listen for treason and search out conspiracy. (A strange place, Hampton Court! You know it's haunted? First, by the nurse of the young Edward VI. She is said to be bricked up in her room, spinning her hand loom for all eternity.

She was a treacherous bitch who tried to kill the young king, but that's another story. The other ghost is Catherine Howard. After she had been arrested for playing the two-backed beast with Culpepper – and me, though I wasn't caught, but there again that's another tale – the king's guards came to take her whilst she was staying at Hampton Court. Catherine heard that Henry was praying in the royal chapel so ran screaming down the corridor. It didn't save her. She went to the block bravely, announcing to the world that she preferred to die the wife of Culpepper than Queen of England. That really infuriated Henry! Good Lord, he was hopping mad!

'Roger,' he whined, the tears falling down his fat, pasty face, 'how could she? How could she?'

Very well, I thought. She was marvellous but I didn't tell the fat bastard that. Anyway, as I have said, that's a tale for another time. But I have seen Catherine's ghost. A white form screaming down moonlit galleries.)

Ah, well, back to that banquet in Hampton Court where I got royally drunk. Henry was there, beginning to get a little fat but still magnificent in his jewel-encrusted cloth of gold and drenched in the perfume of his own making; he had to hide the smell of his ulcerated leg. All right, I'll tell you what happened. I was fascinated by the woman sitting opposite me: Francesca Clinton, Sir Robert's wife. She was a real beauty, or so I thought at the time. She wore her thick, black hair loose and long. It cascaded unbound below her waist. Her skin complemented her hair; she had an olive complexion which shone like burnished gold. Her lips were red, half-open as if waiting to be kissed, displaying teeth as white as ivory, though I noticed one tooth slightly out of line with the others. But like Agnes's, it was her eyes which fascinated me – large, dark, and almond-shaped. Whenever she turned, whenever she spoke, they exuded an excitement which had my young loins stirring. She hardly noticed me but I was fascinated by her. I listened to her voice, rather deep but very sensuous, and turned to Benjamin.

'Is she French?'

'Who?'

'Lady Francesca,' I whispered.

Benjamin stared across the table to where Sir Robert sat, captivated by his wife.

'Of course she is,' he whispered back. 'She is Sir Robert's second wife. They have been married for two years.'

I suddenly remembered that elegant pair of legs wrapped round the royal torso.

'What does the king think of her?' I asked.

'He does not like her,' Benjamin whispered back. 'He does not like the French.'

I nodded and gazed adoringly across the table at those dark, passionate eyes. Of course, I thought, she has olive skin. The legs I saw were white. Suddenly Francesca seemed to notice me. She smiled dazzlingly.

'Master Shallot,' she called in her beautiful French voice, 'my husband says you are to join us in France.'

I just stared back. I would have joined her in Tartary! Lord, when I first met her she was exquisite. I could have sat and stared all evening but Benjamin suddenly realised the drift of my eyes as well as my lechery and, at the appropriate time, seized me by the arm and hustled me from the hall. I went unresistingly. I was drunk as a pig and insisted on stamping on every bloody spider I found on my way back to our chamber.

Chapter 4

The next morning Benjamin shook me awake. I got up, thick-headed, with a cloying mouth. But a cold wash and a cup of malmsey soon put me right. After we had broken fast in the small buttery which adjoined the kitchen, Benjamin dragged me outside to the gardens.

'Where are we off to, master?'

'To see Crispin Hollis and Francis Twynham.'

'Who the hell are they?'

'They are the two messengers, the ones who carry documents to Paris.'

We found them in the stables, tending to the horses; country lads whose constant talk was of saddles, bridles, reins and spurs; what was good horseflesh and what wasn't; what horses should be fed and when they could drink. Benjamin, with his usual charm and tact, drew them into conversation, listening to their voluble descriptions of the horses they had ridden.

'So,' he interrupted, seizing the right moment, 'you carry messages from Westminster to the English embassy in Paris?'

Hollis, a fresh-faced yokel, grinned as he cleaned the gaps between his teeth with a piece of sharp straw.

'From Westminster,' he replied, 'Greenwich, Sheen
. . . wherever the court is.'

'And what route do you take?'

'Dover to Calais, across Normandy to the Porte St
Denis, and either to the Rue des Medeans or across
Paris through the Porte D'Orleans to the Château de
Maubisson.'

'And you stop where?'

'At certain taverns.'

'Nowhere else?'

'Sometimes at the Convent of St Felice.'

'Why there?'

The fellow shrugged. 'You have met Sir Robert
Clinton?'

'We have.'

'And his beautiful wife, Lady Francesca?'

'Of course.'

'Well,' Twynham interrupted with a grin, 'Lady Francesca was schooled there by the nuns. It's a sumptuous
place. Now and again the Lady Francesca asks us to take
the good nuns gifts of embroidery.'

'And that is all?'

'Sometimes a small purse of silver from the coffers of
her husband.'

Benjamin nodded and stared where an ostler was trying
to calm an excited horse.

'And your two companions, the ones in France? Do
they stop there?'

'Again, sometimes. It's an ideal place.'

'But you don't stop there every time?'

'No,' Hollis replied. 'I would say one in every three

times.' He smirked. 'We do not wish to lose a good, soft bed because of our greed.'

'And the pouch you carry?' I asked. 'With the letters and documents?'

Twynham's face became grave with self-importance. 'When we sleep, one of us has it chained to our wrist. No one can touch that bag.'

'But two of your companions were killed?' Benjamin added softly.

Hollis turned and spat a stream of yellow phlegm. 'Yes, I know, but the French protect and afford us every comfort. Those messengers were killed by outlaws. It sometimes happens.' Benjamin nodded and quietly turned the conversation back to horseflesh. As we walked away I looked at him sideways. He had that distant look which showed he was absorbed in solving some problem.

'Master,' I touched him on the shoulder, 'it is strange that these messengers stop at the same convent where the Lady Francesca was educated. Do you think she could be the spy?'

Benjamin ruffled his long, black hair with his hands.

'I doubt it,' he said quietly. 'First Lady Francesca may be beautiful, she may have a sharp wit, but not the power to collect and convey secret information to some spymaster in Paris. Secondly, she would not be privy to any information contained in those letters. Oh, her husband may chatter but I doubt if he gives her a blow by blow account of English activities in France. Thirdly, you have heard the messengers. They only stop at St Felice one out of every three times and, when they do, the bag is chained to their wrists.' He laughed and clapped me on the shoulder. 'And even if the good nuns did seduce them, they would have to break the seal on the pouch as well as my lord cardinal's special seal on each letter, decode the cipher and re-seal them again.' He shook his head. 'No, no, that's impossible.'

Later in the day we received instructions that Sir Robert and his party would be leaving the following morning. The lord cardinal wished us to attend one more of his interminable banquets – and this is where I made a bad situation worse. The banquet began with the usual mumbo-jumbo, except the cardinal dined alone at the high table under a rich cloth of state, his fat body almost hidden by platters of heaped delicacies, whilst all around him stood serving men to refill his goblet, replenish napkins or offer a fresh knife. There was no sign of the king nor, regrettably, Lady Clinton. Suddenly we were disturbed by the roar of many small cannons being fired all at once outside the palace. The gunfire sounded like a burst of thunder. Everyone sprang to their feet but the cardinal's heralds called for silence and he sent his revels master, Henry Guildford, to see what was going on. (Oh, by the way, I never saw Agrippa at these banquets. Indeed, I never saw him eat. Strange, isn't it?) Well, the revels master returned, saying that some masked noble figures had arrived at the water stairs. Wolsey sent the fellow down to escort these strange guests up and we just sat watching the door. Guildford returned leading a large company of masked figures who marched into the hall to the raucous clamour of tambour and fife.

Now these visitors were dressed in simple shepherds' tunics though they were fashioned in stripes of crimson satin and cloth of gold. Visors and artificial beards hid their faces whilst false hair of fine gold wire and black silk covered the rest of their heads. These masquers filed solemnly, two-by-two, down to the high table. Their leader had quiet words with the cardinal, who smiled, clapped his hands, and a green baize-covered table and two chairs were brought in and set down in the middle of the hall. The leading masquer then stood on the dais, whilst a herald challenged anyone in the hall to play this strange man at dice.

Of course, it was a load of mummery, Fat Henry playing at masques and mystery. Oh, we all knew it was him with his stout legs and big arse, but everyone became involved in the pantomime. In theory, no one was supposed to challenge the mysterious figure and, if they did, they were supposed to lose. On that particular occasion matters went wrong. To cut a long story short, drunk as a bishop, I sprang to my feet.

'I accept the challenge!' I yelled, ignoring Benjamin's frantic tugging at my cloak.

The din in the hall stilled. The masked figure stepped ponderously off the dais, sat down at the baize-covered table and indicated with a gloved hand that I should join him. I staggered across. I don't know why. Perhaps it was pure mischief in me. Or was it something else? Perhaps the thought of dice had stirred memories of that terrible evening in the Golden Turk when the Luciferi had trapped me. Anyway, the very devil was in me. The masked figure clapped his hands, a cup of dice was produced. My opponent (of course it was the Great Killer) emptied his purse on the table, so did I, and the game began. I played as if my very life depended upon it. The rest of the hall left their places and gathered around us. I saw Benjamin's anxious eyes but ignored his warning look. I played to win and I did. I won the first purse of gold, then a second, then a third. The joy and gaiety seeped from that hall as the masked player's irritation became obvious. A courtier leaned over and whispered in my ear.

'For God's sake, man, lose!'

But not old Shallot! I threw the dice and almost my every throw beat his until Wolsey, standing behind the king's chair, gave a sign for the trumpeters to blow and the game ended. My opponent drew off his mask and I gazed into the red, sweaty face of the king. Now old Henry was a born actor. Indeed, I wonder if we ever saw the true Henry. (Do you know, I was in the council chamber with Thomas Cromwell when, years later, the northern rebels sent their demands and asked for his removal. Old Henry took his hat off and publicly beat Cromwell, telling him he was a caitiff and a knave and would be sent to the Tower. Of course, Henry was playing games. He wanted more time and the rebels gave him it. Time enough to collect troops and send them north to hang, burn and pillage. By the time they were finished there were ten men hanging from every scaffold north of the Trent.)

So it was that night at Hampton Court. Henry smiled, playing the chivalrous loser. He clapped me on the shoulder, proclaiming I was a great fellow, before sweeping away to join the dancers. I just took my napkin, filled it with all the coins I had won and tied the corners into a knot. Of course, Benjamin hustled me away to a corner by ourselves and that wasn't hard, everyone now distanced themselves from us. The mischief in my veins cooled as I saw the fear in his eyes.

'Roger,' he hissed, 'for the love of God! If you play against the king you always lose!'

'I won,' I quipped. 'By fair means not foul!'

Benjamin pushed his white, anxious face closer. 'No, Roger, the game is not yet over. You will still lose.'

Now, my natural caution exerted itself as I stared round the banqueting hall. Oh, there was dancing, masques and reels, gaily clad courtiers talking in groups, but I caught the fear-filled glances and realised what might happen. The Great Killer hated to be beaten. No one ever challenged Henry and won. The fat bastard's motto was: 'When I play, either I win or you lose!' The napkin now weighed heavy as death in my hands. My mind raced on how the game might proceed. I knew that royal turd. It could be anything from a charge of treason to a nasty accident. Wolsey swept across the room, his purple silk robes billowing round him.

'Master Daunbey, Master Shallot. The king wishes to see you now!'

I caught the stench of fear from the cardinal. A fine sheen of sweat glazed his heavy, quivering jowls. The dark eyes were as hard as slate. He glared at me. I knew why he was fearful. I was a member of his party, one of his retinue, and when the great Henry lashed out it was dangerous even to be in the same room as the king's enemy. We followed the cardinal across the floor. Benjamin nudged me furiously.

'For God's sake, Roger,' he hissed, 'stop this foolishness!'

I had already decided to do that as soon as I entered the darkened chamber where the royal beast sat slouched on a chair. (You had to watch the Great Killer's eyes.

They always reminded me of an angry boar's, small, red-rimmed and vicious – and that's when he was in a good mood! When he lost his temper, and that was often, his cheeks puffed up and his eyes shrank to two small, bottomless black pits. They had that same expression when we entered the room.) Wolsey scuttled to sit down behind him. Benjamin and I needed no second bidding. We fell to our knees, the gold coins clinking ominously in the napkin I clutched.

'Master Shallot, you played well.' The voice was sugar sweet.

'Yes, Your Majesty,' I mumbled, hoping I would not lose control of my bowels or vomit in sheer terror. (I always wore brown breeches.)

'You played against your king and won!'

My mind raced as nimble as a flea in air. 'Of course, Your Majesty,' I stuttered. 'As the wild woman prophesied.'

'What's that?'

I gazed up under my eyebrows. The king was now leaning forward. Wolsey just quivered in terror, shaking like one of the jellies his chefs had so recently served us. Benjamin knelt as if carved from stone.

'What do you mean?' the king repeated ominously.

'Your Majesty,' I stammered, 'when I was young at school in Ipswich, I helped an old lady cross a bridge.' I looked sideways at Benjamin. 'Master, you were with me, you will remember it?'

Benjamin nodded, his eyes fixed on the ground.

'The old woman was a seer,' I continued recklessly. 'She thanked me for my courtesy and prophesied that one day I would play against Europe's greatest prince in

76

a game of hazard, and win. That, she said, would be my moment of glory, to tell my grandchildren,' I added hopefully.

(Oh, what a glorious lie! Shallot at his best, the born story-teller! The only old woman I helped in Ipswich was Bridget the Ancient. I did assist her to cross the river. I pushed the bloody bitch into it after she had cursed me for not handing over every penny in my pockets! But, on reflection, it was a good tale. I liked the bit about grandchildren, a pious hope that the Shallot line did not end there and then!) Well, you could have felt the atmosphere in the room relax as if someone had opened a window, letting in the cool summer breeze. Wolsey's mouth twitched, he once more became the most important person after God. Benjamin's shoulders shook as he controlled the bubble of laughter, but Henry sat back, clapping his hands and grinning from ear to ear like some bloody cat.

'You must tell that to the court!' he roared.

And, without further ado, I was marched back into the hall, placed on the dais, the heralds braying on their trumpets. I repeated my declaration to an admiring court, listening to the plaudits of praise. All the time the Great Killer stood beside me, his hand on my shoulder. When I had finished I turned and, sinking to one knee, dramatically handed the napkin full of gold back to the king. I would have loved to have swung the sodding bag and hit him straight in the balls but the old tight-fist snatched it off me and threw the gold on to the hall floor so he could watch his courtiers scramble. I thought the cunning bastard was finished with me but his hand remained vice-like on my shoulder. For a while he watched his courtiers

77

make fools of themselves, then hissed: 'A word in thy ear, Master Shallot!'

I was force-marched back to the retiring chamber, Benjamin and the cardinal trooping behind us. I wondered what was coming next. Henry sat on the corner of a table, one fat leg swinging.

'I like your wit, Master Shallot,' he said, grinning mischievously at Wolsey. 'I understand you are off to France with Sir Robert Clinton? You are to search out the traitor Raphael and, when you find him, kill him or bring him back for me.'

'Yes, Your Majesty.'

'Look at me, Master Shallot.'

I raised my eyes and stared at that mad, bad face, the fleshy nose, the neatly trimmed gold beard and moustache.

'I hold you responsible, Master Shallot, you and Master Daunbey, for the return of my book from Abbé Gerard. And, one more task . . .'

'Your Majesty?'

The air in the room became positively icy. Henry leaned forward and tweaked my ear playfully. In actual fact the royal bastard's heavy hand sent an arrow of pain down the side of my face.

'Three years ago, Master Shallot, I was in France. I wore a beautiful ring, a love token made of sheer gold. It carried a silver Cupid, the eyes of which were fashioned out of pure diamonds.' The king licked his lips. 'My brother King Francis and I had a wager on a shy damsel at his court. He wagered a necklace of great value so I proffered the ring on who would win her favours first.' Those dry, prim lips pursed in spiteful annoyance. 'My brother Francis won the wager and I handed the ring over. He wears it always, never taking it off, but he said that if I could steal it back without him knowing, then I could keep it. Master Shallot,' he hissed, 'I want that ring back! You, with your skill at hazard, will bring it back to me. You understand?'

'Of course, Your Majesty!'

(Of course I bloody well did! The fat bastard had neatly trapped me. Not only had I to get his damn' book back but regain his ring. If I failed and the French caught me I would hang. If I won and the French caught me I would hang. And, if I failed and returned to England I would hang. I see my chaplain sniggering! The little turd! Mind you, he's right in what he says. When I look back at my golden youth all I can remember is people trying to hang poor old Shallot. For what? For nothing more than being true to himself.)

Henry smiled and dismissed us with a flick of his fingers. I'll be honest, Benjamin and I scuttled out as quickly as two of the cardinal's bloody spiders. We did not speak until we were back in our garret above the gatehouse.

'Master,' I wailed, 'what can I do?'

Benjamin sat on the side of his bed shaking his head. 'You could use your wits,' he replied sharply, 'and keep a close mouth when you are in the presence of princes. Roger, we stand on the edge of darkness. If we are not successful, we will not see England again.'

On that cheerful note he lay down, wrapped himself in a blanket and pretended to fall asleep. I'll be truthful, I sat quivering with terror until dawn. And why not? I had been drawn into the deadly rivalry, both political and personal, which existed between Francis and Henry. They

79

were both arrogant, both lechers, both saw themselves as the answer to all the problems on earth. They took what they wanted and would brook no defiance. The only difference was that Francis did it with more charm. But for me, in that garret at Hampton Court, I felt like a rabbit having to choose between the jaws of the fox and the talons of the eagle.

Late the next morning we left Hampton Court. Benjamin was subdued. He made his farewells to Wolsey and Doctor Agrippa and we joined Clinton's party as they assembled in the great courtyard. The cries of ostlers, grooms, outriders, serjeants and clerks rang out. Horses were saddled, sumpter ponies laden, the marshals of the household imposing order with their white wands of office. I glimpsed Lady Francesca, resplendent in a sea-green dress and cloak and small hat of the same colour, but for the moment, my lust had subsided. All I wanted was to be away from Hampton Court before I further incurred Henry's wrath.

Lord, I was pleased to be free of the place, following the white beaten track first west around London, then south across the downs to Dover. Outriders went first then Sir Robert, Master Benjamin and Lady Clinton. The first two soon became boon companions: they shared a common love of alchemy and an all-absorbing interest in plants and their natural remedies. Often our cavalcade would stop so they could both dismount and study foxgloves, fungi on tree bark, or the different types of mushrooms. Though interested in nature, I was still frightened by the demands of the Great Beast and hung back, watching jealously how the coquettish Lady Francesca seemed to take great interest in Benjamin but remained

impervious to my own presence. Clinton's chief hench-
man, Venner, was an amiable enough fellow but his conversation revolved around bear and cock fighting and the
virtues of one breed of horse over another. There was
not a pretty face in sight so I sulked all the way to Dover.
We paused now and again at some hostelry and, on one
occasion, a Benedictine monastery, I forget its name.
Well, what does it matter? It's only a pile of rubble now
the Great Killer has finished with it.

No, on second thoughts, I wasn't sulking. I thought a
lot about Agnes, her violent death and those of her
family. I was satisfied that the Luciferi had killed her and
I was determined, in my own cowardly way, to exact
revenge once I was in France. Something else nagged at
my mind and gnawed at my soul. An idea whose substance eluded me. Once I was aboard the *Mary of
Westminster* and facing the terrors of the Narrow Seas, I
put the matter aside.

Our cog was a sturdy merchantman escorted by a small
man-of-war. We raised anchor, turned, dipping our sails
three times in honour of the Trinity, and made our way
to the open sea. Two days later, after a peaceful voyage,
we disembarked at Calais – a dreadful place, England's
last foothold in France, nothing more than a glorified
fortress packed with men-at-arms and archers, who staggered the streets in their boiled leather jerkins, drinking
in the many ale houses and generally looking for trouble.

The town was packed with carts and horses for the
Great Killer always kept Calais well fortified. All a waste
of time for his daughter, poor Bloody Mary, lost it to the
French and died of a broken heart. (Oh, by the way, I
was there when she died. I held her hand as the death

81

rattle grew in her scrawny throat. 'Roger,' she whispered. 'My dear, dear Roger. When I die, pluck out my heart and you'll find Calais engraved upon it.' I bowed my head. She thought I was weeping. Nothing of the sort! I was terrified she might see the guilty look in my eyes for I am the man who lost the English Calais. Oh, yes! I was the silly, drunken bastard who left the gate open and let the French in, but that's another story.) We were soon free of Calais and heading south for Paris. The Normandy countryside baked under a warm summer sun. A peaceful journey. Even the scaffold and gibbets at the crossroads were empty; indeed, I even saw two festooned with garlands.

'Strange,' I muttered to Benjamin as we stayed at a tavern on our first night out of Calais.

'What is, Roger?'

'Well,' I answered, glad to have his attention, 'those two messengers who were killed by the Maillotins. It was on the same road we are following now.'

'So?'

'Well, the highway seems clear of thieves and rogues and very well guarded. I have seen at least three troops of cavalry.' I paused and Benjamin just stared blankly back. 'Look, master,' I hurried on, 'I know the Maillotins. They attack in the alleys and runnels of Paris, not plan an ambush in the open countryside.'

Benjamin played with the cup he was drinking from. 'You think it was not the Maillotins who attacked the messengers?'

'Yes.'

'So who did the French hang?'

'God knows!' I snarled, and turned away.

Benjamin patted me on the shoulder. 'Roger, you're out of sorts.'

'Oh, no, not me,' I replied quickly.

'You like Sir Robert?'

'I prefer his wife.'

Benjamin laughed. 'A strange pair,' he mused. 'She's a flirt but he dotes on her. Sir Robert met her when she was a ward of the French court.'

'She seems to like you.'

Benjamin shrugged. 'There's no accounting for taste, Roger.' He smiled, finished his wine, and deftly turned the conversation to other matters.

Just before we entered Paris we left the main road, and, following winding country tracks, approached the Convent of St Felice, its white stone buildings basking in the sunshine amongst soft green fields and small dark copses. A beautiful place, one of those convents which reeked of wealth, security, and its own strange kind of serenity. Everything was clean, precise and in its place. Even the convent yard, just within the great arched gateway, was neatly strewn with white stone pebbles, whilst around the walls small strips of garden full of flowers gave off their own fragrant perfume.

We were left in the guesthouse, drinking chilled white wine, whilst the sisters welcomed Lady Francesca and Sir Robert Clinton in a flurry of joy at seeing their old pupil and protégé. Lady Francesca was treated as a favoured daughter but Sir Robert was idolised, treated with a deference which I found quite surprising. You'd have thought he was some fat cardinal from Rome. The nuns fussed around the Clintons like a group of mother hens. I found it difficult to follow their chatter (you know old

Shallot, nosy as hell and always looking for mischief), but they seemed most concerned about Lady Francesca's health. Anyway, they left us alone.

Lady Clinton went to see old friends whilst Mother Superior, a formidable old bird in her gold-edged habit, took Sir Robert away, her arm linked through his, for quiet chatter in her own private apartment. We stayed for about an hour, then with the sisters' greetings ringing in our ears rejoined our escort outside the walls and continued our journey.

We entered Paris by the Porte St Denis. It was strange to be back there and my memories were not pleasant: starving in the depths of winter, being beaten up, arrested for some misunderstanding and half-hanged at Montfaucon. The scaffold there was the first thing I clapped my eyes on when we entered the stinking streets of Paris. The city fathers had decided to improve the site since I last encountered it. A few corpses swayed in the breeze at the end of a rope but they had built a wall so when the bodies decayed and fell, their sight, if not their stink, was hidden from passersby. We followed the narrow, crooked streets, most of them unpaved and packed with a motley crew of citizens, monks, scholars and a legion of beggars. Stagnant pools of filth made us cover our mouths and noses whilst we kept bobbing our heads to avoid the painted signs which hung outside every house. All the time we were assailed by the noise of a hundred bells and the screams of hawkers and traders who sold everything from a piece of iron to hot chestnuts. We crossed one of the five big bridges built over the Seine and passed under the brooding mass of Notre Dame.

Near the Place des Grèves, or rather the square close

to it, a great crowd had gathered to witness an execution. One of the most horrible sights I had ever seen. A huge vat full of oil was bubbling over a monstrous bonfire and, bound hand and foot inside, stood a criminal being boiled to death. The screams, the smoke and the stench were, perhaps, a prophecy of the horrors which awaited us. Lady Clinton turned pale and would have fainted in the saddle if Benjamin had not caught her, whilst Sir Robert shouted abuse at the outriders, telling them to move on. We left Paris by the Porte D'Orléans and found ourselves back amongst the tilled meadows and windmills which ring the city. The suburbs dwindled and, after an hour's travelling, we turned a bend in the road and there, on the brow of a hill, outlined against a forest, stood the Château de Maubisson, a pleasant sight. It was ringed by a curtain wall protected by a moat spanned by a wooden drawbridge.

We clattered over this into the outer bailey where chickens pecked and pigs rooted for food. The place was busy and alive with noise from the stables, forges and outhouses built against the wall. We rode under another arch, guarded by serjeants-at-arms wearing the royal arms of England; great iron gates were flung open and we passed through these into the inner bailey, stopping before the great four-towered keep which soared up to the skies. Someone had quite recently built a wing on either side of this huge donjon but at each corner of the central building was a tower. Clinton said they were named after four ladies: Yolande, Mary, Isabel and Jeanne.

'From which did Falconer fall?' Benjamin asked.

Clinton pointed to the one on the right nearside. We

all stared up at the great tower which soared six storeys above us.

'So, the castle belongs to the English embassy?' Benjamin asked.

'Yes,' Clinton replied. 'Beyond this tower there is a garden laid out in the French style – some herb banks, a small rabbit warren, and a few hundred bushes of boxwood.' He waved his hand airily. 'Beyond the walls are some vineyards but the weather blights them. Some marshland, then of course the forest.'

He was about to continue when officials of the embassy came down the steps to greet us. There was the usual confusion of grooms taking horses, porters carrying chests, and a sea of faces as haphazard introductions were made. A servant took Benjamin and me off into the main hall, past the great chamber where meals were served, and up a spiral staircase to the third floor above the solar. The chamber given to us was spacious and clean, the walls freshly painted, the wooden floors covered with thick but clean-looking carpets. Two pallet beds had been erected, fresh torch sconces placed in the walls, some stools, a chair, a table and an aumbry, a heavy cupboard for our clothes, provided. Some thick, tallow candles, and jugs and bowls completed the furnishings. The windows were shuttered but one, glazed with horn, afforded a pleasant view of the boxwood garden and a glimpse of the forest-edge.

We spent that afternoon taking our bearings. The château was like many of its kind, stained by war here and there when the English (or the Goddamns, as the French call us) had tried to conquer Northern France, nothing remarkable. We met the officials of the embassy at dinner that same evening.

Now, the hall of the château was a simple affair, a great hearthed fire in the centre with some shields and antlers on the wall for decoration. There was a small gallery at one end which musicians would use and, at the other, against a wooden panelled wall, the dais and high table. Once supper was over and the retainers had withdrawn, the wine jug was passed round and introductions were made. Sir John Dacourt, the ambassador, was squat and florid, with frizzed white hair, light blue eyes, and the most luxuriant curling moustache I have ever clapped eyes on. He was dressed simply in the old-fashioned way with a cote-hardie which fell beneath his knees. He was a soldier of the old school who believed the only good Frenchman was a dead one.

'I don't trust the damn' Frogs!' he boomed. 'Turn your back and the bastards will have you!'

Walter Peckle, the chief clerk, was a young man grown old before his time, with a complexion sallow and unhealthy, sunken cheeks, and eyes which never stopped blinking. His fingers were stained with blue-green ink and he constantly kept scratching what was left of his wispy, greasy, grey hair. Thomas Throgmorton, the physician, was thin as a pikestaff. Of indeterminate age, he had moist grey eyes set in a pale, thin face. His close-cropped hair was hidden under a black velvet skull cap. Michael Millet, Sir John Dacourt's secretarius, was strikingly good-looking. A young man with thick, blond hair which rose in waves from his forehead, and blue liquid eyes. Many a woman would have paid a fortune to have had his eyelashes, thick, long and curling. He was a proper fop: his roses and cream complexion was clean-shaven and a silver pearl dangled from a small gold chain in his right ear lobe. He sat like a woman and talked like one, sending coy glances at all of us. Waldegrave, the chaplain, was small, fat and balding, with the coarsened features and bright red nose of an inveterate drinker. By the time the meal was finished we were all in our cups but Waldegrave had staggered to the meal as drunk as any bishop. He sat next to me and I wrinkled my nose at the sweaty odour emanating from the long, black, food-stained gown he wore.

At first our after-dinner conversation was on general matters but when Lady Francesca withdrew, throwing Benjamin a smile which cut me to the heart, Clinton soon brought matters to order.

'Falconer's death,' he announced as soon as Lady Francesca's high-heeled step faded from the hall, 'was it an accident, suicide or murder?' His words cast a pool of silence. The warmth and cheer evaporated like mist before the sun. We all became aware how dark it was, the torches flickering and the shadows dancing against the bleak, white walls. At the centre of the table, Dacourt looked around.

'If it was suicide,' he trumpeted, 'it's a damn' strange way to go. If it was an accident, then it can't be explained. Check the tower yourself, Sir Robert, you know it well. The wall is crenellated but there are iron bars between the gaps. Falconer would have had to be standing on the very rim to slip and fall to his death. Why should a man do that?'

'Which leaves murder,' my master intervened smoothly.

'Impossible!' Throgmorton, the physician, spoke up.

Benjamin leaned forward and looked down the table at him.

'How, sir! Why do you say that?'

'Oh, our physician knows everything,' Millet quipped tartly. 'He's fond of snooping, especially through the half-open doors of any woman's bedchamber.'

The remark provoked faint laughter and Throgmorton flushed with embarrassment. (Well, as I say, never trust a doctor. It's surprising how many of them love to see a pretty wench stripped down to her shift.) Benjamin, however, refused to be diverted.

'Master Physician, I asked you a question.'

Throgmorton glared once more at Millet, composed himself and ticked the points off on his fingers. 'First, Falconer had the chamber you have now.'

Oh, thank you very much, I thought.

'I have a chamber on the floor above. I saw Falconer go up to the top of the tower. He seemed cheerful enough, with a cup of wine in his hand. I bade him good evening and he smiled back. No one else went up the stairs after him and certainly no one went before.'

'Are there other witnesses?' Benjamin asked.

'Do you doubt my word?' Throgmorton bellowed.

'Tush, Tom!' Millet spoke up, slouching against the table and admiring the cheap, tawdry rings on his fingers. 'I, too, heard Falconer go up.' Millet smiled dazzlingly at Benjamin. 'My humble abode is a garret at the top of this benighted tower.'

Benjamin grinned. 'And you would confirm what the good physician has said?'

'Of course!'

'There's one other matter,' Dacourt boomed, refilling

his goblet. 'The top of the tower is covered with a fine coat of sand and gravel. Millet and I were the first to check that tower, after Falconer's body was discovered by a guard. It bore only the mark of Falconer's boots.'

'And the body?' Benjamin asked.

Throgmorton slurped from his goblet. 'The head was smashed open and the face badly bruised. The neck was so twisted you could lay the chin on either shoulder. Of course, there was bruising throughout his whole body.'

'And the wine he drank?'

'Good claret,' Dacourt boomed. 'Old Falconer liked his tipple. On Easter Monday, as the season of Lent finished and we need no longer abstain from wine, we opened a new bottle. Millet and I were present. We each had a cup before we left.'

'It's a custom here,' Millet added. 'During Lent, we all, as good sons of the Church, abstain from wine. On Easter Monday, we broach the best Bordeaux.'

'So there was nothing strange?' Benjamin asked.

Dacourt looked at me under lowered brows as if recognising my existence for the first time. 'No. Falconer was quiet and secretive but seemed in very good humour, laughing and talking rather garrulously. I did wonder if he had been in his cups before we opened the wine but he assured me he had not.'

'I scrutinised the corpse most carefully,' Throgmorton intervened. 'There was no real smell of ale or wine fumes nor of any other substance.'

'And the cup he drank from?' Benjamin asked, turning his chair slightly to look down the table at Dacourt.

'A pity,' the ambassador replied. 'Smashed to pieces.'

'Why do you say it's a pity?'

'Well, it was one of a set, wondrously carved from pewter. Falconer had four; people call them liturgical cups. You know, each cup bears a picture of one of the Church's four great feasts: Advent, Christmas, Easter and Pentecost.'

'And he was drinking from the Easter one?' I asked.

'Yes,' Dacourt replied. 'But now it's smashed to pieces.'

'Falconer was a very religious man,' Waldegrave slurred. 'Always talking about God. He was affected by the writings of that new teacher in Germany. You know, the monk who has jumped over his monastery wall, Martin Luther.'

(Oh, by the way, I once met Luther and his wife Katherine. He was strange! Brilliant, but still strange. Do you know, he was constipated? Oh, yes, there was nothing wrong with old Luther that a good bowel purge wouldn't have cured.)

'Did he discuss Luther?' Benjamin asked.

'No, not really,' Waldegrave slobbered. 'He was always talking about being saved. About whether he would go to heaven or hell. And if he wasn't talking about the after life, he was talking about birds.'

'Birds? What do you mean?' I asked.

Waldegrave leaned forward and stared blearily at me. 'I mean what I say. He was always watching bloody birds. Be it a duck, a sparrow, a linnet or a thrush. Mind you,' he tapped the side of his fleshy red nose, 'there were other matters.'

The rest of the company groaned in unison at having to listen to a well-known story.

'You see,' Waldegrave squirmed on his fat bottom, 'he came for confession to me. He said he thought he knew who Raphael was. When I asked him what he meant, all he replied was, "It is a grave matter".'

There were further moans and groans at the old toper's repetition of an apparently well-worn story.

'It's time for bed,' Dacourt snapped. 'Sir Robert, you must be tired.' He smiled. 'And the Lady Francesca waits. As for you, Sir Priest,' Dacourt glared at Waldegrave, 'I think you have drunk enough!'

The chaplain just stared back, open-mouthed, and belched like a thunder clap. Dacourt took a step nearer. The priest staggered to his feet and waddled off with an air of drunken disdain.

Dacourt watched him go. 'Bloody priest!' he muttered. 'Him and his jokes.'

'Lord save us!' Millet said languidly. 'If it's not his jokes, he is constantly relating how he fought as a moss trooper on the northern march.' Millet played with a lace cuff. 'The old drunk thinks he knows about horses, and is always trying to get to Sir John's destrier. Have you seen it?' The young man beamed at Benjamin, who shook his head. 'A beautiful horse. Pure air, fierce spirit, with the light tread of a dancer.'

Benjamin looked away and examined his finger nails.

'Sir John, where's Falconer buried?'

'At St Pierre,' Throgmorton the doctor interrupted. 'We couldn't send him back to England. He had no family and the body was a bloody pulp, so we bought a plot in the cemetery of St Pierre in the village of Maubisson.'

'The same church where Abbé Gerard was priest?'

'That's right,' Dacourt boomed. 'Though Abbé Gerard

is no longer with us. He went for a swim in his own carp pond and drowned.'

'Strange,' Clinton mused. He leaned forward in his chair. So far he had been quiet, staring into the darkness, though keeping a careful eye on Sir John.

'What is?' Benjamin asked.

'Well,' Sir Robert also stood up, stretching himself carefully, 'on the Monday after Easter, Falconer dies from a mysterious fall from a tower. Two days later an old priest drowns in his own fish pond.'

'Are you saying there's a connection?' Peckle spoke up.

'No.' Sir Robert just shook his head. 'I just think it's strange.'

Sir John Dacourt gathered his cloak and made to leave.

'One last question?' Benjamin pleaded. 'Falconer's possessions, where are they?'

'His moveables are kept in the vaults below the hall here. What documents he had were handed over to Peckle.'

'You kept them well?' Clinton asked.

'Of course,' Dacourt snapped back.

Oh, dear, I thought, not much love lost here!

'You've seen them already, Sir Robert. Was there anything amiss?'

'No, no, certainly not!' Sir Robert smiled falsely. 'But, as you say, Sir John, the hour is late and it's time for bed.'

Clinton put his goblet down on the table, bade us good night and walked softly away. Dacourt and Millet followed. Benjamin, however, sat staring down the hall. He shivered and pulled his cloak closer about him.

'Master?'

'Yes, Roger, I know, it's time to sleep. Perchance to dream.'

(Oh, by the way, I always remembered that line and later gave it to Will Shakespeare. You will find it in his play *Hamlet* which I helped to finance. It's about a Danish prince who finds out his mother is a murderess and spends his time lolling around, mooning about it. I am not too fond of it but go and judge for yourself. Old Will Shakespeare was forever asking about the murders I'd investigated. Strange, I never told him about the horrors of Maubisson.)

We wandered up the darkened staircase back to our chamber. I lit the candles and stared around curiously. From here, I thought, Falconer had left for his dreadful fall through the night. Benjamin went over to the open window, staring across at the darkened mass of the forest. He shivered at the 'yip, yip' of a fox carried by the cool night wind and jumped at the screech of the huge bats which flickered up and down the castle walls.

'This,' he murmured, 'is truly the valley of death.'

He sat on the edge of the bed and stared up at me.

'You should sleep, Roger. You are going to need your rest. We are in the company of a great assassin. Mark my words: Falconer and the Abbé Gerard were murdered, and things here are not as they appear to be.' He refused to be drawn any further.

I was young, tired, slightly drunk, and didn't give a rat's codpiece so I undressed and, within a few minutes, was lost in the sleep of the just.

Chapter 5

We rose late the next morning. Benjamin appeared to be in better humour and chattered about the history of the château as we broke our fast in the great hall. Afterwards, one of the servants led us down to a vaulted cellar.

'We must examine Falconer's possessions,' Benjamin explained. 'Perhaps the first key to this puzzle will be there.'

Venner was already in the cellar, standing over some coffers and trunks. He grinned in welcome.

'These are Falconer's goods,' he explained. 'But there's nothing much. We have been through them. You have just missed Sir Robert.'

'What will happen to them now?' I asked, my eyes on a cheap silver bracelet.

'Well, Falconer had no heirs so they go to the king.'

I decided to leave the silver bracelet where it was; Fat Harry would skin you alive for taking a crumb of bread from his plate. Venner wandered off and we went through the pathetic pile of possessions: a counter-pane, three dirty bolsters, hose, jerkins, battered boots, more cheap jewellery, a collection of quills and a bar of Castilian soap. As far as I was concerned, the Great Killer was welcome to them. What attracted our attention was the box of pewter cups, each of the three remaining in their small, red-baized compartment. We examined these carefully, especially the deep bowls ornately carved with the appropriate scene: a large dove for Pentecost, the Virgin Mary on the Advent cup, and a child in a manger for Christmas. (You know the sort, they were quite common in England before the Great Killer smashed the monasteries. You drank from each goblet according to the season.) Benjamin sniffed each cup, then the box. 'Nothing,' he exclaimed. 'There's nothing here.'

We went out to take the air in the inner bailey and stood fascinated as four ostlers struggled with the ropes tied to the bridle of a splendid, black war horse. They were trying to back it into a stable but the magnificent beast was all set to charge. The horse stood sixteen hands high, its jet black coat gleaming in the sunlight. Its ears were back in anger, its eyes rolled, and the horse curled its lips, revealing the foam on sharp, yellow teeth. Every so often the animal would rear, lashing out with his sharpened hooves, as the men struggled with a stream of oaths to back it into the stable. Eventually they succeeded, quickly securing both the bottom door and the top flap and, even then, we could hear the horse pounding the thick oaken panels. The ostlers, covered in sweat, walked away, still muttering curses.

'That must be Vulcan, Sir John Dacourt's destrier,' Benjamin remarked. 'Waldegrave must be mad if he thinks he can control such a beast.' He stared across at the wing built to the right of the château. 'I wonder if we should visit the priest? Perhaps he can explain Falconer's macabre joke about graves?' Benjamin grasped me by the arm. 'On second thoughts, let us finish the business in hand.'

We went back, past the hall down a long, stone passage-way to Peckle's chamber. The chief clerk was working there, surrounded by a veritable sea of paper; memor-anda, notes, bills, letters and indentures. He sat with his back to the door, crouched over his desk. The room smelt stale and musty with the pungent odour of the fat tallow candles placed on the desk. All the windows were shut-tered as if we were in the depths of winter. Peckle hardly moved but continued to peer at a document covered in strange cipher markings.

'Good morning, Walter,' Benjamin said, a little too loudly.

The clerk looked round testily. 'Can I help?'

'Well, yes. Do you have Falconer's documents?'

The fellow, sighing dramatically, rose wearily from his chair like an exasperated parent dealing with two naughty children. He dug amongst some papers in the corner and tossed us a canvas bag tied at the top. Benjamin turned and made to leave.

'No! No!' Peckle announced pompously. 'You cannot take them away. You must study them here.'

Benjamin stuck his tongue out at Peckle's back, cleared a space on the floor and squatted there for at least half an hour sifting through the contents of the sack. There wasn't much; a few drawings of birds, quite well done but not of the calibre of the great da Vinci's notebook. (I met the great sculptor once, you know, when I was hiding from the Doge of Venice's assassins. But that's another story.) One strange discovery we did make – scraps of paper bearing the word Raphael. Falconer had apparently been playing with the letters of the name, breaking them up, distancing each from the other. Benjamin studied these carefully, shook his head and tossed them back. We thanked Peckle but he never stirred a hair.

'What do you think, master?' I asked as soon as we were out of the chamber.

'Falconer was murdered.'

'But how? He was alone on the tower and he wasn't drunk.'

Benjamin chewed his lip. 'Falconer was a man who liked birds,' he replied slowly. 'So he goes to the top of the tower to study them.'

'Do you think he discovered who Raphael was?'

'I don't think so but he did believe the word Raphael contained the name of the traitor.'

Benjamin wandered off, saying he wished to speak to Waldegrave, so I decided to take the air in the garden behind the château. I was even more eager when I glimpsed Lady Francesca, magnificent in her dark green velvet dress, with a small hat of the same texture and colour, ornamented with trailing peacock feathers set rakishly on her head. I strolled amongst the box-wood as if I was the keenest of gardeners, taking special interest in the herb banks, the ever-green boxwood, and the multi-coloured flowers where hungry bees searched for honey. The lady was humming a madrigal. She turned quickly at the sound of my footsteps on the gravel.

'Monsieur!' she exclaimed in mock surprise. 'You follow me!'

'To the ends of the earth, Madame,' I replied, fascinated by the sudden rise and fall of her ample bosom. She stepped closer, raising the hem of her dress to reveal thick, white petticoats above black, polished boots. She peered closer.

'You are Shallot, Master Benjamin's manservant?'

'His secretarius, Madame,' I replied more smugly than I intended.

'La, la, secretarius, and an ugly one at that!'

Well, I blushed and stammered.

'Well, well, Master Secretarius,' she continued, 'how can I help you?'

'You are pleased to be back in France, Madame?'

'After two years married to an Englishman, I am more than happy.'

'But you returned only a few weeks ago, during Holy Week?'

Lady Francesca stared at the flowers as if already bored by the conversation. Suddenly she jerked, clutching her stomach as if in pain.

'Madame,' I seized her wrist, 'you are ill?'

Francesca lifted her pale face, no mockery or laughter in those staring dark eyes now.

'Take your hands off me!' she rasped. 'Never, do you understand, *never* touch me!'

She swept by me, leaving old Shallot with the fragrance of her perfume and a deeper knowledge of my true status. I wandered back to the main entrance of the château and found Benjamin, equally disconsolate, sitting on the steps.

'The Lady Francesca seemed upset,' he remarked casually.

I spat into the dust at his feet. 'By the time I'm finished, master, her agitation will be deeper and my hurt will be gone.'

Benjamin rose and, slipping his arm through mine, led me back to the garden, teasing me into a good mood as he explained how he had found Waldegrave drunk as a lord and insensible as a rock in a corner of his opulent chapel. We spent the rest of the day enjoying the strong sunshine. Benjamin seemed fascinated by the edge of the forest, saying he was sure he had glimpsed figures slipping in and out of the trees.

'The château is being watched,' he remarked. 'Perhaps, Roger, we are about to meet our friends, the Luciferi.'

That damn' word brought me back to the harsh reality of my situation: not just the discovery of a traitor or bringing a murderer to book but vengeance for Agnes and, of course, the Herculean task which the Great Killer had assigned me!

We kept to ourselves for the rest of the day, taking food from the buttery and retiring early for we were both still exhausted after our journey from England. As darkness fell, the weather changed. Thick, black rain clouds massed in the sky and, as I fell asleep, rattling raindrops pattered against the wooden shutters. That sleep proved to be the beginning of our troubles.

We were awoken early in the night, a few hours before dawn, by sharp screams, shouted orders, and the sound of running feet. We threw blankets around us and hurried down to the inner bailey, now filling with servants and retainers who splashed amongst the puddles carrying torches. Clinton was there wrapped in a military cloak and Dacourt, looking rather ridiculous in a long night gown, stood near Vulcan's stable. Both the top and bottom doors were flung back and the great war horse had apparently galloped away pursued by grooms. Peckle, Throgmorton and others joined us, though I was surprised to see Millet, the effeminate clerk, dressed as if returning from a visit to the city. We pushed our way into the stable and glimpsed what appeared to be a blood-soaked pile of rags, the gore and slime gleaming in the flickering torch light. Throgmorton was leaning over it, his face turning a greenish-white hue.

'Bring another torch!' Benjamin ordered.

A sleepy-eyed groom pushed one into his hand and swiftly backed away. Benjamin knelt down, bringing the torch closer, and I had to put my hand to my mouth to prevent myself retching. Waldegrave lay there, his body a bloody pulp. His skull had been kicked in and the dark blood seeped out, mingling with the grey sludge of his brains. One eye had popped out from its socket, his chest was a bloody black hole, whilst the lower half of his face had been completely kicked away, revealing stumps of yellow teeth.

'In God's name, what happened?' Benjamin whispered.

'The fool tried to get to the horse. He was always up to these tricks. Only this time Vulcan was too quick and powerful.'

Benjamin stared at the physician. 'He'd tried this before?'

'Yes. As Sir John described the other evening. The old toper still thought he was a horseman.'

'But this is the first time Vulcan attacked him?'

'Yes.' Throgmorton rose, the hem of his cloak over his mouth and nose. 'Sometimes he would try it in the evening but never during the dead of night.'

Benjamin, impervious to the scene, leaned closer and sniffed at what used to be Waldegrave's mouth. Even from where I stood I could smell the strong, stale wine fumes which permeated the stench of the ripped body.

'What actually happened?' I asked Millet, noting how the young man was very much the worse for drink.

The fop shook his head and went outside. He leaned against the stable, sucking in the cool night air like a man surfacing from a deep river.

'Everyone in the château was asleep,' I observed. 'Apart from you?'

The fellow grimaced. 'Yes, apart from me. I had business in the city. Anyway, I returned late. I stabled my own horse and was in the buttery when I heard screams, the crashing of hooves and Vulcan's neighs. I ran back here. Grooms and ostlers were already in the yard. The top half of the stable door was open but Waldegrave had apparently closed the bottom behind him. A groom opened it. The horse shot out like an arrow from a bow.' Millet nodded towards the general direction of the garden.

'I understand he's been cornered there and his attendant is trying to calm him. I came over,' he continued, 'and saw what you have now.' He wiped his mouth with the back of his hand. 'I vomited twice,' he remarked, 'and I think I am going to do so again.'

Hand to mouth, slightly stooping, he hurried away into the darkness. I grinned contemptuously at his retreating back, looked once more at the stable, saw an eyeball glistening on the wet straw and promptly vomited myself. I looked around; Clinton, Dacourt and others now stood near the main steps of the château, Throgmorton with them.

'Master!' I hissed, closing my eyes and leaning against the lintel of the stable. 'What are you doing?'

Benjamin came out, rubbing the side of his face. 'There's nothing we can do, Sir John,' he called across to Dacourt. 'The poor man's body should be removed.'

The ambassador rapped out an order and four servants, their faces masked by cloths soaked in vinegar, hurried across with a linen sheet.

'Take it to the infirmary!' Dacourt ordered.

Benjamin and I watched as Waldegrave's corpse was hoisted on to the sheet.

'One minute!' Benjamin called out.

The servants glared angrily, eager to get the grisly business over and done with. Benjamin seized his torch, brought the flame as near as he could and examined not the wounds, but rather the dead priest's shabby, blood-stained tunic.

'Most interesting,' he murmured. 'Yes, very interest-ing.' He smiled at the servants. 'You may take him away. Come, Roger! The night is not over and we need our sleep.'

Clinton, Throgmorton and the rest tried to draw Benja-min into conversation as we went up the main steps of the château.

'The man was as mad as a Maypole!' Dacourt bellowed. 'A senseless, stupid, drunken act!'

'Waldegrave was undoubtedly drunk,' Benjamin replied. 'He may have been a fool, but I don't think that was an accident.'

'What do you mean?' Peckle jibed.

'I will explain in the morning,' Benjamin answered. 'Sir John, Sir Robert, I bid you good night.'

We returned to our chamber. My queasy stomach had settled and I was agog with curiosity. (I see the chaplain smirking again, probably because I vomited. I'd like to remind him that's nothing to the idiot he made of himself on All Fools Day last when he found the dead stoat I'd placed in the pulpit. Retched like a waterfall he did!) However, Master Benjamin was not in a talkative mood.

'Tomorrow, Roger,' he promised. 'But now I need some sleep.'

I lay for a while waiting for the château to fall silent again before drifting into a demon-filled sleep of black war horses rearing above me, men flying through the night air, and those dreadful corpses laid out so tidily, so neatly, in that beautiful London garden.

We woke early the next morning. Benjamin's stomach seemed to have caught up with his memories for he now looked white-faced and confessed he felt queasy.

'The stupid bastard,' I murmured.

Benjamin shook his head and finished dressing. 'Don't speak ill of the dead, Roger. Waldegrave was murdered. Come, I must see the corpse once more.'

We went down to the white-washed infirmary where I made Benjamin stop at the kitchen for rags soaked in vinegar and herbs. We certainly needed them. The dead priest's body still sprawled beneath his sheet in that small white room. The stomach had begun to swell and the chamber stank with the evil gases which emanated from it. I could take no more but stood by the door whilst once more Benjamin peered at the blood-stained clothing.

'Yes, yes,' he muttered to himself. 'Yes, of course, that's how it was done!'

We left the infirmary, standing for a few minutes outside, drinking in the sweet morning air. Benjamin called a young boy over.

'Listen, lad,' he ordered. 'My compliments to Sir John but tell him Master Daunbey would appreciate his presence here in the courtyard.'

The boy stared blankly back. Benjamin laughed.

'Of course.' He sighed and translated the request into French.

Dacourt joined us a few minutes later, his white moustache bristling with importance, his face a little more puce. I could smell the fresh wine on his breath.

'Sir John, I have a favour to ask.'

'What is it, sir?'

'Would you have the castle searched, particularly the rubbish tips outside the kitchen, for the corpse of a chicken or a pig, some animal slaughtered for no apparent reason?'

Dacourt's eyes looked bulbous.

'Please, Sir John!' Benjamin insisted. 'I have good reason for my request.'

Dacourt shrugged and bawled orders at a servant. He followed Benjamin over to Vulcan's stable.

'The war horse is not there,' the ambassador remarked defensively. 'I have moved it to a small paddock beyond the castle walls.' He kicked the loose cobbles of the yard. 'Some people say he should be destroyed.'

'Why?' Benjamin asked. 'The horse did no wrong.'

'But he killed Waldegrave.'

Benjamin patted the ambassador gently on the

shoulder. 'No, Sir John, he did not, as I will explain in a while. Now, I wish to discover something for myself.'

He went into the stable, closing the bottom part of the door behind him. To do this he had to lean over and push the bolt firmly into place. He then closed the top part and, for a few minutes, remained hidden in the stables.

'What's the madman trying to do?' Dacourt mumbled.

Benjamin threw open the top part of the stable door and grinned maliciously. 'Sir John, you would say I was tall?'

'Yes, of greater stature than most men.'

'Whilst Waldegrave was rather small?'

'Yes.'

'And to close this door, even I, with my considerable height, face difficulties?'

'Yes, yes,' Dacourt muttered. 'I always have to stand on the bottom panel. Why do you ask?'

Benjamin drew back the bolt and came out of the stable.

'I'll tell you why, Sir John, but first I need to break my fast. I should be most grateful if you would discover the results of your search and-gather the rest of our colleagues in the great hall.'

Dacourt threw him an angry glance but, slightly mollified by Benjamin's assertion that Vulcan did not bear the guilt for Waldegrave's death, nodded and stumped off.

We were sitting in the hall finishing off our meal of light ale, freshly baked bread and strips of salted pork, when the others drifted down to join us.

'What's this all about?' Peckle moaned. 'I have work to do. Waldegrave's possessions must be accounted and assessed.'

Millet yawned and slouched against the table. Throgmorton glared angrily at Benjamin as if he recognised a rival. Venner grinned amiably around whilst Clinton, as cool as ever, drummed his fingers soundlessly on the table top. At last Dacourt stormed in.

'You're right!' he bellowed at Benjamin. 'You're damned well right!'

'What's he so right about?' Peckle observed testily.

'One of the servants found a young piglet, throat slashed from ear to ear, on a heap of refuse at the back of the kitchen. The cook didn't order it to be killed and no one will take responsibility for it.'

'How long has it been dead?' Benjamin asked.

'I don't bloody well know!' Dacourt coughed, slumping down in his chair in the centre of the table. 'Sometime yesterday, perhaps. The rats had been at it, the body is already half-gnawed.'

'What is this?' Millet yawned languidly. 'Surely, Sir John, we are not here to discuss the mysterious death of a piglet?'

He smiled appreciatively at the murmur of laughter he'd provoked. Benjamin rapped the top of the table.

'No, we are not here to discuss the death of a pig but the murder of a priest, Richard Waldegrave!'

'Murder!' Throgmorton was the first to react. 'Murder!' he repeated. 'The drunken idiot wandered into Vulcan's stable and got what he deserved. Everyone knows Vulcan is a horse trained for war.'

'But why should he come down in the dead of night?' Millet jibed. 'After all, this is not some lady's chamber, is it, Master Throgmorton?'

'Oh, shut up!' the physician snapped. 'It's obvious this sottish priest tried his luck once too often.'

107

'I agree,' my master replied. 'But, Sir John, has Vulcan ever attacked anyone else?'

Dacourt watched Benjamin attentively, his eyes now not so bulbous but cunning and shrewd. Sir John, I thought, was one of those men who like to play the role of the bluff, hale soldier. He was not Henry VIII's ambassador to France for nothing.

'No,' he replied carefully. 'Old Vulcan is fiery, he can rear, bite and lash out, but pound a man to death? No. Continue, Master Benjamin.'

Benjamin rose. 'Let's play out the little drama again,' he said and, without waiting for a reply, led the group out of the hall into the sunlit courtyard. Benjamin went across to the stable door.

'Look,' he said. 'There are bolts on the outside, top and bottom. Waldegrave opens the top.' Benjamin slid the bolt back. 'And then the bottom.' Again he repeated the action. 'Waldegrave, a short man, goes into the stable. What did he do next?'

'Apparently,' Millet answered, 'closed the bottom half of the door after him.'

'Like this.' Benjamin leaned over the door and pushed the bolt home. 'Now.' He spoke over the door to us. 'Waldegrave was drunk, he stank of wine fumes. He was also a man of short stature; he would have to climb on the beam at the front of the door to push the bolt home. Yes?'

A chorus of assent greeted his question.

'So,' Benjamin continued, 'I am stone sober, taller than Waldegrave, and I find it difficult. It must have been hard for a short, drunken man to do at the dead of night.'

'But he did!' Throgmorton taunted. 'The stable door was found bolted.'

108

Benjamin smiled, opened the stable door and joined us in the yard.

'My good doctor, I agree. But let us say you are correct and Waldegrave is standing in the stable. Vulcan rears, he is out of control. What should Waldegrave have done then?'

'Try to get out?'

'But he didn't. Strange,' Benjamin mused, 'this drunk who can so cleverly bolt the door after him, now finds it impossible to repeat the action to escape from an angry war horse.'

'Perhaps he tried to,' Clinton remarked, scratching the side of his face with a heavy, beringed hand, 'but was struck down by Vulcan.'

'I would like to believe that, Sir Robert. But examine the corpse. All of Waldegrave's injuries are to his face and the front of his body.'

Now the group were attentive. Benjamin spread his hands.

'You see, I don't think Waldegrave would have locked the door behind him. He was drunk. He was of short stature. Gentlemen, we have all drunk too much at times and seen others in their cups. They are careless, they knock over tables and chairs, they leave doors open. But Waldegrave was so precise. He could get into a stable but was unable to get out.'

I just stood admiring my master's sharp wit. Of course, I had reached the same conclusions but he was always better at presenting the facts. He had a way with words, my master. He should have met Shakespeare and Burbage. They would have cast him in many a role in one of their plays. Perhaps Lear, Brutus or Mark Antony. Benjamin was a great orator. In that courtyard of the dreadful castle of Maubisson, he had the rapt attention of those arrogant men.

'Now,' my master continued briskly, 'even if Waldegrave had bolted the door behind him and, let us say, he fell in a dead faint or drunken stupor, Sir John, can you explain why Vulcan would pound his body so mercilessly?'

The ambassador stroked his chin. 'No, I cannot,' he replied. 'Vulcan is trained only to lash out at someone who threatens him.'

'Not a fat, drunken cleric?'

'Come, come!' Peckle snarled. 'Master Benjamin, tell us your conclusion.'

'Sir John, would the smell of blood drive Vulcan to a fury?'

'Of course. It would remind him of battle, of danger.'

Benjamin pointed towards the infirmary. 'Last night I examined Waldegrave's clothing. It was covered in blood and gore which was fresh. However, his tunic was also stained with dried blood.' He paused. 'So, Master Peckle, I will tell you my conclusions. Last night, Waldegrave drank himself into a stupor. Someone had earlier gutted a young pig, and drained off the blood. They went to Waldegrave's chamber and smeared it all over the tunic of our comatose priest. Our murderer then dragged the body silently across the yard, opened the door to Vulcan's stable, placed the sleeping priest on the straw, locked the stable door behind him and slipped quietly away. Vulcan, agitated by dark shapes in the night and inflamed by the stench of blood, was driven to fury. He pounded this strange, blood-stained visitor to his stable, now lying on his back in the straw beneath him. The fury of the attack,

110

at least for a few seconds, drew Waldegrave from his drunken stupor. He screamed, perhaps struggled, but Vulcan lashed out once more with a sharpened hoof, shattering poor Waldegrave's head.' Benjamin folded his arms. 'Sir John, Sir Robert, Waldegrave was barbarously murdered.'

A babble of protest broke out but no one could deny the logic of my master's conclusions. He stilled the clamour with a wave of his hands.

'I should demand that everyone should account for their movements but,' he smiled thinly, 'in the main we all sleep alone and I have no authority to ask.' He clapped me on the shoulder. 'Even my good friend Shallot could not swear that I did not slip out of my chamber to commit this dreadful act.'

The rest of the group just stared wordlessly back. Benjamin shrugged.

'Sir John, I would be grateful for the loan of a groom who will show us the way to Abbé Gerard's Church of St Pierre in Maubisson village.'

Dacourt, lost in his own reverie, nodded and within the hour our horses were saddled and we followed the groom out of the château. Benjamin stopped for a while, staring across at the forest edge.

'We are being watched,' he repeated. 'All the time, we are being watched.'

'The Luciferi, master?'

Benjamin pulled a wry mouth. 'Perhaps, but the danger we face from them is nothing compared to what we face in the château. There is a murderer loose. Waldegrave was killed because of what he knew, something about that pathetic joke.' My master patted his horse absent-mindedly. 'Or was it that?' he continued as if speaking to himself. 'Or because I was the first to show any interest? We shall see. We shall see, eh, Roger?'

Chapter 6

I smiled to hide my own fears. I'll be honest, they weren't caused just by the Luciferi and some maniac loose in the château but by the Great Killer at Hampton Court and his desire to get that bloody ring back. I wanted to broach the matter with my master but he was lost in his own thoughts so I kept my fears hidden as we rode along the lee of the hill.

We wound our way past open fields into shady woods until we entered the neck of a small valley. Nestling at the bottom, on the banks of a sluggish stream, stood Maubisson village: a collection of wattle and daub huts with thatched roofs, two or three of stone and slate, each with its own fenced garden. On the far side of the village was a small water mill, probably used for grinding corn. In the centre of the village green stood a black-spired church, nothing more than a tower and nave hastily thrown together, the type you can see in any village in England or France. It was ringed by its own walls, a cemetery to one side, the priest's house to the other. Even from where we looked you could glimpse the glint of the huge carp pond where Abbé Gerard had drowned.

We rode slowly down the beaten track. Women in thick, serge dresses and wooden clogs gathered at the

113

doors of their houses and watched us pass whilst half-naked children ran behind us, screaming in their patois for a sou or something to eat. A few old men dozed on benches. Around them scrawny-necked chickens pecked at the dust, jostling with thin-flanked pigs for something to eat. We reached the church and rode through the lych gate. Benjamin thanked the groom and told him to return to the château. We tied our horses to a small rail and knocked on the priest's house door.

A young, thin-faced man with brown hair, a sharp needle nose and watery eyes answered. His skin was rather yellow as if he had bile problems or a stone in his kidneys. He was friendly enough, thankfully a Norman born, so Benjamin could converse easily with him whilst I could follow the general gist of their conversation.

'I am the Curé Ricard,' he murmured. 'You are . . . ?'

(I was sure he was going to say 'Goddamn'.)

'English, from the Château of Maubisson.'

'Come in. Come in.'

The curé ushered us in. He lived as poorly as his peasant parishioners. The room was simple. There were a few sticks of furniture and the floor was beaten earth, rather cold despite the summer. A fire burnt in the hearth. Next to it squatted a young girl about fifteen or sixteen years old. Her hair was thick and coarse, her face raw and peeling from work in the sun. She hardly looked up as we entered but continued to stir the huge, black pot which hung above the flames, now and again throwing in a scattering of herbs and the occasional piece of raw, fatty meat.

'My housekeeper,' Ricard shamefully announced.

(Aye, I thought, and I wager she does more than just

114

work in the kitchen, but who am I to judge the poor man's morals? Look at my chaplain! From what I gather he spends more time in the hay loft with young Mabel from the village than he does in his church. Ah, see, he squirms! He thinks I am old and senile. I tell you this, not even the bloody sparrows land on my lawns without my permission.) Anyway, back to the poor priest. At least he did an honest day's work. He told us to sit down and served us vinegar-tasting wine. When he wasn't looking I poured mine on to the floor.

'Monsieur le Curé,' Benjamin began, 'you came here after the Abbé Gerard died?'

'No, Monsieur, I served with him. But the bishop has yet to make up his mind about a successor.'

'So you were here the night he died?'

'Yes and no. On that Wednesday after Easter I was absent from the church. The abbé had allowed me to visit friends. He stayed and cooked his own dinner.' The curé spread his hands. 'Some scraps of beef, he opened a small jar of wine. The abbé liked his claret and he had been fasting during Lent.'

He must have seen the look in my eyes.

'No more than two cups, certainly not enough to make him drunk. Just before dusk one of the villagers, walking through the church grounds, saw the abbé in the garden looking down at the carp pond. I returned after dark.' He looked sideways at the girl stirring the pot. 'Simone and I returned. Abbé Gerard was not to be seen. I went down to the garden. It was a beautiful evening. I thought he might still have been there.' The curé's eyes filled with tears. 'He was floating face down in the carp pond!'

'And there was no mark or sign of violence?'

'No, Monsieur.'

'And the cup and jar of wine?'

'They were found with him in the pond.'

'Ask him where the wine came from,' I demanded.

Benjamin translated my question. The curé shrugged.

'God knows. The abbé may have bought it. But don't forget, Monsieur, it was Easter. Our parishioners, even the people of Maubisson, send us gifts. Fruit, flowers, wine and sweetmeats.'

'Why would the abbé stare at the carp pond?'

The curé laughed abruptly. 'Monsieur, everyone stands by the edge of the water and stares at the fish, that's why we have such ponds. It's a bit like asking why someone looks at the sky or watches the sunset.'

Benjamin smiled. 'A fair point, Monsieur. Can we see this carp pond?'

Ricard led us out into the garden. Really, it was a small orchard, with some apple and pear trees and untended grass. Here and there was the occasional flower bed; the lilies and other wild flowers struggling to thrive amongst the brambles and weeds. In the middle of the garden was a large, deep carp pond. It must have been about two yards deep and three yards across. It was man-made, I glimpsed the grey bricks around the edge, and probably fed by underground streams.

'Tell us again,' Benjamin asked. 'What happened?'

'Well, the abbé was in the water, floating face down.' Ricard wiped his constantly dripping nose. 'I and Simone pulled him out. He must have been dead for hours.'

'Do you think he drowned?'

'He could have had a seizure. Yet the abbé enjoyed

116

good health. He had no fits nor did he suffer from the falling sickness.'

Benjamin sat down on a small bench near the pool and watched the silver, darting carp who swam in dashes of light amongst the water grass and luxuriant lily pads. He half-closed his eyes and listened to plopping sounds in the water for the place swarmed with frogs, and the buzz of the bees as they hunted for honey amongst the flowers.

'Did Abbé Gerard have any enemies?' I asked abruptly.

Ricard shook his head. 'Monsieur, I don't understand.'

'My companion asked,' Benjamin repeated, 'did the Abbé Gerard have any enemies?'

'No, he was a compassionate man, even to me with all my failings.'

'Did he ever talk about his friendship with King Henry of England? You know our king, when he visited Maubisson, often called on Abbé Gerard and used him as a confessor?'

'Others at the château do,' Ricard observed.

I winked at Benjamin. Abbé Gerard, I thought, would be the natural recipient of all sorts of secrets. In an enclosed community such as Maubisson who would want to confess to a drunken idiot like Waldegrave? Apart from Falconer, I thought, and he died.

'The Abbé Gerard,' Benjamin remarked, speaking my thoughts aloud, 'must have known the secrets of many hearts.' He stared up at Ricard. 'But we were talking about our noble King Henry.'

'The abbé often boasted,' Ricard answered, 'about his friendship with King Henry of England. He often described him as a truly Christian Prince.'

117

(It just goes to show you that Henry could fool anyone, and invariably did. At least two of his wives and three of his principal ministers paid the price, not to mention a legion of others whose only reward for speaking their minds was a short journey to the executioner's block on Tower Hill.)

'And King Henry's gift to him?' Benjamin pointedly asked.

'Oh, the abbé was very proud of the gift. A copy of St Augustine's *On Chastity*, I believe. He showed it to me once. I am not a scholar but I saw it was personally annotated by your king. Abbé Gerard usually kept it well hidden.'

'And you never saw it?'

'As I have said, only once.'

'Where is it now?'

'I don't know. You see the abbé had very few possessions. I searched for that but never found it.'

Benjamin stared at the carp pond.

'Monsieur le Curé, since the abbé's death, has anything strange happened here?'

'No. Of course, there was mourning and grief at the abbé's sudden death and his funeral caused disruption in the normal tedium of our lives.' The curé's voice quickened. 'Ah, yes, one incident. The day after the funeral I was out visiting all day. Simone had gone back to her family. On my return I found the doors had been forced. Someone had carefully searched the house from top to bottom but nothing was missing. I did wonder if they were searching for the book. In itself it is valuable, being recently translated from the original Greek and annotated by a king.'

'Did the abbé ever say what would happen to the book after his death?'

'Yes, he joked and said he would take it to heaven with him. How it deserved to go to Paradise.'

'Ask him where the abbé is buried,' I said, an idea half-forming in my mind.

'In our cemetery,' Ricard replied. 'Under the old yew tree. The parishioners bought him a head stone. You can see it there. It's marked simply with his name and the cross of Lorraine.'

'May we see inside the church?' Benjamin asked.

Ricard agreed and was searching for the key on the ring of his belt when we heard the sound of horses and men shouting. We followed the curé back to the kitchen. Simone was standing by the front door which she held ajar, her hand to her mouth. Ricard pushed her aside, stared out then stepped back, his face pale. Benjamin eased by him and I reluctantly followed. The path down to the lych gate was packed with armed men, soldiers in conical steel helmets and tough, leather jerkins. Some wore breastplates, greaves and other pieces of armour, all carried swords and daggers, with shields slung round their necks. They also carried arbalests, huge wicked-looking cross bows, the type used by Genoese; at our appearance they fanned out into a semicircle. Beyond the lych gate I could see their horses milling about, raising small clouds of yellow dust.

'What is the matter?' Benjamin demanded.

'A Goddamn!' one of them replied in a thick, Scottish accent. I peered closer and my stomach curdled. These did not look French and, despite the royal livery of France some of them sported, they were not regular troops. Most were red-haired with thick beards and moustaches. They had the cruel faces of born killers. I stared around. Some carried standards, chevrons, gules and badges. I glimpsed one displaying the Red Lion rampant of Scotland as well as the fleur de lys of France.

'*Le Garde Ecossais!*' Benjamin voiced my thoughts.

I took a step back. These soldiers were the most cruel and professional in the French army, Scottish exiles who served the French crown because of their hatred for England.

(Did you know that whenever the English went to war with France, our soldiers immediately hanged any of these Scottish mercenaries they captured? Indeed, Henry V used to burn them alive. And if any of them captured an Englishman, God help him! I have heard stories of such men taking days to die. These mercenaries were particularly concerned about the skill and accuracy of English archers. The first thing they'd do if they captured one would be to hack off the two forefingers of each hand, the very ones our archers used to pull a long bow. Consequently, our lads, whenever they wished to express their contempt for the French, would show them two fingers. I thought you might find this little aside interesting. My chaplain does. It's a gesture I often use with him when I'm too drunk to argue.)

On that sun-drenched day at Maubisson I kept my fingers well hidden, smiled politely and quietly prayed that these wolves in human flesh were seeking other quarry apart from us. Suddenly the groups divided and a most extraordinary sight sauntered down the path. He was their leader, a soldier, but dressed like a popinjay in multi-coloured hose, a billowing tabard of blue and silver

120

jagged at the edge, a lace-ruffed collar, lambskin gloves and high-heeled Spanish riding boots festooned with bells which tinkled at every step he took. He wore a sort of bonnet on his jet black hair, apparently dyed, and four great eagle feathers were clasped to this. A jewelled necklace round his throat glittered in the sun as did the pearl earrings which hung from fleshy lobes on chains of pure silver. His face was equally extraordinary, pale and soft, smooth like a young girl's, with pursed, prim lips and above them a slightly crooked nose. The eyes were deep-set and shadowed. Is this a woman? I thought, catching a strong whiff of perfume. You see, the fellow didn't walk, he had this strange mincing walk, hips slightly swaying. He was unarmed except for a dagger with a mother-of-pearl handle pushed through an ornately embroidered belt. I stared at that face and something stirred in my memory. Had I seen him before? Yet, surely I would remember such an apparition?

The fellow stopped, one leg pushed slightly forward in a pose which, in other circumstances, I would have found laughable. He peeled one glove off and beckoned like a woman. Ricard stumbled forward.

'Not you!' The voice was soft, well modulated, the command of English perfect.

I had heard that voice before in an alleyway in London. The apparition waved soft, white fingers.

'Go away, you dirty little priest, and close the door behind you!'

Ricard vanished and I wished I could follow him. The apparition smiled lazily at us and beckoned once again.

'Stay where you are!' Benjamin hissed, grabbing my arm.

He didn't have to tell me a second time. I was rooted in terror to the spot. I don't like soldiers and I particularly hate those who dress like women and smile a lot.

Again the apparition smiled. '*Préparez-vous!*'

The command was tossed languidly over his shoulder and immediately loaded crossbows were brought up and aimed at our chests.

'On second thoughts,' I murmured to Benjamin, 'let's do what he asks.'

Benjamin grasped my wrist again. 'I will take one step,' my master called out, 'if you take one.'

The apparition shrugged. '*D'accord*,' he murmured, making a languorous movement with his hand. The crossbows were lowered, he moved forward, so did we. The apparition tapped Benjamin on the chest. 'You are Benjamin Daunbey.' His eyes did not leave Benjamin's. 'And your companion is the creature Shallot.' His eyes flicked coldly over me. 'Creature, we meet again.'

His words confirmed my worst fears. This fellow was one of the Luciferi who had threatened me in London, carried out the dreadful murders of the Ralembergs and put the blame on me. (Now the chaplain thinks I should have sprung at him. If I had loved Agnes so much, surely my passionate nature would have broken all bounds? He does not know old Shallot. Do unto your enemy before he does it unto you, but always make sure his back's turned!)

'My name is 'Sieur Raoul Vauban. I am a clerk in the service of His Most Christian Majesty, King Francis I. We were passing through the village and we heard that the curé had visitors.'

Bloody liar, I thought.

'What are you doing here?' He stared at Benjamin.

'We are the accredited envoys of His Majesty the King of England, and of His Eminence, Cardinal Thomas Wolsey. We are staying at the Château de Maubisson and have brought to the village our royal master's deep condolences on the sudden and tragic death of the Abbé Gerard.'

'No!' Vauban rasped. 'You are spies!'

'Then, Monsieur, we have a lot in common.' Benjamin held open his cloak so the Frenchman could see his sword. 'What is more,' he continued conversationally, 'you must be a member of the Luciferi. Perhaps their principal archangel. Where do you carry that damned candle you always leave at your crimes?'

Well, that shut the bastard up, and, for a few seconds, that infuriating smile disappeared. My master just stood, cool as you like, his arms folded. I could see he had taken an intense dislike to Monsieur Vauban.

'You are not passing through the village,' Benjamin continued. 'You followed us here. You have also been watching the château. Like me, you know the Abbé Gerard was murdered, and you are looking for that book, a gift from our royal master which, by rights, should now be returned to its proper owner.'

Vauban, offended by Benjamin's bluntness, stepped back, his hand falling to his dagger. Once again those bloody crossbows came up and I heard the click of bolts being placed. I edged behind my master, ready to give him support and wondering if Ricard had locked the door behind him. Then, suddenly, Vauban threw back his head and laughed like a girl.

'Monsieur Benjamin! Monsieur Benjamin!' He went up

and clapped my master on the shoulder. 'Why do we quarrel? We are both agents of our royal masters. We have better things to do than kill each other.' He grinned impishly at me. 'We get others to do that for us.'

Well, I could have killed the bastard on the spot but I wasn't armed. He was, and had sixty stout friends to support him. So I smiled pleasantly. Vauban stepped back, hands extended, his expression mock-apologetic.

'Look, we mean no offence. We will escort you back to the château.'

'We don't want that.'

'No, we don't,' I added.

'I insist,' Vauban purred. 'There are rebels, the Maillotins, about.'

Benjamin shook his head. The crossbows came up again.

'Of course, we agree,' I laughed.

'Good,' Vauban replied. 'Let's go.'

We walked down the side of the church and collected our horses.

'I don't like the perverted bastard!' Benjamin hissed.

'Neither do I, master, but keep smiling just in case he changes his mind.'

We mounted and rode back through the lazy summer sunshine, the Scottish troopers massing behind whilst Vauban pushed forward between us. God knows, I thought of Agnes and could have killed him. The bastard chattered pleasantly for a while before suddenly producing a small viol from a bag hanging on his saddle horn. I couldn't believe it. He strummed for a few seconds then broke into a sweet-sounding madrigal known to both my master and myself. (We often sang in St Mary's, Ipswich, my bass a good foil to Benjamin's tenor. Even today there's nothing I like better than to sit in church on Sunday morning and lustily bawl out the hymns.) But on that dusty track outside Maubisson I found the singing macabre. This killer dressed like a popinjay, sweetly singing a madrigal to men he knew were his sworn enemies. He stopped and looked at us.

'I have a good voice, Messieurs?'

'God only knows,' I added sarcastically.

Vauban's eyes narrowed.

'You know this song? You will join me?'

Well, I don't know who was the more insane, he for singing or Benjamin and myself for joining in. Where possible I changed the words, using every filthy, French word I knew. (And believe me there are quite a few!) But Vauban didn't mind. We rode along like three troubadours from some romantic tale. We finished just before we arrived at the main gate of the château.

'I enjoyed that,' Vauban said, leaning forward on his horse. 'Perhaps we can do it again? Our voices modulate well.'

'I would love to,' I replied. 'Perhaps one day you can be our guest again in London.' (In the Tower dungeons, I thought, stretched out on the cruellest rack I can find!)

Vauban positively beamed with pleasure, waved us goodbye like an affectionate friend, then he and his horsemen disappeared in a haze of dust.

Once we were arrived in the inner bailey Benjamin gave full vent to his feelings. He tossed his horse's reins to a groom and went storming off looking for Dacourt. I trailed behind, still shaking from a mixture of fear and anger. Benjamin found the ambassador in a small writing office near the great hall.

'We must meet, Sir John. All of us, now!'

'Why? Why?' Dacourt was flustered.

'Because I want the truth!' Benjamin roared back.

The ambassador dithered so Benjamin stormed out, grasped a frightened servant and made him take us to where Clinton was sitting with the Lady Francesca in a small bower built against the château wall. Lady Francesca smiled and simpered but, when she glimpsed me, her face became as hard as stone. She rose and flounced off in a swish of skirts and a whiff of fragrant perfume. I stood and listened to those sharp, high-heeled shoes clipping along the flagstones. I shook my head and lowered my eyes. I was sure she had been holding a small phial with the letters 'SUL' written on it. I glanced at my master but he was too angry to notice, standing tapping the toe of his boot, waiting for Sir Robert to finish reading a letter.

At last Clinton carefully folded the document.

'Master Daunbey, what is the matter?'

My master leaned forward and in curt, clear tones told him exactly what was the matter.

'What do you want to do?' Sir Robert asked.

'I wish to hold a meeting,' Benjamin rasped. 'Of all the ambassador's staff. I need to get certain matters clear and precise. The French are just laughing at us as we stumble around in a fog.'

Clinton agreed and we all met in the great hall just before dusk. The servants setting the tables ready for supper were summarily dismissed. We all gathered on chairs in a semicircle round the hearth. Dacourt, angry that Benjamin had gone to Sir Robert, slurped noisily from a wine cup, then threw the dregs to hiss in the flames of the fire.

'Master Daunbey,' he grated, 'we are busy men and you have convened this meeting. Why?'

'I am here,' Benjamin answered, 'as the official envoy of Cardinal Wolsey as well as His Majesty the King. We have certain secret tasks to perform.'

I saw Dacourt fidget nervously at his words.

'But our main task is to discover the identity of the traitor Raphael and bring to justice the murderers of Falconer and Waldegrave. I suspect,' Benjamin added, 'they are one and the same person.' He extended a hand. 'Let us summarise. How long has this traitor been in existence?'

'About eighteen months,' Clinton replied. 'But we only learnt he was called Raphael about eight weeks ago, during my visit here before Lent.' He leaned forward in his chair. 'You may remember, Benjamin, I worked with Falconer and obtained that name? Even though it cost us the life of a very good agent.'

'Yes, yes,' Benjamin said. 'Now, I believe Falconer was murdered on Easter Monday?'

A chorus of assent greeted his words.

'He drank some wine from the same bottle you did, Sir John, but he was not in his cups?'

Again there was agreement.

'He was seen going to the top of the tower. The Mary Tower, I believe? And was found dead at the base of it the next morning?'

'Yes,' Peckle stammered. 'We all know this, Master Daunbey.'

'We also know,' Benjamin continued, breathing deeply to contain his anger, 'that on the Wednesday after Falconer was killed, Abbé Gerard from the nearby village also died in mysterious circumstances. Tell me,' he continued, 'did anyone from Maubisson send Abbé Gerard gifts for Easter?'

The group sat silent.

'Well,' Benjamin asked. 'Did anyone?'

Dacourt shuffled his feet. 'I did. I sent him some wine, the best of last year's grapes from Bordeaux, a silver dish of sweet comfits and some marchpane.'

'When was this?'

'On the Saturday before Easter.'

'And what happened to these gifts?'

'Good Lord!' Dacourt bellowed. 'I don't know. The Abbé Gerard was a compassionate, charitable man but one who liked his claret. I suspect he gave the comfits and marchpane to children in the village, sold the silver dish for alms and drank the wine himself. It was only a small, stoppered jar.' Dacourt's voice trailed off. 'Are you saying the wine . . . ? But Throgmorton went down to examine the priest's corpse.'

'Oh, we didn't know that,' I interrupted.

'Well, no,' the physician replied. 'Why should you? I went down to examine the poor priest. There was no sign of poison. The man probably swooned, fell in the water and drowned.'

'Master Benjamin,' Peckle rose to his feet, 'Sir John, we are busy men. Do you have further questions?'

'No,' Benjamin replied crossly.

My master was still very angry and I was intrigued for he was the most gentle of men and very rarely testy or

128

sharp, even with fools. (I have just given my chaplain a good rap across the knuckles; that will teach him to make remarks like, 'And Master Daunbey had good knowledge of fools, having you as a servant.') Anyway, the meeting broke up, though Clinton and his manservant Venner remained seated until the rest had left the hall.

'Tell me,' Clinton asked softly, 'this Vauban – did he know why you were in France?'

'He said we were spies but even a child could deduce that. He also knew we were interested in the Abbé Gerard but, again, that would not require deep perception. Why do you ask, Sir Robert?'

'He never mentioned Raphael?'

'No, he didn't.'

Clinton said, 'So, the Luciferi have still not learnt the true purpose of your mission. You see,' he leaned back in his chair, 'here in the château, Dacourt and the rest of his staff know you wish to catch a spy but, so far, little information has been passed to the Luciferi. Which means . . .'

'Which means exactly what?' I interrupted tartly.

'That the spy here must have special means of conveying such information to his master and has so far failed to use it. If you could discover that, then perhaps we can find out who Raphael is.'

'Nevertheless,' Benjamin answered, 'Vauban did know we were here. I think he was watching the château for days and followed us down to the village.'

'Which brings us to my real point,' Clinton answered. 'Master Venner?'

The servant looked towards the door to make sure there was no one standing there.

'Last night,' Venner asked, 'when Waldegrave's corpse was found, did you notice Millet? He was fully dressed as if he had been out of the château.'

'It could have been a lovers' tryst,' I observed.

'Perhaps,' Venner sneered. 'But Millet's tastes are obvious. He dresses like a woman, the type of tryst he keeps is best hidden under the cloak of darkness.'

'I have raised this matter with Dacourt,' Clinton interrupted. 'He did not even know Millet was absent. I have asked him to keep the matter secret. Perhaps Millet needs to be followed.'

Benjamin rubbed his face with his hands. 'Yes,' he observed drily. 'Millet's conduct and dress last night were suspicious. He could be the spy or his messenger.' He smiled at Clinton. 'And what you say makes sense, Sir Robert. Vauban still does not know the true nature of our mission here.' My master slapped the side of the chair. 'Of course,' he breathed, 'we have been here only a few days. We think Millet was returning. Maybe we were wrong. Perhaps he was on the point of leaving but the fracas caused by Waldegrave's death prevented him.'

Clinton rose to his feet. 'We leave that to you, Master Daunbey. If you wish, Venner could follow him.'

'No, no,' Benjamin replied. 'Leave Master Millet to us.'

I watched Clinton and his manservant leave and once again the business of Agnes's death nagged at my memory. (Do you know, years ago I asked a wise man who lived in a cave outside Alexandria why this happens? Why something should trouble you, yet you are unable to place it or resolve the matter until months later? He answered that we never know what a certain piece of puzzle is until we see the rest and put the piece in place.)

Benjamin and I stayed in the hall whilst the servants returned and finished laying the tables for supper. My master just sat staring into the flames of the fire.

'What is the matter?' I asked. 'Why did Vauban make you so angry?'

'I am puzzled, Roger,' he replied. 'Why were Falconer, the Abbé Gerard and Waldegrave murdered? What is the connection between them? Is their killer Raphael or someone else? How does Raphael convey his secrets to the Luciferi?'

'There is one common theme,' I replied.

'Which is?'

I ticked the points off on my fingers. 'First, the secrets of the King's Council are not revealed until they have reached Maubisson. Now we know the letters are opened by Dacourt and deciphered by Peckle, but Millet is Dacourt's secretary and will be privy to such information. The same could be true of Throgmorton. After all, physicians can wander where they wish and prise secrets from others. Secondly, Falconer was murdered here at Maubisson after broaching a flagon of wine with Dacourt. Thirdly, the Abbé Gerard apparently drowned after drinking claret which was undoubtedly sent to him by Dacourt, though taken down to the village probably by his secretary, Master Millet. Fourthly, Waldegrave was killed by Dacourt's horse, Vulcan.'

'And finally,' Benjamin interrupted, 'Master Millet has a tendency to slip out of the château at night to meet God knows whom.' My master sat rocking himself gently in the chair. 'The common denominators in all these factors, as a mathematician would say, are Dacourt and

131

Millet but, first, we don't know for certain if the wine sent to the Abbé Gerard was in fact the same he was drinking the night he died. Secondly, we don't know if Millet took it. Thirdly, the night Falconer died, Dacourt tasted the same wine he drank.'

'We have only his word for that.'

'Yes, but Throgmorton examined the wine later. He said it was free of any infusion. He also said neither Falconer nor the Abbé Gerard showed any signs of being poisoned.'

I watched my theories slowly crumble.

'And, of course,' I added wearily, 'though Dacourt's horse killed Waldegrave, anyone could have dragged the drunken priest into the stable.'

Benjamin grinned and clapped me on the shoulder. 'I did not say your reasoning was wrong, Roger, only that it was faulty.'

We stayed in the hall and dined with the rest of the company. The conversation was desultory, passing from one banal matter to another. Benjamin did establish that all memoranda, letters and documents sent from Westminster were handled by Dacourt, Peckle and Millet, whilst our mysterious young secretary did take the ambassador's presents down to the Abbé Gerard.

We retired to bed a little more hopeful that some glimmer of light had been shown but, just before I fell asleep, I realised Benjamin hadn't answered my question about disliking Vauban, so I asked him again.

'Go to sleep, Roger,' Benjamin drowsily replied. 'I'll tell you in God's good time, as I will about the secret instructions dear Uncle gave me at Hampton Court.'

132

Chapter 7

They say lightning never strikes twice but it does when old Shallot's around. I could hardly believe it. We were aroused late that night by the most terrible screams and a pounding on the door. I leapt from my bed and threw open the door. (In my youth I was rash. Now, I'd let someone else do it, whilst I checked to see what window I could jump out of!) Peckle stood there, eyes rounded in fear.

'The castle is under attack!' he screamed. 'Maillotins! They are forcing the main gate!'

Benjamin and I seized our arms and rushed out. This time I made sure my master went first and, whilst he ran down the stairs, I scampered like a rabbit to the top of the tower, forcing back the trap door, standing in the same place that poor Falconer had. I looked up. Stars dusted the sky but it was an attacker's moon which slipped treacherously in and out of the clouds. I peered over the battlements. The wind whipped at my hair whilst my stomach lurched in horror at the dreadful sight below. The dark fields in front of the castle were covered in what seemed to be pinpricks of light until I realised they were men carrying torches, streaming towards the main gate. Indeed, most of the fighting was taking place there. I heard the hiss of arrows and the crashing of some makeshift battering ram buckling the beams of the iron-studded gates. The château was ill prepared. I glimpsed half-dressed soldiers seizing crossbows and other armaments and heard Dacourt's voice on the breeze screaming out orders. Most of our archers were massing in the gatehouse, shooting at those trying to force an entry.

I sobbed with fright, even as I addressed the one and only question which confronted me in such a dangerous situation. Was I safe? I huddled down beneath the parapet. What happened if the gate was forced? I could be trapped here at the top of the tower and be either forced to jump or killed like a rat trapped in a barn. I pushed my head over the parapet. Some of the château guards were on the curtain walls, forcing back the scaling ladders placed there. Time, I thought, for me to leave. I looked over to the side wall where the postern gate stood and went cold with terror. More pinpricks of light were moving down there. The attack on the main gate was merely a feint.

'It's time old Shallot moved,' I murmured. 'Perhaps search out Benjamin? Get out of the château, steal a horse and ride straight to Calais?'

I hurried down the tower steps, across the yard and into the outer bailey. The noise was terrible. Our assailants were now shooting fire arrows and these were already causing havoc amongst the defenders. One soldier lay on the ground like a blazing torch. Others had horrible black wounds to their faces and chests. Dacourt stood grasping his sword like some hero from ancient Troy.

'To the walls!' he screamed. 'To the walls! Don't let the banners fall!'

I am sure the silly old bastard had suffered a blow to the head and believed he was playing out a role from some heroic romance. He saw me and yelled: 'Shallot, where have you been? Now is not the time for a faint heart!'

'Piss off!' I shouted, losing my temper. 'The real attack is not here. They are massing against the side wall!'

I waved my sword like a madman, screamed at some men-at-arms to follow me, and raced like a whippet to the postern gate. We arrived to see the tops of the first ladder against the wall. A burly serjeant-at-arms pushed me aside and bravely told 'his lads' to follow him up. I stayed where I was, shouting out orders and near enough to the postern gate if things should go wrong. Our archers caught the bastards just as they began to climb the scaling ladders, whilst men-at-arms, using the long forked poles lying on the parapet walk, shoved them out of the way. I heard screams of anguish, then the attack faded away as suddenly as it came.

Dacourt, Clinton and the rest congregated in the main hall whilst servants lit torches and others brought ale or wine for the conquering heroes. Horses were saddled and scouts sent out. They soon returned, reporting the attackers had vanished, taking their dead and wounded with them. Five of the château soldiers were killed and Benjamin had a small cut high on his cheek. Dacourt estimated we had killed scores of our assailants but only three corpses were dragged in, all of them casualties of the ladder which had been pushed away from the outer wall. They looked scruffy, dirty vermin though surprisingly well armed. Now, I knew the Maillotins, the peasant rebels who lurked in the alleyways and runnels of Paris. I'd lived with them for a while. They were like me, experts in the sudden ambush. Certainly not well armed, organised or brave enough to attack a château in the open countryside.

Dacourt praised my prompt heroic action and I played the role of the modest hero, gulping his wine and giving shrewd assessments of the strategy of the attackers. However, when I doubted that the Maillotins had ever launched such an attack, Dacourt bellowed his disbelief.

'I know these vermin!' he declared. 'They hate the English. They grudge us our victories in France and the occupation of Calais. No, no, the Maillotins were behind this. Or, if not, who is?' His watery blue eyes gazed bulbously at me so I let the fool have his way though Benjamin agreed with me.

'They're too well fed,' he commented. 'And supplied with all the necessary arms. Let's wait till the morning for I am sure Monsieur Vauban had a hand in this.'

Benjamin's words were prophetic. The next morning Vauban and his horde of cavalry trotted into the castle grounds as if they were a welcoming relief. Benjamin and I stayed well away from him as he consulted with Dacourt and Clinton. Only when he had gone did my master ask what had happened.

'Two things,' Dacourt bellowed cheerfully. 'Vauban will leave some of his horsemen camped outside the château walls against further attack. Secondly, tomorrow is His Most Christian Majesty's naming day. We have all been invited to the festivities at his palace of Fontainebleau.' The ambassador grinned at both of us. 'On behalf of all of you, I have accepted.'

Both Benjamin and I wisely kept our mouths shut until we were out of the main hall.

'Vauban wanted that attack,' Benjamin muttered. 'He may wish to kill us all, or some of us.' He stared down and studied one of the fire arrows dropped the previous night.

'Or he could just have wished to have an excuse for placing men near the château to keep us under closer observation.' He smiled sideways at me. 'But at least we will get to Fontainebleau. A chance to meet His Most Christian Majesty!'

'And examine his damned ring!' I replied crossly. 'Master, in God's name what are we to do about that?'

'Nothing,' Benjamin replied. 'At Fontainebleau we do nothing but watch and listen.' He seized me by the arm. 'At no time, Roger, do we make our move there. What are we but simple Englishmen? The French king is well guarded and he covets that ring more than honour itself. Whatever temptations are presented to us, we must not react.'

'And if we fail to take it?' I asked dourly.

Benjamin grinned. 'In that case, my dear Roger, we learn French well and make friends with Monsieur Vauban because we can never return to England.'

We left the château early the following morning, each of us resplendent in whatever finery we could pluck from our wardrobes. Actually, we looked like a group of crows compared to the Lady Francesca who was resplendent in a gown of gold brocade trimmed with lynx skins.

We reached Fontainebleau late that afternoon, and how can I describe it? Its great round towers, the dancing outlines of precise yet beautiful Italian architecture, the splendid red spire of St Hubert's Chapel, the great clock with dogs chasing a stag; on the hour, the bark of the dogs accompanied each chime whilst the stag moved to sound the final chime. Thirteen staircases, hundreds of rooms, alabaster statues of Cupid and Venus with others sculpted in fleshy bronzeness by the French king's Italian artists.

137

All around the palace were cool, lime-shaded gardens full of lilies, violets and wood sorrel; now and again, white-colonnaded courtyards with shimmering pavements of alternating black and white marble stone. The rooms inside were stuffed with the loot from Francis's expeditions into Italy; tapestries, more statues, gold and silver artefacts, jewelled vases, and the softest carpets of pure wool in various hues.

Grooms took our horses, and minions in the blue and gold tabards of the French king led Sir Robert and Lady Francesca away. Dacourt also was provided with his own chamber but we were taken to the top of the palace. Any higher and we would have been on the bloody roof, and squeezed into rather mean, dark garrets. Now I have always been very particular whom I sleep with and I didn't like sharing my room with a possible murderer. I also resented the way Millet was simpering at me. He was wearing more lace than the Lady Francesca!

I'll keep away from you, my fine bucko, I thought, and if I drop anything I'll kick it to the door before I pick it up. (No, my chaplain is wrong. I'm not being unkind. I just find such people strange though I admit some, like Marlowe, have been great friends. What I am saying is, it depends on the person. Marlowe was charming, witty, and very, very funny, but there was something about Millet I didn't like.) Peckle grumbled about the treatment due to envoys but the good physician, Throgmorton, laughed sourly and said he was pleased to be as far away from the Frogs as possible. Servants brought up our baggage, we unpacked, then heard a knocking on the wall outside. Benjamin, who had been sitting on the edge of his trestle bed, got up and opened the door. He looked out and came back, torn between anger and laughter.

'What's the matter, Daunbey?' Throgmorton asked.

'The French have just put a painting up outside our room.'

'Oh, that's nice,' Peckle observed sarcastically. 'What is it? A picture of the French defeat at Agincourt?'

Benjamin shook his head. '*La Belle Jardinière.*'

'So what?' I muttered. 'What the hell are they doing?'

'The painting's by Raphael,' Benjamin replied. 'They are mocking us.'

Do you know, that's the first time I began to wonder about the name Raphael. Why did the spy use it? Why not Ragwort? Or Fat Cheeks? Why Raphael? The name of an angel, an archangel to be sure, and therefore linked to Vauban's motley crew, but also the name of a great Italian painter. Our debate on this intended insult by the French was summarily ended: a wand-bearing chamberlain told us to assemble in the great hall below for the rare privilege of an audience with His Most Christian Majesty.

Dacourt and the Clintons were waiting for us, Sir Robert dressed in cream silken hose, darted below the knees, and padded doublet and breeches of dark sea blue; Lady Francesca was clothed all in white, a small, lace veil over her lovely hair, pearls clasped round her neck. I gasped at her beauty and, like the rest, threw envious glances at her most fortunate husband. Dacourt, however, was dressed as if he didn't give a damn, in sloppy jerkin and breeches which would have shamed an intelligent plough boy. Millet giggled and, whispering to the old soldier that his points were undone, asked did he wish to astonish the French with his apparent prowess? Dacourt laughed gruffly and turned surreptitiously away to adjust his dress.

The snotty-nosed chamberlain tapped his wand on the floor and we were led along marble corridors, through chambers being prepared for the great banquet, past nobles draped in velvet and cloth of gold, retainers in blue, violet and scarlet liveries, all chatting merrily in French. They stood aside and let us pass, though we heard the sniggers and laughter caused by their little jokes. We stopped before a great, gold-embossed door and the chamberlain turned.

'You are,' he announced in English, 'to be ushered into the presence of His Most Christian Majesty.'

(Most Christian Majesty . . . that was the biggest lie, especially when Francis was allied to the Ottoman Turks, who were devils incarnate. You wait till you read my later journals. I still wake trembling at the horrors I suffered at Suleiman's silk-draped, terror-filled court.) Anyway, at Fontainebleau the doors were thrown open so we could feast our eyes on this Most Christian of Kings. We all trooped in, two by two, as if we were the animals going into Noah's bloody ark. The room shimmered with light, a treasure house of precious cloths and beautiful jewels. At the far end I glimpsed a small crowd who stopped talking and drew apart at our approach. I glimpsed a cloth of state under which two figures sat on thrones and then the devil Vauban appeared.

He looked gorgeous, dressed in a pink silk gown with a gold-tasselled cord round his waist. He wore blue leggings and his feet were pushed into soft leather buskins. His chest gleamed like a mirror as the thick, cheap jewellery draped across it caught the sunlight. Down each arm, from shoulder to sleeve, gleamed those bloody little bells which tinkled every time he moved. He smiled effusively, gave a

140

mock bow, and went to stand beside one of the thrones.

'May I present,' he announced, 'Sir Robert Clinton and his wife, the Lady Francesca, Sir John Dacourt and the other English envoys.'

By now I had forgotten Vauban and was surreptitiously staring at the two seated figures. Francis and his Queen Claude perched like waxen images under a cloth of state of red silk, the oriflamme. The thrones they sat on were fluted and heavily decorated with clusters of mother-of-pearl along the back and arms.

We all bowed, then Dacourt began the usual boring, diplomatic speech bearing messages from Francis's 'brother' the King of England. I noticed a flicker of a smile cross the French king's face at the usual flowery hypocrisies; Francis hated Henry and the English king responded in kind. In a way I preferred Francis. He was a big-nosed bastard with heavy-lidded eyes, high forehead and a weak mouth which he hid beneath a moustache and beard. He was dressed in cloth of gold from head to toe, a simple crown on his head, and I could see he was as bored as I by Dacourt's vapid pleasantries.

You see, Francis was the Salamander King, that wondrous creature of magic which was surrounded by fire but never burnt. Someone had called him this more as an insult than a compliment but Francis took a liking to it and you will find salamanders carved all over his palaces. You know, he shouldn't have been king. He was fortunate enough to marry Louis XII's only daughter and so became the appointed successor. And what a change! Old Louis, feeble and doddering, choking on his own spit. Henry VIII saw him off or, more truthfully, his sister Mary did. You see she was as hot for the joys of the bed as her brother,

141

the Great Killer. She was married for three months to poor old Louis before he collapsed and died of exhaustion and Mary went home to marry the love of her life, Charles Brandon, Duke of Suffolk. If she had been married to Francis, Mary might have had a harder time for he was a consummate bed player. As one of his courtiers later whispered to me, 'He slips readily into the gardens of others and drinks water from many fountains.' Oh, yes, Francis was ardent, he had his own *petite bande*, a group of young blondes led by Madame D'Estampes who joined in the antics on the black satin sheets of his bed. Do you know, at Fontainebleau he set up a system of mirrors so he could watch his young ladies pose and inspect them from every angle, whilst his palaces were full of secret passageways with peep-holes in every bedroom for Francis was deeply interested in the sexual exploits of others.

(Poor Francis! Yes, I say 'poor'. At Fontainebleau he was full of the juices of spring but that's before he caught syphilis and his nether parts began to drop off. He got it from *La Belle Fertonière*: her husband knew she had syphilis and allowed Francis to seduce her. King Francis became so rotten that when they took his corpse to St Denis they had to put it in a lead coffin. It still stank and his nobles were so keen to avoid the putrid smell, they sent waxen images of themselves to the church. Can you imagine it? A church full of wax statues mourning a waxen image?)

Ah, the passage of time! When I met Francis on the first occasion in that throne room, life had not turned sour for him. He was still the great lover, and the woman beside him was the reason for his constant philandering. Queen Claude – or 'Clod' as the courtiers called her – was fat, lame and revolting. Yet she had a kind heart! (Ah, there goes my clerk, the clever little fool: 'You're no better than Henry VIII!' he cries. 'You, too, regard women as objects of lust!' What the hell does the little hypocrite know? Don't you worry, some of the women I've met have proved to be the most formidable of foes. Like little Catherine de Medici who married King Francis's son, Henry. She practised the black arts. Oh, yes, I know about the secret metal box she owned; her turreted chamber at Blois with its magic mirror which told her the future; and her employment of that terrible prophet Nostradamus who prophesied the end of the world. I'll tell you some other time about Catherine's special squad of ladies, the *Escadron Volant*, whom she used to seduce her opponents. I'll finish with this about women: they make the best of friends and the worst of enemies! A man forgives and forgets. A woman can forgive but she never forgets. You mark Shallot's words!)

Now in that room at Fontainebleau so many years ago, I studied Francis but my eyes were drawn to that bloody ring which sparkled on the fourth finger of his left hand. I knew it was the one Henry wanted back. The French king, his elbows resting on the arms of the throne, kept playing with the ring, taking it on and off, twirling it around, whilst throwing heavy-lidded glances and the soupçon of a smirk at Benjamin and myself. Beside him Vauban seemed to share the joke; that extraordinary bastard leaned against the arm of the throne as if he was the king's brother, openly stifling a yawn at Dacourt's ponderous phrases.

The ambassador, however, kept rambling on. Lord, I thought, he'll never shut up. I even considered swooning so as to get out of the room when suddenly a secret door just behind the throne was thrown open and the most incredible sight emerged: a man, black as night, well over two yards high. A crimson turban was wrapped round his head, the upper part of his body was bare except for gold bands round his arms and wrists. He wore white, baggy trousers which billowed like silken sails and red, high-heeled, velvet slippers with ornately curled toes. Dacourt stopped speaking and gaped like a carp. The big, black mameluke was an eye-catching sight but the beasts which went before him on silver chains were really alarming. Two great cats, amber-eyed, with tufted ears and spotted skins of burnished gold, padded as soft as death across the polished floor. The French king suddenly stirred, laughed and clapped his hands.

'Akim, you're late!'

The mameluke grinned vacuously, his mouth opening like a great, red cavern. I closed my eyes in disgust. Where the tongue should have been was a rag of skin.

'Monsieur Dacourt,' Francis announced in perfect English, 'I apologise for the tardy arrival and abrupt interruption of your eloquent speech by Akim and his cats. By the way, I call them Gabriel and Raphael. They are a gift from the Pasha of North Africa.' The king waved the mameluke to a small stool next to Queen Claude who continued to sit there as if carved from stone.

It was then that I noticed something suspicious. Never once had the French king offered a seat to Lady Francesca, who stood gazing at the monarch, an awed, frightened expression on her beautiful face. What really intrigued me was that Francis always honoured women but on this occasion he studiously ignored the Lady Francesca. Indeed, the only persons the French king seemed

144

interested in were Vauban and that stupid, smiling mameluke.

'*Asseyez*,' Francis said. 'Sit down! Sit down!'

The mameluke obeyed, still grinning vacuously, though his eyes were hard as marble and I caught a gleam of the great scimitar which swung from his side. He sat down, those bloody cats on either side of him, stretching and yawning, their lips drawn back revealing sharp, white teeth. Of course, the mameluke had been deliberately late. Francis had planned that either to impress or terrify us, I don't know which. At last Dacourt finished his tedious speech and stopped boring everyone. Vauban tucked his hands in the voluminous sleeves of his gown and stepped forward. He looked like a benevolent father confessor about to impart some doleful news.

'Monsieur Dacourt,' he began, 'you speak as eloquently as an archangel.' He paused and smiled broadly.

I heard Clinton hiss with anger at this baiting about a French spy at the English court.

'A speech even the Archangel Raphael would have envied,' Vauban continued. 'St Paul said he might have the tongue of an angel, Monsieur Dacourt, you certainly have that. Nevertheless,' his smile disappeared, 'we are concerned by the contrast between the words of your royal master in England and his secret preparations for war.'

'That's a lie!' Clinton interrupted.

Vauban spread his hands. 'Monsieur, why should I lie? We have information that the English king intends to erect a huge mirror on the south coast so that he can see which ships sail from French ports.'

'Nonsense!' Benjamin muttered.

'No, Monsieur, not nonsense. Your uncle, His Eminence

145

the Cardinal, is ordering large quantities of wheat, malt and hops, organising cohorts of bakers, brewers and under-brewers to work on them; vast amounts of fodder for horses and dried meat for soldiers; whilst iron, lead, copper and saltpetre, not to mention six thousand horse-shoes, three hundred thousand horse-shoe nails, six thousand pounds of rope and twenty thousand suits of armour, are all pouring into Calais.' Vauban stood, one leg slightly forward, ticking the points off on his fingers like some housewife checking the stores.

I glanced sideways at Dacourt. His face had gone deathly pale and was covered in a fine sheen of sweat.

'But,' Vauban clapped his hands, 'perhaps Henry of England intends to help us against our enemies? However, to assure us of his good intentions,' he sighed deeply, 'it would take an archangel to come from Heaven.' He glanced sideways at his royal master, who allowed a flicker of a smile across his face. 'Monsieur Dacourt, Monsieur Clinton,' Vauban continued, 'this meeting is over but His Most Christian Majesty requires your attendance at the banquet tonight as well as the festivities tomorrow.'

Well, Dacourt literally swept from the room. Even his ears seemed to bristle in anger. Clinton seemed subdued whilst the rest of the entourage, with the exception of Benjamin, looked positively frightened. Once we were all away from the audience chamber, Clinton summarily dismissed the Lady Francesca who swept off in a flurry of flowing, perfumed lace.

'Let us go into the garden,' he murmured. 'It is the only damned place no spies can lurk!'

It was late in the day and we all sat near one of the small fountains, taking advantage of the shade against the hot

146

afternoon sun. A servant brought us glasses of cool, white wine and we sipped them, taking stock of our recent interview with the king.

'That bastard was baiting us!' Dacourt blurted out. 'The references to angels, archangels and Raphael! Vauban was reminding us that he has someone close to the heart of the English council.'

'Yes, and they proved that,' Millet piped up.

'What do you mean?' Benjamin asked carefully.

'For goodness' sake, Daunbey!' Throgmorton sourly replied. 'Didn't you notice those two bloody cats, the jewelled collars round their necks? They were part of Henry's gift to the same Pasha of North Africa. Only the French heard about the ship. Galleys from Marseilles captured it as soon as it was through the Straits of Gibraltar.'

'There's more than that,' Peckle intervened. 'He knew about our king's war preparations, even to the detail of how many horse-shoe nails.'

'Who would have known that?' Benjamin interrupted.

'The king, his council in London, and we at the embassy.'

'And the business of the mirror?' I asked.

'Oh, that's correct,' Dacourt snorted. 'But the fellow who proposed it took the money and fled.'

'One thing is very clear,' Benjamin persisted. 'The French, because of Raphael, control this game and are openly baiting us. I suggest, gentlemen, we keep our mouths closed and our eyes and ears open.' He rose. 'Sir John, Sir Robert, we must change for the banquet.' He indicated with his head that I should follow.

Once we were out of earshot, he pulled me into the

shadow of a wall. 'And what did you learn, Roger?'

'The French king is laughing at us.'

'And apart from that?'

'Raphael was involved in the deaths of Falconer and Abbé Gerard.'

Benjamin pursed his lips. 'I agree. And what else?'

'The French king does not like the Lady Francesca. There seems to be some tension there.'

Benjamin scratched the back of his head. 'Yes, yes, I noticed that too. I wonder about that lady. Sometimes she does not seem at all well. She's secretive, flirts openly, but actually says nothing.'

'When I surprised her at the château, she had a phial, or something similar in her hand.'

'What do you mean?'

'Some kind of medicine. I saw the letters SUL. Then there's the business of the ring.'

Benjamin grinned at me.

'It's your problem as well!' I added.

'I wonder about that ring.' Benjamin stared across to where a group of courtiers had stopped by a fountain, talking to each other in high-pitched voices which even drowned the strident screams of the peacocks.

'Master, you were going to say?'

'Well, there's a story that Agrippa raised a demon who worked for Wolsey and this demon is controlled by a magical ring.' He laughed. 'I just wondered if the ring Francis has is the one of popular legend? Or it could be a present from our Henry's dead brother and, though I speak in riddles, the king's brother is the cause of our present problems . . .'

(I see my chaplain snorting with laughter about the

148

magic ring. He doesn't know what he's talking about. We may live in more enlightened days but one of Wolsey's enemies, the Duke of Norfolk, actually hired a conjuror to make him a cloak of invisibility from linen and buckram cloth, treated with horse bones, chalk and powdered glass. Oh, I don't know whether it worked. If I thought it did I would get one myself and go up to the hay loft and see why my chaplain takes the apple-cheeked, full-bosomed Mabel there to instruct her.)

Ah, well, at Fontainebleau I was more concerned with practical realities. Benjamin and I returned to our chamber to prepare for the great feast. My master instructed me to keep careful note of the rest of our companions and watch if any tried to slip away.

That evening banquet was memorable! The banqueting hall was a sea of light and silk; thousands of torches, ten times that number of beeswax candles, silver plate, Venetian glass, and every type of food: sea hogs, beef and garlic, fawn in a ginger salt, and subtle confectionery in the shapes of figures and birds. Naturally, we got the Archangel Raphael sculptured in sugar and wax! Dacourt, Millet and the Clintons were invited to the great table on the dais. We were shoved far down the hall near the door just under the gallery where hordes of musicians played viol, sackbuts and tambours, whilst young boys from the Abbey of St Denis sang sweet carols until some of the guests began to pelt them with sugared almonds and sponge cakes. There were the usual masques and drinking contests but, for once, I kept sober, carefully watching my companions.

Towards the end of the evening the king and his council moved amongst us. I saw Lady Clinton deep in conversation with Vauban, whilst Sir Robert was involved in a fierce dispute with a physician over the elements of certain chemicals. Benjamin remained sombre, watching everything around him. Suddenly, Vauban was between us, placing his hands on our shoulders. My master flinched but Vauban was amity personified.

'You like Paris, Master Daunbey?'

'No,' Benjamin lied, pressing his leg against mine.

I followed his glance: Millet had disappeared. Vauban, however, seemed intent on distracting us.

'Oh, surely you like Paris? You must come to my home near the Rue des Moines behind the cathedral of Notre Dame. It stands in its own grounds. I call it La Pleasaunce.'

'You live there alone?' my master asked.

'Oh, no, Monsieur. I have a family.'

I caught the note of pride in Vauban's voice.

'Little angels,' he murmured.

Now, I had had enough of this baiting so I threw him an angry glance.

'Monsieur Shallot, you are surprised I have a family?'

'No, Vauban, I am not. Even Nero had one. What would surprise me is that you had parents!'

His smile dropped, as did his hand to his dagger hilt.

'One day, Monsieur, you will pay for that remark.'

'As you will,' I snarled back.

I watched him walk away whilst Benjamin calmed me by refilling my wine goblet.

'Master, I hate that man!'

'So do I, Roger, and for the same reason.' Benjamin's eyes softened. 'I know about Agnes,' he said gently. 'Vauban was behind her death. But he's a dangerous man, Roger. You have insulted him and he will exact a price.'

150

'I don't give a damn!' I replied. 'I only wish I could place him. I have seen his face before.'

'Well, naturally, in London.'

'No, no, all I saw were his paid thugs. I may have heard his voice but I never clapped eyes on him that I can remember until that day outside Abbé Gerard's church. What is more immediately interesting,' I continued, 'is Master Millet's disappearance. I wonder where, and I wonder why?'

We sat and waited. It must have been over an hour before Millet returned. He was followed by a young, French courtier who immediately went up to Vauban, now beside the king, and whispered heatedly into his ear. Vauban grinned, and not for the first time I began to wonder if our Master Millet was Raphael.

Chapter 8

The feasting and masquerades must have lasted for many hours but we retired early to our beds and in the morning joined our companions in the gardens for a light collation of watered wine and freshly baked bread. Most of our conversation was about the feast the night before. Throgmorton and Peckle had drunk too much, Clinton was describing his dispute with the French physician to a bored Dacourt, Master Millet looked worried, white-faced and red-eyed. Lady Francesca joined us, looking as cold and beautiful as a spring morning. Benjamin complimented her on the perfume she was wearing which drew a snort of laughter from Throgmorton.

'All perfumes smell the same,' he jibed. 'They could be sulphur and mercury for all I care.'

Lady Francesca threw him a dagger-glance and was on the point of replying when a royal herald entered the gardens to summon us to the great courtyard to see the king's justice being done. Sir Robert turned to his wife.

'You, my dear, are excused.' His face became severe. 'I insist. It's best if you return to your chamber and see that all is well.'

I was surprised. I had never seen Sir Robert look so angry or, indeed, Lady Francesca so submissive as she trotted off. Sir Robert whispered something to Venner then stared round at us all.

'What we are going to see,' he announced, 'is not a pleasant sight, but we are in France.' He made a face. 'Convention must be followed. If royal justice is to be done, then all males above the age of eighteen who are attendant upon the king must be present.'

I hadn't any idea what he was talking about, more bemused by Lady Francesca's sudden departure; the others, however, looked strained and nervous and I caught Master Benjamin gulping anxiously. We re-entered the palace, passed down sun-dappled corridors and came out above a great courtyard. We found ourselves on a balcony which stood over a porticoed colonnade, beneath us a great black-and-white stone courtyard. The king, flanked by leading notables, was seated on a throne like a Roman Emperor about to watch some gladiatorial display. The rest of the court whispered nervously, with catches of high laughter and forced bonhomie, clearly apprehensive of what was to happen.

I'll tell you this, it was a nightmare. A herald blew a sharp, shrill blast on his trumpet, a door in the courtyard opened and a small procession filed out, led by the master executioner dressed in black from head to toe. Behind him walked a royal serjeant-at-arms and other assistants. Again a short, sharp burst of the trumpet and a line of chained, condemned men were led out. They looked like prisoners the world over; dirty, dishevelled, haggard, bare-foot, and heavily manacled both at wrist and ankle.

The serjeant-at-arms read out a list of crimes. I couldn't understand everything he said but the word *trahaison*, treason, was repeated. Justice was then dispensed. Now,

154

our Great Killer in England was fond of sending wives and friends to the block – poor John Fisher, Bishop of Rochester, had to watch his own scaffold being built – but Henry always kept well away from the killing ground. He was dancing when Boleyn died and hunting when poor Catherine Howard was hustled off to her death on Tower Green. But Francis wanted to see justice done. His court was like that, moving from brilliant scholarship to the stark, bleak horrors of the Dark Ages. (Oh, by the way, he got worse. Men tied in bull-skins were baited to death by dogs. The French palaces became Murder's own playground. One of Francis's sons was killed by a strange poison fused in water. The assassin was torn apart by horses. Another was murdered whilst playing snow-balls when someone threw a linen cupboard out of a window above him and crushed his skull. Catherine de Medici, Francis's daughter-in-law, liked to have the bodies of her opponents brought fresh from the scaffold so she could inspect them, and specialised in putting her prisoners in wooden cages suspended from beams. I know, I spent a bloody week in one of them, but that's another story.)

On that sunny morning in Fontainebleau I certainly saw the dark side of Francis's court. Two men were quickly garotted, their last gasps sounding like a thunder clap in that silent courtyard. Two more had their noses slit and ears cropped whilst the fifth, poor wretch, had his lips and eyes sewn together. He would then be put in a huge sack with two starving mongrels and thrown into the nearest river. Sentence was carried out in a deathly silence broken only by the shrieks and groans of the prisoners, the grunting of the executioner, and the stifled

155

sobs of some of the courtiers. Benjamin turned his back but I stood as if rooted to the spot, fascinated by the horrors being perpetrated.

I could see why Sir Robert Clinton had told Lady Francesca to withdraw, or at least I thought I did. Eventually the macabre show was over: the trumpet shrilled, the executioner's assistant cleared the courtyard, whilst others began to wash the blood and gore away until it seemed as if the strangulations and mutilations were all part of a bad dream. A herald shouted we were to return to the square to see a show of a different kind. The French king rose, clapped his hands. The courtiers, most of them like me pallid and a little green about the gills, went back to their different pursuits. Very few expressed a desire for anything to eat or drink. Benjamin tugged me by the sleeve and we left Dacourt and the rest murmuring about French severity compared to the clemency of the English king. I found that really amusing!

Benjamin led me back to the gardens. 'What do you think, Roger?' he asked.

'Barbaric,' I replied.

Benjamin stared up at the blue sky. 'No man should be dealt with like those poor captives.' He narrowed his eyes. 'Our French king must have read Machiavelli. Those executions were meant as a warning: no matter how beautiful the palace is, how generous the prince, how gorgeous the garden, the king will not be brooked.'

'Do you think he was warning us, master?'

'Perhaps. He may know we wish to seize that ring. Of course, it could be a general threat. I wonder who our spy is?' he murmured, changing the subject.

'Millet went missing last night.'

156

'Yes, and I noticed he slipped away during the executions. He whispered to Dacourt that he felt sick but our good friend Vauban was also missing and I find that strange. Vauban strikes me as a man who would like to watch others die.'

'We know one thing, master.'

'Which is?'

'The spy and the murderer are one and the same person.'

'Yes, I can see that. It must have been someone in the château the night Falconer died and someone who could take a poisoned flask of wine down to Abbé Gerard.' Benjamin chewed his lip. 'It would also seem that our good Monsieur Vauban and his Luciferi only reveal their knowledge of English secrets when letters reach France.'

'So that rules out Robert Clinton, his wife and his servant?'

'Why?'

'Well, they were in England when Gerard and Falconer died.'

'True, true,' Benjamin murmured. 'But I wonder about the Lady Francesca. Why do royal messengers take presents to that convent?'

'And why does the spy use the name Raphael?' I asked. 'Oh, I know, master, it's the name of an archangel, but Falconer seemed fascinated by it and I wonder if the actual name contains any clue to this mystery?'

We talked for a while, sitting in a quiet garden bower, sifting through names and wondering about the identity of this traitor and assassin until Venner arrived.

'Sir Robert Clinton requires your presence!' he shouted good-naturedly, catching sight of us. 'The French king has another masque. Don't worry,' he grinned, 'I don't think it's a repetition of this morning's horrors.'

We followed Venner back as he chattered gaily about the boar he'd glimpsed in a cage in another part of the palace grounds.

'A magnificent beast,' he murmured. 'The French king captured it himself. He's as obsessed with the hunt as he is with the ladies. Did you know that when his favourite greyhound died he had the dog's corpse skinned and a pair of gloves specially fashioned for him which he wore for months to remind him of the animal?'

'I hope he doesn't have *us* skinned!' I retorted. 'What's he going to do, make us fight the boar?'

(All I can say is that many a true word is spoken in jest!)

We found the rest of the courtiers reassembled on the balcony overlooking the courtyard. Millet had rejoined our group. He still looked pallid and the front of his doublet was stained with vomit. The rest, however, were chatting happily, drinking and eating from the different dishes being carried round by young girls dressed in cloth of gold. Lady Francesca was also there, teasing Dacourt about his moustache, whilst Sir Robert was loudly lecturing Throgmorton on the veracity of the science of alchemy. He turned and waved at us to join him, drawing Benjamin into the debate, whilst I stood and stared around.

The French king lounged on his throne, his fat queen beside him, whilst on his other side stood Vauban, whispering softly in his master's ear. He looked up, caught sight of me, grinned and waved as if we were old friends. I looked away. The courtyard below had been cleaned

158

and life-sized mannequins placed there. Now, let me describe what happened and be precise about the details. I was standing overlooking the courtyard, a drop of about twelve feet but protected by a thick, oaken palisade which rose about waist high. Behind me the rest of our group talked and chattered whilst servants bustled about. A trumpet sounded, the door below was once again thrown open and the most gigantic boar I have ever seen bounded into the courtyard. He looked as if he had swept in from hell itself; massive shoulders where the muscles hunched, a high ridge of hair bristling down the line of his spine, powerful, black hindquarters and a face as ugly as my chaplain's. Most notable were a huge, wet snout and white, cruel tusks which curved up like scimitars. Even from where I stood I could see the rage blazing in those eyes and throbbing in every muscle of that brutish body.

The beast stood pawing the ground, his breath coming in short gasps, and I caught a whiff of the foul stench. A deathly hush fell as everyone pushed towards the palisade, necks strained, all eyes on this terrible beast. For a few seconds he stood, head swaying slightly from side to side then he caught a glimpse of the gaily caparisoned mannequins and charged wildly at them. He moved his massive bulk with the speed and grace of a greyhound, smashing the statues over, then turning to rip them to pieces with those cruel tusks. The crowd 'Oohed' and 'Ahed', following with a ripple of applause. The beast stopped, his head came up and he glared in fury at his tormentors.

I was fascinated. I was leaning forward like the rest when someone gave me a vicious shove in the middle of my back and I tilted head first over the parapet. Oh, I was supposed to fall to the courtyard below but fear always sharpens old Shallot's wits. Even as I fell, I gripped a rib of stone which ran just beneath the parapet. I could hear the shouting and screaming. Benjamin called my name. I scrabbled for a better grip even as I heard the boar charge and stop just below me, craning its neck, head swaying from side to side, those wicked tusks narrowly missing the heels of my boots.

'Roger, my hand!' Benjamin was leaning over the parapet, arm extended.

Bruised and shaken, I eased my grip to grasp his hand – and slipped. It was only a few feet yet I seemed to be dropping for miles. The boar, startled, galloped away, turned, and stared at me. It lowered its head, its hooves stirred, and suddenly it threw itself into a furious charge. There was nowhere to run. I just stared in terror at this huge, black beast bearing down on me. Suddenly a crossbow bolt whirred and the boar stopped as if stunned. I saw the snout go down for another charge, then the boar collapsed on to its side. Only then did I glimpse the bolt embedded deeply just above the beast's eyes. I heard the applause, shouts of 'Well done!', and looked up. Benjamin stood holding a crossbow, probably snatched from one of the guards. Beside him, Vauban stood grinning down at me.

'Monsieur Shallot!' he called out. 'You were supposed to watch the show, not become part of it!'

This remark was translated back into French and evoked bellows of laughter. I just crouched. I daren't stand. I was in a state of terror, fearful lest I wet myself or collapse in a gibbering heap.

'Monsieur,' I called, 'I thank you for your concern.'

Vauban shrugged. 'Everyone, Monsieur Shallot,' he retorted, 'has a guardian angel to watch over him. Perhaps Master Daunbey is yours!'

The door in the courtyard opened and Benjamin strode out. He pulled me up by the arm as if I was a child and gently led me away from well-wishers, Dacourt's party and the rest, into a little chamber along the corridor. He made me sit and left for a few minutes, bringing back a huge, deep-bowled wine cup filled to the brim.

'Drink that!' he ordered. 'But drink it slowly!'

'Vauban and his bloody angels,' I moaned. 'I was pushed! Deliberately pushed! For God's sake, master, who was it?'

'I don't know. We were all at the edge of the balcony leaning over the parapet. There were servants going backwards and forwards. I was further down on your left. You just seemed to slide over the parapet. I thought you were gone.'

'Some bastard pushed me,' I repeated. 'But why?'

Benjamin just looked out of the window and shook his head. 'Apparently you know something, Roger. The question is, what?'

We were interrupted by a knock on the door and Clinton and Dacourt came in.

'Shallot, you've recovered?' Clinton asked.

'Oh, yes, as fine as a flower in spring,' I snarled. 'I'll be even better when my bowels stop churning and my legs have some strength.'

Sir Robert grinned. 'You were pushed,' he remarked quietly.

'Nonsense!' Dacourt interrupted.

161

'No, no, he was pushed,' Clinton repeated. 'By whom or why I don't know but it's time we left here. I have paid my compliments to His Most Christian Majesty!' The words were spat out. 'And I think it's time we were on the road.' Clinton stopped at the door and looked back. 'Do you know who pushed you, Roger?'

'No, but if I did, the bastard would be lying on top of that damn' boar!'

Clinton made a face. Dacourt glared over at me and followed him out.

'Come on, Roger,' Benjamin murmured. 'I have a feeling more horrors are about to occur.'

We left Fontainebleau just as the great, ornate clock was striking the first half-hour after mid-day. The excitement of my accident had died down. Venner was most solicitous and, whilst Benjamin kept to himself, Clinton's manservant rode along beside me, generously offering a wineskin he had filched from the kitchen. Dacourt and the Clintons went ahead whilst a few of Vauban's horsemen, red-bearded rascals in armour, guarded our front and rear. We wound down the white dusty lanes. The sun was hot, and in the heat of the day even the birds kept quiet and cooled themselves in the green darkness of the surrounding forest. After two hours' riding we stopped. Clinton said his horse was rather lame and asked Throgmorton to check it out. Venner laid out cloths beneath some trees and spread pastries and freshly baked bread, wrapped in linen cloths, which his master had commandeered from the royal kitchens. Small, horn-glazed goblets were distributed and Clinton produced a sealed flagon of wine.

'A present from Monsieur Vauban,' he remarked

quietly. 'The best of the claret from the first year of His Majesty's reign.'

He tore open the seal and half-filled his goblet. The sun danced on the many rings on his fingers. We were seated in a semicircle. Lady Francesca was wearing a broad-brimmed hat with a lace veil protecting her skin against the heat and dust.

'Be careful, Sir Robert!' Benjamin suddenly called out.

Clinton stopped, the goblet halfway to his lips, whilst everyone stared at my master.

'What happened to Roger this morning,' he continued, 'was no accident. Falconer died after drinking wine, as did the Abbé Gerard. How do we know that His Most Christian Majesty's gift is not poisoned?'

I stared back. Vauban's horsemen had also stopped. Most of them had dismounted and were lying in the shade of the trees, talking softly in their strange, sing-song accents. A prickle of fear ran along my spine. Despite the wine I had gulped at Fontainebleau, I still felt threatened, pursued by some silent, vindictive fury. Clinton narrowed his eyes and sniffed at the wine.

'The seal was unbroken,' he observed. 'I do not think His Most Christian Majesty would like to explain to his brother of England why his envoys died after drinking some wine, especially provided by the French king.' Sir Robert smiled, sipped the wine and smacked his lips. 'If that's poisoned,' he announced, 'then I'll drink it every day.'

The tension abated, the wine was served, Clinton pouring it, Venner passing it along. Throgmorton rejoined us, announcing that there was nothing wrong with Clinton's horse. The food was served and duly tasted but Clinton's

163

remark had abated our suspicions and we gossiped about what we had seen at the French court. Lady Francesca, however, remained silent, sipping at her wine but refusing to touch any of the food. We continued our journey and must have ridden for another hour when Throgmorton reined in, holding his stomach, his mouth gaping and his face deathly pale, hair matted with sweat.

'These pains,' he croaked. 'Oh, my lord!'

We gathered round him. Throgmorton suddenly vomited, his face turning a blueish tinge.

'I have been poisoned,' he whispered. 'This is poison!'

He stretched out a hand towards Benjamin and, before we could help, slid out of the saddle and crashed to the earth, his horse sheering away in fright. We dismounted and stood round him. For a few seconds Throgmorton lashed out like a landed fish, in short sharp convulsions, vomiting and retching, gasping for air. He scrambled on all fours like a dog, his back arched, then he collapsed, eyes and mouth open.

Lady Francesca turned away, her gloved hand pushing part of her lace veil to her mouth as if she, too, wanted to be sick. Peckle, Millet and Venner just stood like frightened children, Dacourt loudly cursed whilst Clinton helped my master try to find some pulse in the now prostrate doctor.

'He's dead,' Benjamin observed. 'Sir John, I would be grateful if you could keep Vauban's riders away. Tell them the good doctor has suffered a heart seizure.'

'Has he?' Clinton asked.

Benjamin turned the body over and sniffed at the dead man's gaping mouth. 'No seizure, Sir Robert. Look at the livid skin and blue lips. Throgmorton was poisoned, probably with white or red arsenic. If he had vomited earlier, perhaps he might have lived.'

'Would arsenic act so quickly?' Clinton queried and I remembered his keen interest in such matters. 'Surely not, Master Daunbey, the dose would have to be powerful. I suspect it was mixed with something else, something which struck at Throgmorton's heart.'

My master chewed his lip and gently touched the dead man's damp cheek. 'Perhaps you are right, Sir Robert.'

'I know I am; arsenic and perhaps digitalis or deadly nightshade. But when? We all drank the same wine and who could know which piece of food Throgmorton would choose?'

Clinton had the baskets containing the food and wine unpacked. The rest of what was left was carefully examined, including the wine flask and the cups though these had been washed clean in a nearby brook: no trace of poison was found. Clinton stared at the sky, blood red in the sunset.

'We must continue,' he ordered. 'We should be off the roads before nightfall. Maubisson is only another hour.'

Poor Throgmorton's body was tossed across his horse and our sombre journey continued like something from a macabre dream. We rode along the country track, winding between dark woods, lush green fields, past hamlets betrayed only by faint spirals of smoke. Vauban's colourful riders clustered around us: Lady Clinton masked; Sir Robert Clinton and my master deep in conversation; the rest riding silently; and, at the back, led by poor Venner, Throgmorton's dreadful cadaver strapped to his horse as if Death himself was trailing us to Maubisson.

We found the château sleeping lazily under the warm

evening sun. Vauban's men went back to their camp before the walls as we clattered across the drawbridge and Dacourt bellowed for servants. Throgmorton's body was sheeted and carried to lie beside that of Waldegrave in the small chapel, Dacourt issuing strict orders that they both be taken down to the cemetery in the village and given summary burial.

The ambassador then ordered us all into the hall where the food baskets were laid out on the table whilst Clinton instructed us to take the same positions as we had during Throgmorton's final, dreadful meal. A wine flagon was ordered and, in a sinister imitation of our picnic, the wine served. Yet we could clarify nothing.

'Was it the food?' Benjamin queried. 'Or the wine which was poisoned? If it was the food, then how did the murderer know which piece poor Throgmorton would take? We all drank the wine and no one knew which cup he would drink from.'

The discussion continued. Had it been an article of Throgmorton's clothing? Peckle and Venner were sent to check, but returned none the wiser.

'The French could have done it,' Clinton observed. 'Before Throgmorton left Fontainebleau.'

'No,' Benjamin countered. 'Throgmorton did not begin to sweat until he had stopped to eat and drink with us. One of us here is the poisoner.'

My master's words stilled all the clamour and debate. Lady Francesca leaned forward, her beautiful face lined and pallid.

'But why?' she asked. 'Why poor Throgmorton? How do we know,' she continued, 'that he was the intended victim? Perhaps his death was a mistake and the poison

166

intended for someone else?'

Lady Francesca's shrewd remark hit home. We all became suspicious of each other. There were mumbled excuses and the meeting broke up. Benjamin and I returned to our chamber and my master lay on his bed staring up at the ceiling.

'Lady Francesca could be correct,' he began. 'Perhaps Throgmorton's death was a blunder.' He continued to stare at the rafters. 'So far,' he said, 'Vauban and his Luciferi control this game. All we do is jerk like puppets at the end of their strings. Perhaps it is time we took matters into our own hands?'

'And do what?' I asked. 'Storm the Louvre Palace, seize Vauban and torture him until he tells us all? Knowing that sadistic bastard,' I added, 'he'd probably like that!'

Benjamin smiled lazily. 'A worthy suggestion, Roger. But we should ignore Vauban, he only receives the information. We hunt the man or woman who supplies him with it, and should follow our suspicions.'

'Such as?'

'Well, Master Millet for a start. He creeps out of here at night. He goes missing during the French king's ostentatious banquet.' Benjamin swung his long legs off the bed and peered up at me. 'And by the way, that banquet gave me an idea. Anyway, Millet's our quarry. I doubt if he will leave Maubisson tonight but tomorrow, Roger, you will slip through Vauban's men, wait in the forest and follow him into Paris.'

'Oh, thank you,' I replied. 'Just what old Shallot needs! Wandering around the smelly streets of Paris with Vauban and his bloody Luciferi following me!'

'You know Paris.'

'Yes, I know bloody Paris!' I wailed. 'Because I stayed there for months, starving and freezing, before being half-hanged at Montfaucon!'

'Look,' Benjamin rose and placed a hand on my shoulder, 'I want you to go to Paris. We have to see where Millet goes and whom he meets. You know the old haunts of the Maillotins. You knew one of their leaders, Broussac. First, try and see if he or his comrades were involved in the attack here. Secondly,' his long face broke into a smile, 'I want you to hire the most expensive courtesan in Paris, someone fresh, someone unknown, someone who will catch the eye of the king.'

Now I was perplexed.

'What do we do, master? Send her into King Francis's bedchamber to ask for the ring?'

'No, no! In a week's time we celebrate the Feast of St John the Baptist, patron saint of England. I am going to persuade Dacourt and Clinton to open the coffers and arrange a lavish banquet at which King Francis will be the guest of honour. Our girl will be there.' He shrugged. 'We leave the rest to chance.'

'And if it doesn't work?'

'If it does not work, my dear Roger, we'll try something else. But Francis will come, and with him Vauban. We'll have an opportunity to watch the French and see if anything happens. For the rest . . .' He became brisk, undid a small coffer and pulled out a fresh roll of parchment, ink horn and quill, and sat down at the small table, pen poised. 'Let us list again,' he said, 'what we know. For eighteen months a spy at the English court has been selling secrets to the French. He or she uses the name

Raphael. Two months ago, just before Lent, Clinton and the Lady Francesca came here, and Sir Robert, together with Falconer, tried to find out who Raphael is. Falconer lost one of his best spies in Paris but not before the name Raphael was handed over. Clinton, with his wife, then left for England.

'The messengers travelling to and from the English court regularly stop off at the convent where the Lady Francesca was educated. There's nothing suspicious about that. Lady Francesca was apparently devoted to them; they send her gifts and she reciprocates.' Benjamin paused, his quill scratching across the parchment as he listed his conclusions. 'Now,' he looked up at me, 'these couriers are also of interest to us. Two of them were butchered outside the convent on the road to Paris though the diplomatic bags they carried were not tampered with but handed over intact to the English embassy. All became quiet until, just after Easter, Falconer shared some wine with Dacourt. He was then seen happily walking up to the top of the tower but later found dead at the bottom. The wine was not poisoned, Falconer was not drunk, and he was alone on the tower. So how did he die?'

Benjamin stared at me but I just shook my head.

'About the same time,' my master continued, 'a respected priest, Abbé Gerard, was found floating face down in his own carp pond. Abbé Gerard was once confessor to our king and Henry gave him a copy of St Augustine's work *On Chastity*. That book has now disappeared but Vauban and his Luciferi would love to find it.

'Finally, we have the business of the ring. Henry has made our task more difficult by demanding its return, but

169

so far we meet with little success in this or anything else. Raphael is still giving our secrets to his masters. You were nearly killed at Fontainebleau whilst both Walde-grave and Throgmorton have died in mysterious circum-stances.' Benjamin paused and drew a deep breath. 'What else do we know? That Millet is acting suspiciously. Anything else?'

'We do know,' I said, 'that the killer must be someone in the embassy here. The secrets appear to be revealed only when despatches arrive at Maubisson or at the embassy house in Paris. But you are right, master, the only clue we have is Millet's suspicious behaviour.'

Chapter 9

Early the next day, I strapped a money belt round my waist and armed myself with a fearsome sword and dagger. I saddled my horse and, slipping through a postern gate, managed to ride round Vauban's men, along the country tracks, towards the main road into Paris. Millet would have to follow the same route for his nocturnal journey and all I had to do was leave the road, lurk amongst the trees and watch for him to arrive. Naturally, this meant a tedious wait, broken only by the consolation of an occasional sip from a wineskin and tender thoughts of my dear, dead Agnes. I became quite maudlin, so locked in my misery I almost missed the faint clip-clop of hooves on the gravelled track. My long wait was rewarded: Millet, dressed from head to toe like a courtier, was riding into Paris without a care in the world.

I let him go and, following Benjamin's instructions, waited for a quarter of an hour before I took up a slow pursuit. As we approached the Porte D'Orléans the task became easier as the thoroughfares became clogged with wandering friars, pedlars, tradesmen, country bumpkins, wandering scholars, troubadours, and even a few Egyptians with their gaudily painted caravans and a tame bear which danced to the tune of a reedy flute. Millet was easy to keep in sight. He stabled his horse at a tavern just within the gateway. I followed suit, then tracked him through the winding streets of Paris.

The city teemed with noise and clamour. Every rogue in Christendom seemed to have gathered to join his fellows and they swarmed like fleas on a turd: musicians; students in their tight hose and protuberant cod-pieces; relic-sellers; rag-pickers with their wheelbarrows full of scraps of cloth; knights; porters; priests; hawkers and beggars; young nobles with falcons on their wrists, riding through all this din in order to train their birds not to stir or flutter at any noise. The gibbets were well hung. Near the Grand Pont the spire of a church had collapsed and was surrounded by a mass of onlookers. Carts full of produce forced their way through from the Seine, jostling with huge carriages pulled by two palfreys which could take six people sitting alongside each other on a bench. The late evening rang with the sound of bells from dozens of churches, rivalled by the shrieks of the urchins who pelted a convoy of carts full of criminals, each with a halter round his neck, as they made their way down to the city gaol.

All the time I kept one eye on Master Millet's colourful jerkin as he wound through the fetid streets, sauntering daintily around piles of refuse and ducking carefully to avoid the painted signs which hung outside the houses, at times so clustered together they blocked out the sun. We crossed the Petit Pont on to the Ile de la Cité. For a while my quarry sauntered under the towering mass of Notre Dame where stone gargoyles snarled above us. He stopped at a wine shop. I waited outside, realising that Master Millet was killing time. When he came out he walked straight into the nearby cemetery of Holy Innocents Church.

The graveyard was massive, like a huge paddock, surrounded by a high, brick wall. It was a favourite meeting place for Parisians; lovers lounged in the long grass whilst hucksters laid their wares out on the tops of weather-beaten tombstones. A strange place, this cemetery! The mud there was so foul some claimed it was mixed with sulphur, and it had become a favourite burial place because the corpses interred there decomposed quickly. One wag said it took only nine days. The bodies were buried just a few inches beneath the soil and I saw two dogs fighting over some deceased person's thigh bone. Most of the weather-worn tombstones had collapsed and the few wooden crosses leaned drunkenly to one side. In the centre was a huge watch light, a thick tallow candle placed on a high stone plinth, protected by a metal hood, which was lit every night to fend off evil spirits. Little arches had been built into the cemetery wall where the more wealthy had their remains interred in the pious hope that their bones would not become the meal of some scavenging dog. Above these arches was a huge open loft or garret. Every so often the cemetery would be cleared of all its remains to make way for fresh corpses. The bones collected would be tossed into this garret and, when I saw it, the pile was at least two yards deep. In fact, the French had a joke: for a Christian, Paradise was heaven, but for a dog Paradise was a charnel house at Holy Innocents!

Millet sauntered round this macabre place. I watched him carefully. So far he had met no one. I was confident he had not seen me but, at the same time, I was uneasy.

I felt sure I was being watched but, when I turned sharply or hid behind corners, I noticed nothing untoward. At last Millet went into Holy Innocents Church. I followed and stood admiring the Dance of Death carved in the stone work. (Believe me, if you are full of the joys of spring, that carving will soon remind you that in the midst of life we are in death. The sculptor must have had a genius all of his own, for Death and his squadron of devils danced in a drunken stone frenzy along the frieze, collecting kings, emperors, popes, bishops, and I suppose, when the time is right, even old Shallot.) A bell sounded, its hollow boom sounding out above the grave-yard, and I glimpsed Millet coming out of the church, so I hid in the shadows and let him go by. I noticed others in the cemetery had begun to stir and wondered if the bell was the curfew when the graveyard must be locked.

Millet, however, followed by other fops and dandies, left the cemetery by a small postern door and made his way up an alleyway to a dingy-looking tavern with the sign of a golden sickle above it. Inside, the taproom was large, spacious, clean and well swept. Each table was hidden in a shadowy alcove and the wine was served by young boys dressed in tight hose and short jerkins who had the looks, hair style and walk of saucy young wenches. Their lips were carmine-painted and the one who served me wore more face powder than any self-respecting whore in London would have used. I ordered wine and carefully watched the other side of the room where Millet was sitting.

Now, in my youth I may have been inexperienced but I had no illusions about the Golden Sickle or Millet's presence there. It was a molly-shop, or so the denizens

174

of Southwark would have termed it: a drinking house where young men, or old, who liked other men could meet kindred spirits in a warm, intimate and secure spot. Believe me, they had to be careful! The laws against sodomy and buggery were as cruel in Paris as they were in London. If caught, the culprit could face hanging, disembowelling and castration – though I suppose, by the time you reach the last, you'd really be past caring. Now I do not sit in judgement. I just report things as they are, not as they should be. Indeed, to be perfectly honest, I always felt sorry for the likes of Millet: their lives were an eternal nightmare, waiting for the traitor or paid informer to turn them in.

I wanted to see who Millet was meeting. Certain men did approach his table but he summarily dismissed them. (There goes my chaplain again. 'Did any approach you?' he sneers. Well, I've never claimed to be an Adonis. Yes, one did approach me, and no, contrary to my chaplain's opinion, he wasn't blind, just as drunk as a bishop's donkey!) An hour passed. I had to be careful I didn't become tipsy for the drink was heavy and rich.

At last a young man came in, covered from head to toe in a long, black cloak, the hood pulled well forward. He sauntered up to Millet. Our young Horatio smiled at him and the stranger sat down. He pulled back his hood and I gasped. You see, I have an excellent memory for faces and I was sure I had glimpsed the man amongst Vauban's entourage at Fontainebleau. Millet and he talked for a while then rose and left the tavern. I followed a few minutes later but, when I reached the darkened alleyway beyond, they had disappeared and, despite my curses and hurrying to and fro, I had lost them. I stumbled

175

round the church of Holy Innocents for a while but my search was fruitless so I decided to fulfil the second part of my master's instructions.

Now, if you have read the earlier instalment of my memoirs, you will recall that the previous year I'd spent some time in Paris as the enforced guest of the Maillotins, or 'Club-Men' as they called themselves. They were the bottom layer of Parisian society who constantly plotted and conspired to bring about a bloody revolution and create God's kingdom here, where justice and prosperity would reign and the meek would surely inherit the earth. Of course, they were idiots or dreamers. As far as I can see, the only earth the meek inherit is a shallow hole in the likes of Holy Innocents graveyard, and even then the dogs make sure they don't have that for long. Now, I had become friendly with the Maillotins, especially two of their leaders, Capote and Broussac. Capote had died, choking his life out on the gallows of Montfaucon. I hoped Broussac had not yet received his just reward as I slipped like a cat along the dark, foul, smelly alleyways of Paris to the tavern where he and his court of whores always assembled.

I was not disappointed. Broussac was in the same corner, drinking himself stupid, surrounded by some of the most loud-mouthed harridans of the city. At first he didn't recognise me, but isn't silver wonderful? I produced two coins and Broussac's red, beery, dark-whiskered face broke into a gap-toothed grin and those wicked eyes danced with merriment.

'Of course,' he bellowed, throwing one smelly arm round my neck and planting wine-drenched kisses on my cheeks. 'Ladies,' he shouted, 'may I present Master

176

Roger Shallot, the only good Goddamn – the only *man* who was hanged at Montfaucon and survived to tell the tale!'

I told the noisy bastard to shut his mouth as I did not want to be arrested by the Provosts as a spy. Another piece of silver was produced. Broussac became as sober as a priest, ordered a fresh jug of wine, two of the establishment's cleaner cups, and a table far enough away from any would-be eavesdropper.

'Listen, Broussac,' I began. 'Forget old times. Here's a coin. Answer one question: the attack on Maubisson, did the Maillotins organise it?'

Broussac grabbed the coin.

'No,' he replied. 'We did not. We never leave the streets of Paris. But, for another coin, I can tell you who did.'

I flicked a further piece of silver across the table. Broussac clutched it and it disappeared in a twinkling of an eye. I don't know how he did it, whether he had purses in his sleeves: one minute he had it in his hairy paw, the next it was gone.

'Well, come on,' I demanded. 'Who the hell did?'

'Look around you, Monsieur.'

'That's no answer.'

He saw my hand go to my knife.

'Now, now,' he purred like some benevolent cat. 'Come on, old friend, what are you going to do? Draw on poor Broussac? If you do, you'll never leave this tavern alive. As it is, you still might not!'

I looked around. In the poor light of the smelly, tallow candles, every customer resembled a rat on two legs. Their thin, pallid or yellowing faces, greedy looks and sharp glances proved Broussac right and I cursed myself. I was in the devil's own kitchen and these were his scullions: dice-coggers, coin-flickers, pickpockets, pimps, conjurors (most of them failed), footpads and nightwalkers. Indeed, in any other circumstances, I would have felt very much at home but I'd been so eager to see Broussac I had blundered in and now began to wonder how I would get out. He leaned over and seized my wrist.

'Don't worry,' he whispered as if reading my thoughts. 'You're Broussac's friend. I have given you the kiss of friendship.'

'Aye, and so did Judas!'

Broussac threw back his head and bellowed with laughter until his devil's eyes disappeared in rolls of flesh.

'Listen, Broussac,' I continued, 'I have no wish to quarrel but I asked you a question and paid you good silver!'

'And I gave you fair answer. These villains took part in the attack on Maubisson. They were hired by bully-boys and organised by some great lord, I don't know who.'

I knew I would get no further. 'There's something else,' I hastily added. 'I need a whore.'

'Don't we all, my friend?'

'No, I want a high-ranking courtesan brought to the Château Maubisson within three days. She is to assume a new name and tell no one her true identity. If you do this you will be richly rewarded.'

Broussac's smile widened as if he could almost hear the chink of coins falling in his purse. He rose and beckoned me to follow.

'Come, we cannot talk here.'

We went upstairs to a small, dust-laden chamber where

Broussac ordered some stools and fresh wine, shouting for the best, not the vinegared water I had been sipping down in the tap room. A slattern, having lit candles, hurried up with this. Broussac, his face as serious as a father confessor, leaned forward.

'How much?' he asked.

'For your expenses, two hundred pounds.'

'Sterling?'

'No, *livres tournois* or fifty pounds sterling, in freshly minted coins.'

'And for the whore?'

'Four hundred pounds, *livres tournois* or one hundred pounds sterling.'

'Where's the money?'

I emptied the contents of one small purse into his grimy paw. 'There's twenty-five pounds. Before you get the rest the girl must be with us, suitably clad, and bringing one fresh gown with her. She must be,' I continued, 'beautiful, wholesome and pleasing. Not one of your doxies,' I added. 'I want a courtesan, someone skilled in the social arts and graces.'

The old rogue heard me out.

'One final thing,' I added. 'I want to leave here and reach Maubisson without let or hindrance. I have seen the pack of weasels below. I don't want to be followed and quietly knocked on the head.'

Broussac smiled, rose, and pointed to the wafer-thin pallet bed in the corner. 'Tonight, rest here. Tomorrow,' he picked up the wine jug and cup, 'you will be safely back at Maubisson.'

He left, closing the door quietly behind him, and I heard the bolts being pulled across. That night I slept the sleep of the just. You see, I trusted Broussac. He'd walk to Cathay and back if he thought there was enough profit in it for him. The next morning he roused me, his manner all servile. I broke my fast on bread and wine, and Broussac, true to his word, led me through the streets of Paris to the Porte D'Orléans, not leaving me until the turrets of Maubisson showed above the trees.

My return provoked little interest. Benjamin scrutinised my face and immediately hustled me to a quiet part of the garden where he let me speak freely.

'The king will be here in four days' time. We have a suitable lady friend?' he asked.

'She will arrive in three days.'

Benjamin nodded and bit his lip in excitement. 'Good, that will give us time to prepare. And the rest?'

I described exactly what had happened to Millet. Benjamin shook his head. 'You are sure it was one of Vauban's men?' he asked.

'As certain as I am of sitting here.'

Benjamin stood and half-cocked his head, listening to the liquid song of a wood pigeon. 'Too simple,' he murmured. 'Far too simple. Oh, I believe you, Roger. Master Millet is a man who likes the best of both worlds, but you say he went to the tavern and turned others away?'

'Yes.'

'Perhaps,' Benjamin continued, 'we are only thinking what we are supposed to think.' He smiled and clapped me on the shoulder. 'As for the château, nothing untoward has happened here.' He crouched, plucked a wild flower, raised it to his nose and sniffed the sweet fragrance. 'Mind you,' he said absent-mindedly, 'I have been thinking.'

'About what?'

'About the Abbé Gerard. Perhaps it's time we visited the church.'

'Is Millet back?' I asked.

'Oh, yes. Why do you ask?'

'Well, if that bastard can rest,' I wailed, 'why can't I?'

'Come, come, Roger, time is passing. Dacourt has received letters from His Majesty the King and Cardinal Wolsey. Both Henry and my dear uncle expect results and, so far, we can report on nothing.' Benjamin gazed up at the blue sky. 'Vauban's guards are still there,' he said, 'scattered round the castle, but they are great eaters and drinkers and Dacourt has generously supplied them with a cask of malmsey. They'll either be drunk or sleeping it off, so we'll leave now.'

'I'm hungry,' I moaned, 'thirsty and tired.'

Benjamin's smile faded. He came close and pushed his long face into mine. 'Roger, I tell you this: if we are not successful in these matters, we'll have more to worry about than meat or drink!'

Well, you know me, put like that I had little choice. I re-saddled my horse and within the hour we'd slipped through a postern gate, following the path round the lee of the hill and down to the church of Maubisson village. Curé Ricard was not pleased to see us. The poor fellow had scarcely recovered from the fright of Vauban's visits. Oh, he invited us in, but only the sound of Benjamin's clinking purse made him a more genial host. His housekeeper served us bowls of pottage, liberally garnished with peppers and peas, and watery beer he must have made himself.

'I suppose,' the yellow-skinned priest began, 'there's

no crime in talking to people who patronise our church?'

'What do you mean?'

'Well, the English envoys, Sir John Dacourt and Sir Robert Clinton, often came here to watch the Abbé Gerard celebrate Mass. They gave him gifts and the old priest liked to hear the gossip of the English court.'

'Did they ever ask about His Majesty's book?'

'You mean St Augustine's work *On Chastity*? No, they did not.'

'But Vauban has?'

'Well, yes,' Ricard stammered. 'He has, but I tell you, masters, it can't be found. I say again the same to you as I have to them. The Abbé Gerard claimed he would take it to heaven, that it would be with him in Paradise.'

The priest looked nervously over his shoulder at the silent girl who crouched before the hearth as if carved from stone.

'The abbé was like that,' he continued in a half-whisper. 'He was always making little jokes.'

'What did the abbé do?' I asked curiously. 'I mean, he had the care of souls, the duties of this parish, but what was he interested in? After all,' I glanced slyly at the girl, 'everyone needs some respite from the tedium of life.'

Ricard sniffed and pointed to huge copies of the Bible which lay chained to a heavy lectern in the far corner.

'He studied scripture. He claims to have heard the lectures of Erasmus and Coelet. He was forever translating different passages from the Gospels.'

'Was he a Lutheran?'

'Of course not!' Ricard snorted. 'But he had his theories.'

'About what?'

182

'About miracles. He was fascinated by the miracles of Christ and speculated whether Jesus performed them because he was God or because he was a perfect man.'

'May I have a look?' Benjamin asked and, without waiting for an answer, rose and went over to open the great Bible.

'The New Testament,' Ricard called out. 'He was forever studying the New Testament.'

Benjamin nodded and found the place easily enough; the pages were worn by many thumb prints. For a while he stood and studied the book in silence, then he smiled and waved me closer.

'Look,' he whispered.

Benjamin was studying a chapter from St Matthew's gospel, where Christ walked on the waters during the storm on Galilee Lake. Now, my master was a biblical scholar, hence his speed and dexterity in finding the place, but he'd been helped by the Abbé Gerard who'd carefully underlined each word and scribbled his own commentary in the margin. Benjamin peered at this and translated it for me.

'Did Jesus really walk on water?' the abbé had written. 'Or did the sea of Galilee have shallows?'

'What does it mean?' I asked.

Benjamin made a face. 'There are some scholars,' he whispered, turning his back so Ricard, who was craning his neck, couldn't hear him, 'who maintain that certain of the miracles in the New Testament can be explained by natural phenomena. Now Jesus walking on the waves is one of these: they claim the Sea of Galilee is very shallow and what the apostles thought was Christ walking

183

on the waters was really Christ walking along some sand bank.'

'Very interesting,' I answered. 'But do they explain how Jesus stilled the storm? And can you tell me, master, what this has got to do with our present problem?'

Benjamin smiled and closed the Bible. 'Master Ricard, may we look at your carp pond again?'

The curé waved his hand airily. 'You know where it is. By all means.'

We went out. In the late afternoon sunshine the overgrown garden hummed with the buzz of hunting bees. Benjamin led me to the edge of the carp pond.

'Isn't it strange?' he mused. 'Poor Giles Falconer was interested in birds and their flight and he falls from a tower. The Abbé Gerard was interested in miracles, particularly the one about Christ walking on the water, and he drowns. Waldegrave was keen on horses, and he is pounded to death by a horse's hooves. Do you see the connection, Roger?'

'Not yet,' I snarled. 'But give me another decade and I will!'

Benjamin nudged me gently. 'Come,' he said. 'Let's see the abbé's church. Perhaps that will yield a few secrets.'

The curé was only too willing to show us around. The church was large and lonely, surrounded and shaded by great elms which dominated the cemetery, extending their majestic branches in benediction over the sleeping dead. The large, low porch was guarded by a Norman doorway, heavy and oaken and studded with nails. Ricard unlocked this and we followed him inside. Despite the sunshine it was gloomy and the curé had to light some of the sconce torches. We stood and gazed around. Heavy arches rose into the darkness and between them arrow-slit windows, without glass or horn, dazzled white in the sunlight. At the far end was the chancel where the windows were of rich glass; the sunlight illuminated their noble colouring and lit up the black oak of the altar and other sanctuary furniture. It was a simple church. The walls were unpainted; the rood screen, uncarved, was nothing more than a wooden panel. Ricard pointed out the church's two notable features: the stone, sculpted baptismal font and the ornately carved choir screen above our heads. Benjamin looked at everything carefully as if trying to search out the Abbé Gerard's hiding-place.

'He can't have hidden his book here,' I said. 'This is scarcely Paradise.' I shivered. 'The place would frighten a ghost.'

Benjamin smiled absent-mindedly and stared up at the choir loft.

'A fine church,' he murmured. 'And the Abbé Gerard is buried where?'

'I told you,' Ricard answered crossly. 'In the church-yard, under one of the yew trees.'

We followed him back into the warm sunlight along the coffin wall and across the overgrown grass where a simple, white headstone, marked with the cross of Lor-raine, stood next to a stunted yew tree. We studied the simple inscription. Benjamin made pleasant conversation, then prepared to leave. We shook Ricard's hand, col-lected our horses, and made what I thought was our way back to the château. Outside the village, however, Benjamin suddenly left the track, pushing his reluctant horse in amongst the trees.

'Master, have you left your senses?' I called.

Benjamin just waved me forward and I followed him into the forest darkness. God knows the place must not have changed in a thousand years. It was like entering some vast, green cathedral: trees stood like pillars and their rich foliage spanned out to hide the summer sun. Only when we entered a small glade, silent except for the bubbling of a brook which snaked through the green darkness, did Benjamin dismount and unhook the heavy saddle-bags he had swung across his horse's neck.

'In sweet God's name!' I murmured, almost frightened to raise my voice and break the stillness. 'Have you lost your wits, master?'

Benjamin stretched and gazed around.

'I found this spot when you were in Paris,' he remarked. 'It's secluded, near the road, and there's water to drink.'

'So?'

'So, Roger, we stay here until darkness. Then we go back to Abbé Gerard's grave. The coffin won't be buried deep. We'll disinter it and see what secrets the grave reveals.'

'Master, you're insane!' I yelped. 'This is France. Vauban's men are everywhere and the sentence for grave robbing is, I presume, the same as in England. Death by hanging!'

'Tush, Roger, we won't be seen.'

'And what are we supposed to use?' I shouted. 'Our hands and teeth?'

Benjamin kicked one of the sacks.

'There are small spades and mattocks here. They'll suffice.'

Now my master was like that; once he'd decided on

186

the course of action, and that long face became resolute and those soft eyes hard, there was no turning him. We would stay in that damned forest and dig up poor, bloody Abbé Gerard whatever the outcome. He'd brought some food, bread and fruit, and we drank from the brook as we waited for the sun to set. The hours seemed to drag by. Benjamin gave me a lecture on the different types of trees and plants around us until I nodded off to sleep.

When I awoke, the sun was setting and Benjamin was staring at the bubbling waters of the brook and muttering something about men who walk on water. We both fell silent as the sun finally set and the forest became a different place; the silence became more oppressive, broken only by the rustling of animals in the undergrowth, the hoot of hunting owls and the blood-tingling screams of the bats which flitted amongst the trees. A hunter's moon rose, slipping in between the white wisps of clouds, bathing everything in a ghostly light. I sat and softly cursed those princes and prelates who had brought me to this haunted woodland to lurk like some animal whilst preparing to rob a grave.

'It's wrong,' I piously announced.

'No, it's not,' Benjamin replied. 'All sin, my dear Roger, lies in the will. I have nothing but the greatest respect and reverence for the Abbé Gerard but the king requires that book.'

'Why?' I snapped. 'Why the bloody hell does the fat bastard want it?'

'If I find it, I'll tell you,' Benjamin promised. 'Come, it's time we moved.'

We tethered and hobbled our horses, removed the spades and mattocks from the sacks and crept back on to the track. Every step we took only increased my fear as the twigs cracked like thunder under our booted feet and the night birds screeched horribly at our unwarranted intrusion. We found the path back to the church, crept over the wall, and froze as we heard the howl of a dog. We checked the priest's house. No lights burned so we returned to the graveyard, following the line of the church, jumping and starting when birds nestling in the eaves stirred and rustled their wings. We crept across the cemetery and stopped as a heavy-feathered owl swooped low to seize its shrieking victim in the long grass. At last, we reached the abbé's headstone and I began to dig like some demented mole.

'The sooner we finish our ghastly task,' I reasoned, 'the sooner I get back to my warm bed!'

Now and again Benjamin struck a tinder to ensure all was going well. At last my shovel scraped the coffin lid. I pressed again and heard the welcoming thud of metal on wood.

'We don't want it out,' Benjamin whispered.

So we continued digging around, clearing the earth on either side of the long, oblong coffin. Then both Benjamin and I, one of us working each side, bent down and began releasing the wooden pegs which screeched like ghosts protesting at their eternal dream being disturbed. I quietly cursed. The sound seemed so strident I was sure they could hear it in Maubisson. The pegs were removed more quickly than I had expected.

'Let's see,' Benjamin said. 'Let's see. I wonder . . . ?'

'What's the matter?' I asked.

'Nothing,' he murmured. 'Lift the lid.'

It came away easily and Benjamin's suspicions were

confirmed. We were not the first ones to open this coffin. Despite the summer heat the soil had been loose, the coffin pegs easily removed. Inside, the decaying, garish skeleton was lying haphazardly; the head and neck, to which pieces of dried flesh still hung, were skewed to one side whilst the rotting, white gauze which had once covered the corpse had been pulled back and bundled at the bottom of the coffin.

'Vauban,' Benjamin whispered. 'The bastard has been here before us.' He poked around in the coffin, softly exclaiming as his fingers touched rotting pieces of flesh. He tapped the bottom and sides. 'Nothing,' he concluded. 'But let us at least pay the abbé some last courtesy.'

Despite my protests, Benjamin insisted that we re-arrange the skeleton in a more reverent position and that we say the Requiem.

Lord, I could have cursed! Here we were at the dead of night in a lonely cemetery in France, disturbing the remains of a dead priest, only to make sure his skeleton was comfortable and say a prayer for his soul. Yet my master was like that. I'll be honest: given half a chance I'd have left the grave as it was, jumped over the wall and run like a whippet back to Maubisson. Nonetheless, I helped. We re-sealed the coffin, ploughed the earth back in, flattening it carefully though anyone with half a brain could see it had been disturbed. We then left to collect our horses in the forest.

Oh Lord, I was relieved to see them. We put our spades back in the sack, mounted, and were about to leave the forest when a twig cracked behind us. I froze like a statue.

189

'Monsieur Daunbey! Monsieur Shallot!' the voice purred from the darkness around us. 'What a waste of time. You'll never find that book!'

190

Chapter 10

I just kicked my horse into a gallop, leaving Benjamin no choice but to follow. I tell you this, if that had been a race against the speediest horses in King Henry's stable, I would have won by a length and a half! I didn't rein in until my horse clattered over the wooden drawbridge of the château and I yelled at the guards to let us through. Of course, our dramatic arrival caused a little fuss but Benjamin smoothed things over with Dacourt and the captain of the guard. Then he hustled me up to our chamber.

'Who was that?' I whispered hoarsely.

I was squatting on my bed, wiping the sweat from my face and neck. Benjamin pushed a brimming cup of wine into my trembling hands.

'Vauban, I suppose,' he answered. 'Though I didn't stay to find out. I suspect he has been watching us since we left here this afternoon.' He sat on a corner of the rickety table. 'I am tired, Roger,' he continued. 'I am tired of providing Monsieur Vauban with such amusement.'

'Let's question Millet,' I demanded. 'Let's get the bastard down to the dungeons and apply a few hot irons!'

Benjamin shook his head. 'What good would that do, Roger? If I was tortured I could confess to being Raphael, to murdering Falconer, Waldegrave and Throgmorton.

191

Indeed, I'd confess to anything just to stop the pain.' He grinned sheepishly at me. 'No, Roger, as I sometimes say, three things will solve this. Observation, deduction and proof!'

'And luck!' I intervened.

'Yes, Roger,' he replied wearily, dropping his cloak and kicking off his boots. 'Luck or fortune.' He smiled brightly. 'And, of course, our opponents may make a mistake.'

We spent the next two days considering possible culprits from every point on the compass, but could reach no conclusions. The Clintons? Why should they be traitors? Moreover, Falconer and Abbé Gerard had died whilst they were in England. Dacourt? Again, lack of motive, and the same applied to Peckle, leaving only Millet as a probability. On the whereabouts of Abbé Gerard's famous book we were like hapless gamblers who constantly drew a blank card, yet we still had confidence in our plans to steal King Francis's ring.

The rest of the household at Maubisson now became involved in frenetic preparations for the French king's visit: rooms were swept, hangings cleaned, fresh rushes laid, whilst servants were sent out to buy supplies of flour, meat, sugar, salt, fresh casks of wine, and the château kitchens were thronged with sweating scullions gutting, preparing and roasting what the huntsmen brought in. Of course, Broussac arrived at Maubisson. I could have laughed like a jester: he turned up clean, well shaven, and dressed in the sober garb of a clerk – filched, I suppose, from some poor bastard who made the mistake of drinking in the same tavern as he. His companion was hooded and cloaked. She revealed herself only after Benjamin and I had hurried them up to our chamber. Now, I tell you this, if Broussac was a beast (and he was a veritable hog), his companion was Beauty in warm flesh. She was small, petite, like a miniature Venus. Her hair was silver, or was it gold? I forget now. But I know it shone, glittered in the candlelight of our room. Her figure was perfectly formed and her eyes were violet, or were they green? Good Lord, my memory's slipping, but her mouth was made for kissing. She had skin like alabaster with a touch of rose in her cheeks and, when she smiled, she had all the merriment of the devil incarnate.

'Messieurs,' Broussac grandly announced, 'may I introduce Mademoiselle . . .' he stuttered '. . . Beatrice. Yes, Beatrice de Cordelière.'

'Is that her real name?' I asked.

'No, it isn't,' the girl replied in perfect English. Those beautiful eyes caught mine. In one glance I knew that I was looking at a kindred spirit, a Shallot in petticoats.

'My name is my own concern,' she continued evenly. 'And, if you wish to question me, ask me directly. I am here at Monsieur Broussac's request, and because I will be well paid. But if I don't like what I see or hear, then I'll be gone within the hour.'

Benjamin took the girl's hand, raised it to his lips and kissed it softly. 'Mademoiselle,' he apologised, 'we have been so long without such beautiful company that we forget our manners.' The subtle flatterer threw a sharp glance at me. 'So,' he continued, 'I shall tell you why we invited you here. But first, Monsieur Broussac,' a bag of silver suddenly appeared in my master's hand and disappeared just as quickly up Broussac's sleeve, 'we have no further need to delay you. You are a busy man and Roger will see you safely to the château gates.'

Broussac took the hint, grinned wickedly at the girl and, with me trailing behind, we left the beauty with Benjamin as I hurriedly escorted the beast back to the château gates.

'Where did you find such a woman?' I whispered.

Broussac tapped the side of his fleshy nose, 'Ask no questions, Master Shallot, and you'll get no lies.'

And, without a shake of his hand or a backward glance, the old rogue trotted off across the drawbridge. I ran like a greyhound back to our chamber, only pausing outside to regain my breath and resume my usual serene demeanour. Inside, Benjamin and Beatrice were seated on the edge of his bed, quietly conversing in Latin as if they had known each other for years.

'Ah, Roger.'

'Ah, Benjamin,' I answered, and sat down on the edge of my bed, determined not to move.

'I have told Beatrice why we need her and she has agreed, on three conditions. First, she is allowed to keep any gowns or jewellery we give her. Secondly, she is paid half before she meets the king and half after.'

'And thirdly?' I rasped, gazing at the little minx's face.

She had the face of an angel but the eyes of a tax-collector.

'Thirdly,' Benjamin continued evenly, trying to stifle his laughter, 'Mistress Beatrice has declared that we are both personable young men with whom she is prepared to spend the next few days, but the nights she keeps to herself!'

I gazed speechlessly at this girl with the face of a sixteen year old and the shrewd mind of a merchant.

'She need have no worries about that,' I mumbled. 'And if she comes anywhere near my chamber,' I added discourteously, 'I'll take my strap to her.'

Beatrice leaned forward, her eyes clear pools of innocence.

'Oh, yes please,' she murmured. 'Such masterfulness!'

Then she sat back and burst into peals of laughter.

Benjamin joined in and, to be honest, I soon saw the funny part. She was not being insulting. She was here to carry out a task and nothing else. In a way, I respected her honesty and in doing so broke Shallot's second golden rule: Never judge a book by its cover.

(I see my little chaplain flinching on his stool, his little bum waggling with pleasure. 'You mean to say you never seduced her?' he cries lustily. If he's not careful I'll take my strap to *his* arse. Believe me, by the time I've finished this story he'll be a damn' sight more careful and reflect a little further before yielding to the lusts of the flesh with young Mabel in the hay loft.)

Anyway, Beatrice, Benjamin and myself soon became sworn companions and friends. Of course, her arrival at the château created innumerable questions and consternation. The men goggled and Lady Francesca glowered at the presence of a possible rival to her own beauty. I rather enjoyed that and spent most of my time making the most elaborate courtesies to our Lady Beatrice. Benjamin, however, pressed ahead with his plans. The day before the French king was to arrive, he whisked young Beatrice off to Les Halles in Paris to buy gowns, petticoats, shifts, a lace veil, perfume and jewellery (which he assured me was imitation). I reluctantly stayed at the château, being dragooned by Dacourt and Clinton into helping with the preparations for the king's arrival. Benjamin and Beatrice returned later that evening but the young minx kept to herself in a chamber specially provided by Dacourt. I was tempted to pursue and show her the true ardour of my feelings but Benjamin had strictly cautioned me.

'Roger,' he insisted, 'Beatrice is here for one task and one task only. She is to be the companion of King Francis and be seduced as Mademoiselle Beatrice de Cordelière, the daughter of a local bourgeois merchant. She is to be the king's companion, ensnare his affections and, in doing so, seize the ring.'

'How will she do that?' I jibed. 'Just ask old Long Nose to hand it over?'

'No, I will give her an imitation one, an exact replica of what Francis wears. Or at least what I think it looks like. Anyway, it will be exact enough to cause sufficient confusion and allow the girl to steal it.' Benjamin shrugged. 'And, if the French king finds out, we will say Mistress Beatrice has gone: we are the envoys of Henry of England and cannot guarantee the honesty of Francis's subjects.'

Such a brilliant plan! My master used all his ingenuity and subtlety to prepare it and everything augured well for its success. The vanguard of the French king's party arrived early on the morning of the Feast of St John the Baptist. Outriders, trumpeters and heralds came first, bearing the blue, silver and gold banners of Valois clustered around the sacred oriflamme, the King's own personal banner. Behind these, the multi-coloured pennants of other nobles in his retinue snapped and fluttered in the early morning breeze. They cluttered across the drawbridge followed by chamberlains, stewards of the household, officers of the royal buttery, kitchen and scullery. These inspected the apartments prepared for Francis and made a thorough search of the kitchens, cellar and corridors to ensure all was safe. They unpacked their caskets and chests, supplying us with fresh cloths to hang on the walls and insisting that in France their king walked on carpets not rushes. We left these minions alone, unable to make any sense of their constant demands, though Dacourt was sharp enough to place armed guards on his chancery, muniment, library and other writing rooms.

'We don't,' he snorted with laughter, 'want any spies digging up any juicy morsel!'

'There's no need to,' a dry-voiced Peckle answered, pushing back his soiled hair with ink-grimed fingers. 'The French seem to know our secrets before we do.'

His words stilled the clamour of conversation. So intent had we all been on the French king's arrival we had forgotten Throgmorton's and Waldegrave's recent deaths. I scrutinised Peckle carefully. He was the one man who kept well away from the rest, spending every waking hour in his writing office, only joining us for meals or a short walk in the garden. Was he the spy? I wondered. The industrious clerk who kept secrets to himself. I glanced at Millet. His languid, white face betrayed no emotion. Benjamin and I had kept our suspicions about him to ourselves; my master concluding that, for the time being, there was little to be gained by confronting him. But what about Millet's master? I wondered. The bluff, hearty soldier? Or even Clinton, with his courtly ways and mysterious French wife? Or the ubiquitous and ever cheerful servant, Venner, who ate like a horse but drank so sparingly, always insisting on watering his wine?

Further speculation about the identity of the murderer ceased at the faint blare of trumpets and a retainer burst in, shouting down the sun-dappled hall that the French royal party had been sighted. We went to watch King

Francis (or old Long Nose) arrive, preceded by halberdiers, archers and members of the *Garde Ecossais* in plumed helmets and light brigandines. I stayed well out of view. I glimpsed the king's long face under a scarlet bonnet and, beside him in a surprisingly sober grey gown, the heavy-lidded eyes and secret face of Monsieur Vauban. I remembered that strange voice in the forest calling out to us and, in spite of the sunshine, I shivered.

The usual boring speeches were made: the French party, Vauban included, swept off to the apartments set aside for them in one of the wings of the château whilst I, following my master's instructions, kept a careful eye on the embassy household, trying to glimpse anything untoward. My vigil proved fruitless. Dacourt and the Clintons joined the French king; Peckle, grumbling to himself, went back to his chancery; whilst Millet and Venner, after dancing attendance on their respective masters, played a noisy game of bowls and quoits in one of the corridors. That in itself was worthy of any comic drama because the château was now packed with Frenchmen who, if they had no noble blood in their veins, were left to their own devices to find quarters. Time and again Venner and Millet would set up the quoits, only to be disturbed by troops of grumbling Frenchmen. At last both men gave up hope and, followed by me, trailed off to the relative peace of the garden.

Just before sunset a strange silence fell over the château as everyone prepared for the great banquet. Now Dacourt had done us proud. The old hall had been swept, cleaned, polished, and hung with new drapes. White cloths shimmered over the old trestle tables and the long room was lit by thousands of small, white, wax candles. When I glimpsed these I grinned for they were exact replicas of the candles used by the Luciferi, but then I remembered Agnes and all my merriment faded. Benjamin and I stood at the entrance of the hall waiting for Beatrice to join us. At last, just before the French king swept in, she came tripping along, looking absolutely ravishing in a demure dress of rose damask trimmed with lace at neck and cuff, whilst a pure white gauze veil hid her lustrous hair. Rings sparkled on her fingers and what was supposed to be an amethyst pendant dazzled the eye and drew attention to her soft, ripe breasts.

Oh, she was a minx, coyly glancing at us beneath lowered eyelashes, acting the innocent, speaking as sweetly and softly as a young novice. Her long eyelashes fluttered. I even saw a faint blush on those ivory cheeks. The trumpets sounded and we stepped aside as Francis and his court swept into the hall. The king was dressed in doublet and hose of beaten cloth of gold. His courtiers were no less exotic, garbed in German-style jackets of crimson and purple satin, or red velvet doublets open and laced with silver chains. Others had fur-lined cloaks slung over their shoulders, and hats trimmed with pheasant feathers perched jauntily on their heads. There were no ladies with them. (I later learnt King Francis kept his harem at home and on his travels just took whatever female caught his eye.)

This group marched up to the high table where Clinton and Dacourt were waiting to receive them. Vauban was with them. His hair oiled and perfumed, he was dressed in black velvet lined with sables, whilst the studs and buttons on his doublet must have been mother-of-pearl. A man well rewarded by his king, I thought, and no wonder. The Luciferi had been most successful in crushing dissent at home and ferreting out the secrets of other powers. Once the French king and his courtiers were seated at the horse-shoe-shaped table on the great dais, we lesser mortals took our seats. Benjamin had arranged that Beatrice sit between us in a place most likely to catch the French king's eye. I leaned over and hissed, 'Master, do the rest know why Beatrice is here?'

Benjamin shook his head. 'No, I told them I have taken a fancy to her,' he whispered back hoarsely. 'And you know the English, Roger. They'd rather die of curiosity than ask a question!'

I gazed at Vauban's face and wondered if he suspected. The bastard smiled beautifully down at us, raising his hand slightly as if acknowledging old friends and trusted comrades. Once more the heralds appeared, titles were proclaimed, trumpets blared, and the lavish banquet began. Beef, plover, pheasant, quail, pike, carp, dishes of vegetables and huge hogs' heads were served on a dazzling array of platters whilst the wine flowed like water. I suppose I drank to quell my fears though Benjamin's plan worked brilliantly. Once the feast was over, the tables were cleared and there was the usual, stupid mummery about George and the Dragon and Robin of the Greenwood. After that the musicians struck up and the dancing soon became daring and merry. King Francis, of course, swooped on young Beatrice like a hawk on some plump pigeon. He seemed captivated by her and we had to sit and watch old Long Nose work his evil ways.

Eventually I was dragged off to bed by Benjamin who appeared to have drunk as much as I had. We both sat on the floor of our chamber, sang a two-voiced madrigal and then promptly passed out. I was awoken early the next morning by a servant rapping on the door.

'Master Shallot! Master Shallot!'

I tossed a cloak round me and flung open the door.

'What is it, man?'

'The young Lady Beatrice. She has left the castle. She asked me to give you this.'

He handed me a sealed leather purse.

'There are no coins in it,' the insolent fellow said. 'Just a ring.'

I gazed in utter joy, resealed the pouch and, despite the heavy wine fumes which still cloyed my brain, raced down the stairs and across the courtyard where the servant's news was confirmed by a guard.

'By herself?' I asked. 'That's rather dangerous.'

The fellow gave me a weary smile. 'Exactly what I said,' he replied. 'But she said others would meet her.'

I hurried back up to my room to arouse Benjamin.

'Master,' I hissed. 'Master, we have the ring!'

He opened his sleep-laden eyes and stretched out a hand.

'Show me.'

Benjamin opened the purse, took one look inside and fell back with a loud groan. 'The stupid woman,' he moaned. 'All she has done is return the replica I gave her!'

'It can't be! She's left. You haven't paid her the second half of the sum!'

Benjamin sat up, shaking his head. 'Yes, I did. She demanded it last night before the banquet, saying otherwise she would refuse to proceed any further.' He shrugged. 'So I gave her the money.'

'Now the little trollop's disappeared!' I wailed. 'And we are left like two coneys in the hay!'

We both washed and dressed and went down to the courtyard where the French king, looking a little more tired than he had the previous evening, was preparing to leave, his household minions swirling around him. Vauban, dressed in a monkish cowl, sauntered across.

'Good day, Messieurs.'

The bastard seemed as fresh as a spring morning.

'On behalf of my master, I thank you for the comfort and solace provided by Mistress Beatrice.' He looked slyly over his shoulder at King Francis. 'I understand she was most accomplished in her arts.' He leaned closer and shook his head, a solemn look on his face. Once again I tried to remember where I had seen him before.

'But you should be careful,' he continued in a mocking half-whisper. 'She is not what she claims to be. One of my men recognised her as a member of the dreaded Luciferi who often works alongside another rogue named Broussac. Do you know him, Shallot?'

I could have driven my fist into his impish face as the enormity of his trap became apparent. The rogue turned away, muttering, 'Lackaday, lackaday, whom can we trust?'

He sauntered back to join his master who, raising his ungloved hand, allowed that damned ring to dazzle in the sunlight. We stood like two fools and watched them depart. Dacourt, Clinton and Peckle swaggered over to congratulate Benjamin on the success of the occasion. My master just glowered at them, grabbed me by the arm and walked away.

'Enough of this tomfoolery!' he snarled.

We followed the French cavalcade across the drawbridge and stood watching them disappear in a cloud of dust.

'We were tricked!' Benjamin announced sourly. 'Vauban was manoeuvring us all the time. Broussac must be a member of the Luciferi. He's probably their spy amongst the Maillotins and would have been the organising spirit behind the recent attack on the château. The same applies to Mistress Beatrice.'

'So, Master, we are back at the beginning?'

Benjamin turned and winked. 'Not quite, Roger. Last night's wine loosened my memory.' He stood staring into the distance. 'Let's go back to the Abbé Gerard.'

'Must we?' I groaned. 'Why?'

'The abbé was a man who liked the new learning. A friend of King Henry VIII of England who had given him a book. The abbé said he would take the book with him to Paradise. Now, he died unexpectedly so he could not have burnt it but he had hidden it away where no one else could find it. We did think it might have been buried along with him but,' he grinned sheepishly at me, 'we found nothing at all. Now, last night I remembered the choir loft, for two reasons.' He ticked off the points on his fingers. 'First, the slang word for a gallery can be a "Paradise". Secondly, did you notice the carving on the choir screen?'

'No, it was too bloody dark!' I grumbled.

'It was Adam and Eve in the Garden of Eden.'

'In other words, Paradise!' I exclaimed.

Benjamin turned and clapped me on the shoulder. 'So, my learned friend, we shall return to the church. Vauban and his royal master will be laughing their heads off all the way back to Paris, thinking we are still too half-drugged with wine to do anything.'

I needed no second bidding and two hours later we confronted the Curé Ricard in his stone-flagged kitchen.

Benjamin showed him two gold coins drawn from our dwindling supply of money supplied by the cardinal. The priest's eyes bulged in excitement.

'These are yours,' Benjamin began, 'on a number of conditions. You allow us to go into the church, do what we have to, and after we leave, repair any damage we cause. I assure you it won't be much. Finally, if you value your life, tell no one what has happened.'

Of course, the fellow agreed: he would have sold us the church and the house for the money we offered. Benjamin grasped the keys and we half-ran to open the door, locked it behind us and hastily mounted the wooden spiral staircase. Now the choir screen was really a balustrade with oaken panelling on either side. Benjamin had brought both dagger and crowbar and, within the hour, he had carefully prised loose one side of the screen and there, behind the carving of Adam and Eve in their Paradise, wedged between the two slats, was a small, leatherbound book. Benjamin seized it, stuffed it down his doublet and replaced the screen as best he could. We collected our horses and galloped back to Maubisson as if the devil himself was pursuing us.

We found everyone at the château still recovering from the rigours of the previous evening. Only after we had unlocked the door of our own chamber did Benjamin bring the book out and carefully examine it. At last he closed it and cradled it in his lap.

'I did promise you, Roger, that when we found this book I would explain why it is so important and what secret instructions my uncle gave me at Hampton Court. This,' Benjamin paused and drew a deep breath, 'is St Augustine's work *On Chastity*. Inside it are annotations

204

by our king; one of these is most significant.' Benjamin opened the book and pointed to where the royal hand had scrawled in the margin: '*Quando Katerina devenit uxor mea, virgo intacta est.*'

'When Queen Catherine became my wife,' I translated, 'she was a virgin.' I shrugged. 'So?'

Benjamin looked down at the book. 'My uncle has advised me that our royal master wishes to divorce his wife, Catherine of Aragon.'

I just stared dumbstruck as I recalled the sad, dark face of Henry's Spanish wife.

'On what grounds?' I stuttered.

Benjamin made a face. 'You may recall, Roger, that Catherine was formally betrothed and married to Henry's elder brother Arthur in December 1501. Five months later he died at the Palace of Ludlow. Arthur was always a sickly boy and our royal master became heir-apparent. Now the old King Henry VII did not wish to give up either the alliance with Spain or Catherine's very generous dowry.'

(By the way, I knew my master wasn't lying. The old king was a proper, tight-fisted, pinch-pursed man who counted every penny and never paid a bill. I have seen his household books in the Tower muniment room. He used to check and sign every page. He could tell to the last farthing how much the royal exchequer held and how much it was owed. I can confidently assure you that it was the only time in the history of our kingdom that the royal exchequer had more going in than going out. The great Elizabeth, when she visits me, tells me in hushed tones how she still finds caches of gold hidden away by her miserly grandfather in secret compartments in palaces all over the country.

Anyway, in that dusty chamber at Maubisson the seeds of such greed began to germinate. The opening of a wound which sent hundreds to a bloody death, provoked the northern shires to rebellion and led to the suppression of every convent, monastery and abbey in England. It snatched old Thomas More from his Chelsea home, his walks by the river with his tame fox, ferret and weasel, and sent him to the headsman's block. I had a premonition of all this and shivered as I remembered Doctor Agrippa's famous prophecy of how Henry would become the Mould-warp, or Dark One, who would plunge his realm into a sea of blood.)

'How could he divorce Catherine?' I spluttered. 'She has borne him children!'

'Yes, but only the girl Mary has survived,' Benjamin replied. 'Our king wants a male heir and every one of Catherine's boys has died within a week of birth.'

(Oh, by the way, that's correct. On one occasion when Venetian assassins were pursuing me through the streets of London I hid in the crypt of Westminster Abbey. I crawled through some fallen masonry and entered a dark, mysterious tomb where little coffins lay on slabs like ghastly presents in some grisly shop. I later discovered these were the still-born children of Catherine of Aragon, God give them rest. I must have counted at least six.)

'Anyway,' Benjamin continued, 'Henry now believes that the deaths of his sons are God's judgement on him for marrying his brother's widow in contradiction of Leviticus Chapter 20, Verse 21: "Thou shalt not marry thy brother's widow".'

(The Great Beast loved quoting this verse. For those who are interested in such matters there's another verse in

206

the same book which says that you *should* marry your brother's widow. It just goes to prove the old saying that even the devil can quote scripture. I hope my chaplain takes note of that. He is fond of garnishing his sermons with verses from the Bible.)

'Yes, but was Catherine a virgin when she married Henry?'

'Of course she was,' Benjamin replied. 'Arthur was a sickly boy, constantly suffering from a flux in the bowels and bringing up yellow sputum. On the morning after his wedding night he shouted for a glass of wine, saying it was hot work being in Spain all night, but that was just boasting. He was incapable of the sexual act. Catherine always maintained she was a virgin, and her second husband,' Benjamin waved the book in front of my nose, 'has corroborated this. So now . . .'

'Now,' I continued, 'our royal liar has changed his mind. He is going to obtain a divorce and, naturally, he wants that book back.'

Benjamin pulled a face. 'Exactly. This is the only proof that Henry knew his wife was a virgin. Destroy this and he can push his case at Rome for an annulment.'

'And what about Spain?'

'Catherine's parents are dead and Henry wants to desert the Spanish alliance.'

'And the good cardinal?' I asked.

Benjamin looked at the floor. 'He opposes the divorce.'

I stared at my master carefully. 'Why?' I asked. 'Wolsey couldn't give a damn about anyone.'

Benjamin cleared his throat. 'My uncle has always believed that he will lose power and control over the king due to a woman. He quotes the ancient prophecy: "When

207

the cow rideth the bull, then priest beware thy skull'', but he has to acquiesce.'

'Is there anyone else?'

'What do you mean?'

'Has our royal bull met his cow?'

'No, not yet.'

Benjamin was speaking the truth. Henry had a string of mistresses: Bessie Blount, Mary Boleyn, and the occasional court wench who caught his eye. However, by the time they lowered Fat Henry's rotting corpse into a special, lead-lined coffin (you see, his body had burst and they had almost to pour it in), he had murdered three of his six wives and was intent on killing the last when death claimed him. In that musty chamber at Maubisson, so many years ago, the first few scenes of that dreadful play were about to begin.

Benjamin took the book and hid it under the wooden lavarium.

'Now we know why the king wanted that book back. And the French, of course, would love to hold it. They suspect our king's intentions: can you imagine Henry protesting the invalidity of his marriage when his opponents could produce such irrefutable proof written in Henry's own hand that Catherine was "*virgo intacta*"?'

We both started at a loud rap on the door.

'Come in! Come in!' I snapped.

I expected a servant or Dacourt but the benevolent Doctor Agrippa waddled into the room, swathed in his usual black cloak, his fat face smiling like some friendly friar.

'Good morrow, gentlemen, I come from Calais to find the château like the Valley of the Dead.'

He unclasped his cloak and sat down beside me, relishing our dumbstruck looks. He stretched out his short, fat legs. His leather riding boots were covered in a fine dust.

'Well,' he announced, 'aren't you pleased to see me?'

Of course we weren't but we didn't say that.

'For heaven's sake!' he shouted good-naturedly. 'Don't I get a cup of wine?'

I hastened to obey whilst Benjamin, regaining his wits, leaned over and clasped the doctor's hand.

'Why are you here?' Benjamin asked.

'I was sent by the cardinal.' Agrippa took the brimming cup and smiled his acceptance. 'So, what progress has been made?'

'None.'

'Do you know who Raphael is?'

'No.'

'And the murderer of Falconer and others?'

Benjamin smiled wearily. 'Yes and no.'

'Which means?'

'The good news is that we are sure the murderer is Raphael.'

'And the bad news,' Agrippa finished, the smile fading from his face, 'is that you do not know who Raphael is.' He sipped from the wine goblet. 'And the ring?'

'I am afraid not.'

'And the king's book? His gift to the Abbé Gerard?'

'No,' Benjamin lied, with a warning glance at me.

Agrippa stirred restlessly; his eyes changed to the colour of small, black pebbles and his fragrant perfume of musk and ambergris was masked by that hot, molten smell you sometimes catch in a kitchen when an empty pan is left

209

over the flames too long. The good doctor's body tensed with fury.

'This is not pleasing,' he grated. 'His Eminence the Cardinal is most perturbed, and someone,' he glanced sideways at me, 'will feel the royal wrath.' He smiled as if trying to shake off his irritation. 'The cardinal is most anxious,' he continued wearily. 'The king cannot fart without the French knowing about it. God knows what might happen!'

'Such as?' Benjamin asked.

Agrippa shrugged. 'Let us speak candidly. We all know our royal master. He will not be brooked in any matter. If he thinks the spy is here he will send troops from Calais. Everyone will be arrested, accused of treason, and face summary execution.'

'But we could all be innocent!' I yelled.

'King Henry will leave that to God to decide.'

I stared through the sunlit window and shivered. Agrippa was right. Henry had the malice to do that. (I always remember his instructions to old Thomas Cromwell about the abbot of a large monastery who resisted royal oppression. 'Give him a fair trial!' Henry had snapped. 'Then hang him high over his own main gate!')

'Does that include you, good doctor?' Benjamin asked.

Agrippa grinned. 'Let me put it this way, Master Daunbey. I am certainly not going to go home to report such failure. If the worst comes to the worst, I'll saddle my horse, slip out of some postern gate and go.' He raised his head and screwed up his eyes. 'Yes, I could follow the sun south to Italy and take ship to Byzantium.'

'Byzantium's gone,' I remarked. 'The Turks took it seventy years ago.'

Agrippa stared at me, his eyes now liquid clear. 'I know,' he replied. 'I was there.'

I gazed back in disbelief.

'I was there,' he said, 'when the Turks found a gate open and stormed into the city. I stood beside Michael Palaeologus, the last Roman Emperor. He died drenched in his own blood and that of his attackers.'

(By the way, I half-believed Agrippa. Only two years ago when I was in London I saw him waving at me from an upstairs window; he hadn't aged a day but, when I looked again, he had gone.)

'Lackaday!' Agrippa murmured. 'We have little time left. The king has sent letters under secret seal to his captain at Calais. We have a month to clear this business up.'

'But Dacourt and Clinton are his friends,' Benjamin stammered. 'Surely the king wouldn't hurt them? Dacourt fought with him at the battle of Spurs, and Clinton and his first wife were often Henry's hosts at their manor in Hampstead.'

'King Henry VIII has only one friend,' Agrippa answered, 'and his name is Henry VIII. Never forget that, Master Daunbey.' He rose. 'If you do, like others you will pay for it with your life. I leave you to your plotting, gentlemen. If there is anything I can do to help?' He let his words hang in the air, gathered his cloak and slipped out of the room.

'Is Clinton one of the king's friends?' I asked.

'Of course. My uncle told you that.'

'And his first wife?'

'Sir Robert loved her to distraction. She died of a tumour, a malignant abscess, some years ago. Our problem,' Benjamin continued evenly, 'is what do we do next?'

'We could challenge Millet?'

'And prove nothing.' Benjamin licked his lips. 'There is one loose strand,' he said.

'Which is?'

'The Lady Francesca. When we visited the convent on our way to Paris we noticed how the sisters there adored Sir Robert and were very fond of their former pupil.'

'What's suspicious about that?'

'Nothing, except they gave her a gift just before we left. I have talked to the messengers. They not only take presents from Lady Francesca to the nuns, but carry their gifts to her.'

'You think there's something wrong in that?'

Benjamin shuffled his feet. 'I don't know. I would like to know more about her.'

(My heart sank to my boots. I had a suspicion what would come next.)

'Would you go, Roger?'

'Go where?'

'To the Lady Francesca's home town, St Germain-en-Laye. It's only a few miles south of Paris.'

'And do what?'

'Ask a few questions about her.' Benjamin shrugged. 'Who knows? Perhaps the woman we know is not the same Lady Francesca who lived there.'

'That's impossible,' I snapped.

'Stranger things have happened.' Benjamin leaned forward. 'You must go. At the moment it's all we have, that and the book.'

'And what about the bloody ring?' I asked.

Benjamin just gazed blankly back and my despair deepened.

Chapter 11

After an uneventful journey I arrived in St Germain late in the afternoon of the following day. The village was a rambling, sprawling place, a high-steepled church at the centre with cottages and the houses of the more prosperous peasants around it. Each stood in its own plot of ground guarded by rickety fences. The streets were dusty, full of screaming children, some of them almost naked, and the women dressed so alike in their grey gowns that they looked like members of some religious order. Most of the men were working in the fields but the *auberge*, or tavern, a two-storeyed building with a bush pushed under in its straw eaves, was doing a brisk trade.

I entered its smelly darkness; there were only two windows and the place stank of cow dung. The beaten earthen floor was covered with scraps of rubbish which three scavenging pigs were obligingly eating. I have always found that garrulous old men are the best source of gossip so I pretended to be a student, the offspring of a French mother and an English father, off to the university of the Sorbonne in Paris to continue my studies in law. Like any stranger I was greeted with obvious hostility but silver creates universal friendship. Drinks were ordered, jokes and funny stories shared about the Goddamns, and then I changed the conversation to the great house I had passed by on my way into the village.

Now, my master told me that Francesca's maiden name was Sauvigne and, as sure as God made little fishes, the old men described the beautiful daughter who once lived there.

'A grand family,' one toothless oldster ponderously stated.

'Are they still there?'

'Well, the old ones are gone.'

'And Francesca?'

'Oh, she was sent off to a convent outside Paris.'

'And who is the seigneur now?'

'Well, in the absence of a male heir, the title went to a distant cousin.'

'Not Francesca?'

The old man shook his head. 'She would never have inherited the title.' He turned and spat. 'You know the customs amongst the great ones. Their sons go to war or court and the women either marry or go to convents. Mind you, she was a very pretty girl.'

'How do you mean?'

The old man gave me a detailed description of the Lady Francesca and I felt a twinge of disappointment at one of my master's theories being so brutally shattered: the woman the old man described could be no other person than Sir Robert Clinton's wife.

'It's strange she wasn't married off earlier?' I queried. 'I mean, such a beautiful woman?'

'Oh, but she was!'

'No, she was not!' another interrupted. 'She was betrothed to a young soldier, the Seigneur de Gahers.'

214

'And what happened?'

'Well, de Gahers went to Italy in the king's army and distinguished himself most bravely in the march on Naples.'

'And he was killed there?'

'Oh, no, he came back laden with honours, but within a year he died of some wasting illness. The Lady Francesca was heartbroken. She refused any further offers of marriage. She must have been about sixteen summers then, so her parents despatched her to the convent.'

The old man turned and spat a stream of yellow phlegm straight between the ears of one of the pigs. The beast snorted in anger and turned away. (And the French have the cheek to call us English dirty!) Well, there was nothing more to be gained. I had spent enough silver and the old men were becoming suspicious, so I slept in a small copse outside the village and then made my way back to Maubisson.

The château had recovered from the French king's visit. Peckle was sitting in the courtyard, sheaves of paper in his hand, Millet and Dacourt, the former as bland as ever, were closeted together in the great hall, whilst Clinton and Doctor Agrippa were deep in conversation. I did wonder if the good doctor was warning everyone else about the king's impending wrath. My master was poring over strips of parchment in our chamber, each bearing a name as he tried to make some sense out of what had happened.

'Your journey was successful, Roger?'

I told him what I had learnt. He gave a sigh of exasperation, threw his pen on to the table and went and lay down on the bed, staring up at the ceiling.

'Did you notice anything untoward?' he asked. 'As you came back into the château?'

'No, why?'

Benjamin propped himself up on his elbow and began to curl his hair around his fingers, one of his favourite mannerisms when he was deep in thought.

'Vauban has withdrawn his men,' he replied. 'A sure sign that the bastard is cocksure we will learn nothing new.' Benjamin threw himself back on the bed and just lay there, staring, as I unpacked my saddle-bags and rested after my journey.

'You said Lady Francesca was betrothed to Seigneur de Gahers?'

'Yes.'

Benjamin got to his feet. 'Stay there, Roger. I need to speak with our two messengers. I wonder if they want to earn some extra silver?'

I thought he'd return but he didn't so I looked about for something to read. I studied what Benjamin had been writing but he had been using some secret cipher known only to himself. I remembered Abbé Gerard's book so retrieved it from its hiding place, bolted the door, and went lazily through its pages, more interested in the king's annotations than anything else. I chuckled to myself. If Fat Henry thought of getting a divorce from Catherine of Aragon then this book would certainly prove him a liar. I had no illusions as to what would happen once the fat bastard got hold of it. The book would be burnt and Henry left free to tell whatever lies he wished. I turned to the loose leaves at the back which, as was the custom, Abbé Gerard had used for his own personal notes. I noticed that the dead priest had written there, 'Chantry Masses to be sung for the souls of the lately departed.' As would be expected these included names of relatives of those at the

English embassy. Some I did not recognise, others were quite fresh: a sister of Millet's, John Dacourt's wife, Catherine Stout, as well as that of Sir Robert Clinton's first wife, Clare Harpale. I was disturbed by Benjamin's return. When I unbolted the door he took the book off me.

'What have you been doing, master?'

'Oh, this and that.'

He lay on the bed sifting through the pages of the book, leaving me to my own thoughts.

The next few days dragged by. Benjamin claimed he was waiting for news and went back to his secret writing but I could see from his frayed temper he was making very little progress. Doctor Agrippa's presence only deepened his gloom, and everyone else's. Dacourt became openly nervous, Peckle buried himself in his work and Millet was one of those stupid young men who think music is the solution to every problem. Even Sir Robert Clinton looked agitated as if he realised his friendship with the king would not save him from the royal wrath. Old Dacourt, to lighten the mood, hired a troupe of acrobats, the usual mummers and clowns who entertained great lords and ladies in their halls and bowers. If anything, these idiots only deepened our gloom, their laughter and merriment ringing hollow in the dour atmosphere of the hall.

But isn't it strange how little things can cause the most devastating changes? I am reminded of that childhood rhyme:

> For want of a nail,
> the shoe was lost,
> For want of a shoe,

217

the horse was lost.
For want of a horse,
the rider was lost.
For want of a rider,
the battle was lost.

In this case it was a mongrel dog, an intelligent little beast who, under instructions, could draw painted letters from a small bucket and spell simple words like 'bone' or 'meat'. Sometimes he got them mixed up and this caused unwarranted merriment but it reminded me of poor Falconer's absorption with the name Raphael. A notion occurred to me but I dismissed it until I was alone with my master. I told him and he sat down as if poleaxed.

'I can't believe it! No,' he stuttered eventually. 'It's not possible!'

He rose and paced up and down the room.

'What is it, master?'

'Shut up, Roger, and let me think.'

The pacing continued. He sat down at his desk and began scribbling madly on any available piece of parchment. He was still writing when I fell into a fitful sleep.

The next morning a red-eyed Benjamin shook me awake.

'Look, Roger,' he said, almost dragging me from the bed. 'You are to dress, go down and join the rest and break fast with them in the hall. You are to draw them into conversation and ask John Dacourt whether his late wife's name was Catherine Stout, but watch Millet and ask him a question: did he have a sister called Gabriel who has recently died?'

'But what's the use?' I asked.

'Oh,' Benjamin jibed, 'his name's Michael, the name of an archangel, his sister was Gabriel, the name of another, and Raphael's the name of a third!'

'But . . .'

'Shush!' Benjamin raised a finger to his lips. 'Please, Roger, just do it. But make sure they are all there.'

I wandered down to the great hall and sat making idle conversation until the rest joined us. I turned the talk to the Abbé Gerard.

'When I was at his house,' I lied, 'I saw his list of Masses for the dead. Sir John, your late wife was the Lady Catherine Stout?'

Well, old Dacourt's eyes immediately brimmed with tears.

'Yes, yes,' he mumbled, tipping his nose into his cup of watered wine. 'She died five years ago. The old abbé and she were friends.'

'And you, Michael? I see you also paid for masses for your sister Gabriel?'

Millet looked self-conscious.

'Yes, she died about eight months ago when the sweating sickness visited Lincoln.'

'Michael and Gabriel,' I smiled. 'The names of arch-angels.'

Oh, I tell you this, I felt as if I had put a noose round that young man's neck. He writhed in embarrassment. Dacourt looked up sharply, Clinton became agitated, whilst Peckle's eyes narrowed. I saw the cloud of suspicion grow.

'It was a conceit of my father's,' Millet blurted out as if he couldn't stand the silence and unspoken accusations. He laughed. 'We cannot be responsible for what our parents do, eh, Shallot?'

I let the subtle insult pass and changed the conversation to other matters. Yet, whatever my master had intended, his arrow had struck home. I left the hall and went back to report what had been said. Benjamin finished shaving himself, washed his hands carefully in the pewter bowl on the lavarium and grinned as he dried himself.

'Soon, my dear Roger, a new game will begin. Or, as we say in Ipswich, you have shaken the tree, let's see what falls out.'

The first real change was Millet's exclusion by the rest of the embassy staff as if he was already marked out. Dacourt gave him more menial tasks and, when these were finished, the dandified fop spent most of the time in his own chamber. The real game, however, began two days later when Dacourt summoned Benjamin and myself to his chamber. The old soldier glared at us accusingly.

'It would appear,' he began, 'you have made great friends at the French court.'

'We have no friends at the French court,' Benjamin quietly replied.

'Well, sir, it appears that you have.' Dacourt waved a small piece of white parchment with a purple seal on the end. 'An invitation from His Most Christian Majesty, despatched under his signet seal, inviting you to his palace at the Tour de Nesle in Paris to discuss the matter of a certain ring.' Dacourt glanced at the parchment. 'Of course, this was not written by the king but his creature, Vauban.'

Benjamin snatched the parchment from his hand and, with me peering over his shoulder, studied it carefully. Dacourt had not given us the full message. King Francis said he wished to discuss the matter of the ring: 'As well as other matters attendant upon it, which could ease the ring's speedy return to His Most Christian Majesty's royal brother, King Henry of England.'

'What does it mean?' Dacourt snapped.

Benjamin handed the parchment back. 'I suggest, Sir John, you keep this matter to yourself. And whilst we are gone, be most careful what happens here at Maubisson.'

We left the ambassador standing open-mouthed. Benjamin hustled me back through the corridors to our chamber.

'Pack now!' he snapped. 'We leave for Paris immediately. And we go well armed. Roger, I urge you to eat or drink nothing, to touch nothing, and to stay close by me until we are out of the château.' He raised one bony finger to his lips. 'Trust me, Roger, and be most careful, for we are to face a most ruthless and skilful enemy.'

'Then why are we going?' I asked.

'My dear Roger, we have no choice. If we stay we are in great danger. You must realise that. And how can we face our own master if there is a letter on record, held by the English ambassador in Paris, that King Francis offered to negotiate over King Henry's ring and we refused?'

Benjamin dragged our saddle-bags from their peg on the wall.

'A clever plan,' he murmured. 'We don't control the game yet, Roger, so we must dance to the tune that's being played.' He started pushing clothes into one of the bags.

'Do you think King Francis wishes to negotiate?'

Benjamin made a face. 'God knows. He may well do. Francis is like our own master, duplicitous. On the one hand he declares Henry is his brother. On the other, Uncle told me that the French king has even consulted an astrologer on how to kill Henry. Francis has already sent assassins to England who, by careful and crafty means, tried to kill the king but were caught and summarily hanged.' Benjamin threw the saddle-bag on to the bed. 'This may be a trick or Francis could be trying to save his master spy, Raphael.' He smiled thinly. 'Be well armed and remember, Roger, when you go to sup with the devil you always take a long spoon!'

We entered Paris just before curfew and made our way through its streets, smelling even fouler after a violent summer thunder storm, to a comfortable tavern near the Latin Quarter. We dined in silence, Benjamin in one of his withdrawn moods, mumbling to himself as if I wasn't there. The following morning, as the church bells were clanging the hour for lauds, we presented ourselves at the ornate gateway to the king's palace at the Tour de Nesle on the right bank of the Seine. A strange building, towers and turrets soaring into the sky, it was half-fortress, half-palace with extensive gardens and orchards all enclosed by a high-bricked, crenellated wall. (A place cursed, or so Benjamin told me, for it was here two hundred years earlier that Philip IV's three daughters-in-law secretly met their lovers. I mean, it's rare enough for a princess to put the cuckold's horns on her husband but these three beauties successfully duped each of Philip's sons with their secret assignations with young knights of the court. But at last Philip found out and the princesses were bricked up in cells and allowed to starve to death; the young men were pulled apart by wild horses in the very courtyard we crossed.)

I thought of the story Benjamin had whispered to me as we followed an arrogant chamberlain into the palace proper, along silk-draped corridors to a small audience chamber where, of course, Master Lucifer himself, Monsieur Vauban, was awaiting us. He was dressed in his usual ostentatious finery: lace ruffs and cuffs, high-heeled boots, a short gown which fell to just beneath his knees, and those bloody bells which tinkled every time he moved. His hair was oiled. I am sure he had some cosmetic on his face and he reeked of perfume. Mind you, the bastard could be charming. He rose from behind his desk and clasped our hands.

'Monsieur Daunbey, Monsieur Shallot, I am so pleased. Come! Come!'

He waved us through another door, I thought we were going to see the king. Instead, he took us into a small chamber, the walls and ceiling painted completely blue and decorated with silver crescents and stars. On the small dais at the far end a veritable banquet had been laid out for us. A collation of cold meats, breasts of chicken, slices of lamb, jellies, quince tarts, and a jug of chilled white wine. Like some devil inviting us to temptation, Vauban bowed and mockingly gestured.

'Come, Messieurs, you are our guests.'

We heard a sound. I turned and froze in terror: seated in the far corner of the room was the great, black mameluke. He just squatted there on a stool and, crouching before him, their gold chains wrapped round one of his muscular hands, were those two damned cats, cool amber eyes studying us lazily.

'What's he doing here?' I whispered.

'I didn't see him,' Benjamin murmured back.

'Oh, he always sits there,' Vauban replied. 'Always in a corner just inside the door. People often walk in and scream in terror when they catch sight of him. But he's harmless enough. Where I go, Akim goes!' Vauban pointed to our sword belts. 'Messieurs, if you please, you must take those off. In the presence of the king, no one is allowed to wear arms.'

'Where is His Most Christian Majesty?' Benjamin tartly asked.

Vauban shrugged. 'In a little while, Monsieur Daunbey. Your sword belts, please.'

We had no choice but to unbuckle them. Vauban received them as carefully as a trained servant and laid them gently on a chest. Do you know, looking back, I don't think I've ever attended such a strange banquet. We sat eating and drinking only what Vauban ate and drank; that archangel of the Luciferi served us with a mocking deference; and all the time the cruel-faced mameluke and his predatory cats watched us unblinkingly. Vauban was courtesy itself.

'Will Monsieur try this dish? Master Roger, some wine?' And all the time, on one banal subject or another.

Benjamin remained cool despite the beads of sweat on his brow and the flicker of fear in his eyes. I was terrified. Here we were in the midst of our enemies, naked to their malice, being entertained by a man who hid his ruthlessness beneath a polished veneer of courtly manners. The afternoon passed without a sign of the king though once, and I thought it may have been due to fear, I looked at the portrait hanging on the far wall and was sure I saw the eyes move. When I looked again, all I glimpsed was the glassy look of some long dead courtier framed for ever in a dusty oil painting.

'Monsieur Vauban,' Benjamin interrupted the archangel's meaningless chatter, 'we were invited here to discuss the matter of the ring. The day is passing.'

'Ah, yes, the ring.' Vauban smiled. 'You have heard the story about it?'

And, without waiting for an answer, he launched into a long, detailed story of the friendly rivalry which had existed between the two kings and how His Most Christian Majesty wished it to be returned. At last even he tired of wasting time.

'Come,' he invited. 'Let us walk in the garden.'

He led us off down a darkened passageway and I realised it was almost dusk. Behind us, padding like three figures of death, came the mameluke and the two great leopards swaying on their chains.

The gardens behind the Tour de Nesle were cool and fragrant under a red-streaked sky. Vauban took us along narrow, winding paths between raised flower beds and into a small orchard. Now, at first, I thought the pieces of cloth hanging from the trees were some subtle decoration but, on closer scrutiny, I nearly fainted with terror. The orchard was small and enclosed, the trees closely grouped together, and from the branches of many hung a number of corpses, the only consolation being that their faces were hidden beneath black, leather hoods. Vauban just ignored them and kept up his inane chatter but Benjamin stopped and stared around this small forest of the damned.

'What is this?' he whispered.

Vauban looked surprised and stared up at the trees as if he was some proud fruiterer.

'Oh, these,' he declared. 'These are the fruits, the crop of my hard work. They were members of His Most Christian Majesty's household who believed they could steal from the royal treasury or make profits by selling secrets to the agents of foreign powers.' He studied the legs of one corpse and tapped it playfully on the foot so the remains danced evilly and the branch from which they hung creaked and groaned. 'This is Reynard,' Vauban continued. 'He was a squire in the chancery and thought he would make a little profit in telling what he knew to Venetian spies.' Vauban stepped back as if expecting our applause.

I just looked away, pinching my nostrils with my fingers, for beneath the sweet smell of apple I caught the sickly stench of corruption.

'The marshal of the royal household always hangs them here,' Vauban continued. 'Anyone guilty of lese-majesty ends his time in my orchard.'

We walked on, the mameluke and his cats still padding behind. We came to the edge of the steps and stretching out below us, about a mile across, was an intricate maze.

'Do you like it?' Vauban asked. 'The hedges are of boxwood and privet. It was first laid out by Louis XI whom you English call the Spider King. Do you know the story of the maze?'

Benjamin shook his head wordlessly.

'Louis wanted to go on crusade to the Holy Land.' Vauban spread his hands. 'But you know the burdens of high office. He was unable to keep his vow, so instead he laid out this maze and every Good Friday crawled on his knees to the centre to make his devotions. Come, let me show you, then we will see the king.'

We followed him down and entered the narrow tunnels of the maze. On each side of us, the boxwood hedges stretched up about three yards high. The paths were narrow, about half a yard across, so we were forced to follow Vauban in single file. My terror increased when I heard the mameluke pad softly behind us and the purring of the great cats as they pulled at the ends of their chains. Still talking, Vauban led us round one corner after another until I had lost all sense of direction, whilst above us the sky darkened and the sun began to set. Benjamin looked around and threw one anxious glance at me. I shared his fears. We were now in the thick of Vauban's treachery.

At last we reached the centre of the maze. A small circle, the ground pebble-dashed, in the middle a simple, wooden cross and two stone benches. Vauban sat on one of these and gently wiped the sweat from his brow with the silken cuff of his sleeve. He looked up and breathed in the evening air.

'I love coming here,' he said quietly. 'Only I know the way in and the way out.'

Benjamin sat next to him whilst I stared round. There was no sign of the mameluke and his cats.

'And you don't intend us to leave, do you, Monsieur Vauban?'

The Frenchman smiled and I saw his hand go to where his dagger was hidden.

'My master wanted you to be killed immediately,' he answered, his face becoming serious. 'But you are like me, Master Daunbey. We work in the shadows of the great ones. Our game is one of luck and chance.' He rose and went to one of the entrances. 'It's all a game.' He bowed slightly. '*Bonne chance, Messieurs!*'

And, before we could object or say anything, he slipped down the darkened path. I ran after him but he just disappeared. All I could hear was faint, mocking laughter and the tinkling of those bloody bells.

'Come back, Roger,' Benjamin murmured.

'We have been trapped!' I wailed.

'Yes, Roger, we have been trapped. But if we escape we will know who the murderer is, though I am still a little puzzled as to how some of the deaths were arranged.' He squinted up at the darkening sky. 'We were invited here because Raphael has seen through our little charade at Maubisson. Vauban has left us to die. He is probably drafting the letter to our royal master, saying we left the palace safely and that he cannot be accountable for our movements after that. We are supposed to disappear, but how?'

I stood and shivered with fear for the thought hadn't occurred to me. How could we be in danger in the centre of a maze? Vauban could be trying to ridicule us and we could spend most of the night trying to get out, but there must be something more than that. I heard the eerie shriek of peacocks from the lawns then a gust of evening breeze fanned the stench from that horrible orchard and its rotting human fruit. Old Shallot's courage just ebbed away. Benjamin played with the top of his boot.

'Master, what are we to do?'

A twig cracked. Benjamin rose quickly and pushed me down a path. He ignored my protests and shoved me on, turning up and down the paths of the maze. He was using the setting sun as a pointer, determined to put as much distance between us and the centre of the maze as possible. At last, breathless, we stopped and Benjamin put his hand over my mouth.

'Who else came into the maze?' he whispered. Benjamin saw the terror in my eyes and smiled thinly. 'Yes, indeed. The mameluke,' he whispered. 'He and those damned cats. Roger, we are being hunted!'

'But how?' I hissed. 'They will need our scent.'

'Where's your sword belt, Roger? They have our scent, as well as our weapons.'

We stood, ears straining into the darkness. We heard a faint snap followed by a soft, silken sound and the low, deep purr of one of the cats.

Now, I have been hunted by wolves in frozen Paris and outside Muscovy; by killer dogs in the catacombs of Rome; and by Venetian assassins in the old Roman sewers of London. Yet none was more macabre than that dreadful hunt on a balmy summer's evening through a dark green maze under the night skies of Paris. Now and again we could hear the sound of merry voices on the evening breeze and, every so often, the slither of soft-soled shoes over twigs and pebbles, the pad of clawed feet and the deep-throated purr of the hunting leopards. What is more we couldn't run. There was nowhere to run to. No fixed point of safety. And that's what Vauban intended. We would run until we dropped then wait for the mameluke and his leopards to capture us. The sweat streamed down our faces. My heart began to thud like a drum and my terror only increased when I realised we were using paths we had already been down. The green box hedges closed in like the thickest walls of a prison. I suppose my presence gave my master some form of courage for, when I glanced at his sweat-soaked face, the usually calm features were twisted into a snarl of rage.

We paused, caught our breath and hurried on. We turned a corner and there, squatting on all fours, was one of the leopards, eyes blazing, ears pulled back, its great tail twitching. For a few seconds it just sat there, the muscles of its golden back rippling, then it rose and the purr became a snarl. Benjamin seized me by the shoulder and we ran. We came to a crossroads in the maze.

Benjamin unhooked his cloak and threw it to the ground.

'Leave it!' he gasped. 'It will delay the cat.'

We hurried on, the blood pounding in our ears, our hearts hammering, breath coming in short coughs, until we were forced to stop, gasping and retching.

'Let's think,' Benjamin whispered. 'We *are* armed.' He slid one sweat-soaked hand down into his boots and pulled out the long, thin, Italian stiletto he kept there.

'Anything else?' I asked.

Benjamin shook his head. 'That's all, Roger, and our wits.' He looked up at the top of the hedge. 'Come on, up you go!'

'Master, the leopards will follow.'

'No, they won't. The hedge will take our weight, the branches are intertwined. Spread yourself as if you were on a frozen lake.'

Benjamin cupped his hand for my boot and, gasping and panting, I swung up on to the hedge, lying face down. The sharp branches, freshly shorn, bit into my stomach, crotch, legs and chest. I had to protect my face with my hands as I inched my way to the edge. I lowered my hand and, God knows how, pulled Benjamin up to lie just behind me. For a few seconds we lay there, catching our breath. I was too terrified to move but Benjamin, half-raising himself, stared out over the maze.

'We are fortunate, Roger. This hedge is slightly higher than the rest. If we go forward as the crow flies, keeping the sun as our guide, we could reach the edge of the maze near the palace wall.' He looked round and chuckled. 'What is more pleasing,' he gasped, falling back on to his stomach, 'is that the mameluke is well behind us, though God knows where the leopards are!'

Chapter 12

We learnt soon enough. The beasts were puzzled by the lack of scent but, by chance, one of them caught sight of us edging our way along the top of the hedge and, snarling with fury, threw itself at us. However, the boxwood was too high and the pathways of the maze so narrow the cat had no room for a spring. All it could do was dash itself against the sharp-branched hedge. It gave that up but stalked alongside us, ears flat in fury, snarling and giving that strange blood-chilling bark. Benjamin, grasping his knife, urged me on.

'Take off your doublet, Roger,' he gasped.

Gasping and struggling, cut by the branches of the maze, I tossed the doublet down and the leopard stayed long enough to tear and rend it to pieces. We must have spent an hour crawling towards that wall. Now and again one of the leopards would catch up with us and either Benjamin or I tossed down some article of clothing. It may have saved us from the leopards but left us more vulnerable to the sharp-edged boxwood branches. My hands, chest and stomach were now scored with pin-pricks and gashes whilst Benjamin had an ugly cut just under his right eye.

'Thank God!' he murmured.

231

'What for?' I snarled.

'Thank God the mameluke unleashed the leopards and didn't hunt with them.'

At last we reached the edge of the maze and collapsed on to the ground, little more than two sweat-soaked, bloody heaps.

'Come on, Roger,' Benjamin whispered. 'The wall!'

We had hardly begun our run when the mameluke slipped, like the shadow of death, from one of the pathways of the maze, his great, two-handled scimitar held back over his shoulder. He came tip-toeing like a dancer towards us. Benjamin pushed me on, slipped to one knee and, bringing the stiletto back, threw it with all his force. I turned, half-slipping, and saw the dagger take the mameluke just under his throat, sinking deep into his left shoulder. Not a killing blow but the creature dropped to his knees, eyes staring, mouth open, the great scimitar slipping out of his hands. Benjamin raced forward and picked this up and before the mameluke, caught in his own circle of pain, could react, sliced the man's head clean from his shoulders.

I heard the dull thud as the head hit the ground like a ball and turned away at the dark red arc of blood which spouted yards into the air. Then Benjamin was beside me, cursing at me for not running on. We reached the wall. The brickwork was loose and gouged my hands and knees as we clambered to the top. Surprisingly, there were no guards about. Vauban must have been fully confident in his mameluke and his leopards. I looked back towards that dreadful maze and, just before I jumped to the ground, I glimpsed the first leopard leave the maze and pad like a ghost towards the ghastly, decapitated corpse.

(Ah, I am sorry, my chaplain has interrupted. He cannot believe we crawled across the top of boxwood hedges. If I was young enough I would prove it now, and if he doesn't keep a civil tongue in his head I'll get him to demonstrate to all and sundry that it is possible. Is that why you sit at the centre of a maze? he asks. Well, yes, I suppose it is. I learnt something that dreadful summer's day. If you want protection, to be really safe, sit at the centre of a maze. Even if your enemy gets in, he may never get out alive. All the great villains of history sat at the centre of a maze, be it in a garden or a palace. Catherine de Medici, Madame Serpent, had her palace at Chambard turned into a labyrinth of false passageways, secret tunnels and corridors of moving floors containing oubliettes through which her hapless victims would disappear.)

Anyway, enough of that. Benjamin and I were sore, bloodied, our nerves stretched like the strings of a lyre, but we had one advantage, best summed up in that Irish prayer: 'Oh, Lord, make my enemies arrogant.' Vauban was arrogant; he thought we would die in the maze and, come morning, our bloody, tattered corpses would be sewn in bags filled with stones and thrown into the Seine. That's why there were no guards, no witnesses who could be bought with English silver. I can just imagine how Vauban would have tripped gaily down to Maubisson to express the deep condolences of His Most Christian Majesty at the abrupt and mysterious disappearance of two English envoys.

As matters turned out we returned to Maubisson only by the skin of our teeth. We had lost our weapons and our horses, whilst one of Benjamin's boots and both of mine were now in the proud possession of Vauban's bloody cats. We posed as beggars, and that wasn't hard, slipping through the Porte St Denis just before curfew, begging a ride with a carter and reaching Maubisson late the following morning. An alert sentry sent for Dacourt. He came down, huffing and puffing, but Benjamin was strangely silent, refusing to talk to him about our unkempt appearance. Dacourt muttered something about Venner but Benjamin brusquely interrupted.

'Sir John,' he rasped, 'I wish to see Doctor Agrippa – now!'

Something in my master's tone made the old soldier obey with alacrity and we had barely reached our chamber when Agrippa joined us. He was dressed in black the same as ever, but his jovial smile was belied by his hard, enigmatic eyes. Benjamin cut his florid salutations short.

'Doctor Agrippa, you bear warrants from the king and my uncle. Don't lie,' Benjamin warned. 'I know my uncle and I know you. You bear blank warrants which give you the power of life and death, as well as authority over all the king's subjects. So, I want the château sealed, every gate and door locked, archers placed on the parapets. No one is to come in or leave without your permission. Have the messengers returned?'

Agrippa nodded, his eyes narrowed.

'They must stay here, but send some trusted man to Calais with secret messages. Tell the commander of the garrison there to have troops of horsemen ready and mustered near the Pale.'

'And I have something to tell you,' Agrippa replied.

'Not now, Doctor, please, I beg you. If you do what I ask, we shall trap Raphael.'

Agrippa shrugged and waddled off.

Benjamin waited till the sound of his footsteps faded. 'Come on, Roger, we need to see those messengers. Go and find them. Tell them to come here and bring whatever reply or package they were given at the convent.'

I found both men sunning themselves in a small paddock near the stables. They seemed unwilling to break their rest but, when I clinked my purse, they promptly rose, disappeared and returned carrying a small canvas bag sealed at the top. I took the pair of them back to my master, who locked the chamber door behind them and almost snatched the bag from the surprised messenger's hand.

'What's the hurry, master?' the man grumbled.

Benjamin nodded at me. I produced two pieces of silver and handed them over.

'You were given this at the convent?'

'Yes, for the Lady Clinton.'

'But,' Benjamin interrupted brusquely, 'on the king's orders you did not tell anyone about it?'

'No, master, we kept it hidden. No one knows where we went or what we brought back.'

Benjamin smiled. 'Good! Then let's keep it like that. Do you understand? Good. You may go.'

As soon as they were gone, Benjamin opened the bag and took out a small package. He ripped open the thick yellow parchment and we both stared in disbelief at the small red and gold quilted cushion which lay there. My master picked it up, weighing it carefully in his hands.

'Your knife, Roger.'

He took it, slashed the cushion open, crowing with delight at the small phial he found hidden there.

'What is it, master?'

Benjamin held it up against the light. 'Oh, I think I know,' he murmured. 'But for the time being, Roger, let's leave it.' He hid the phial under his mattress. 'First things first, Roger. Let's cleanse ourselves of the stink of Vauban's leopards and that bloody maze.'

Servants were summoned with buckets of hot water and we carefully washed ourselves, Benjamin pouring coarse wine over the cuts and abrasions on my hands, arms and legs until I felt as if I had been stuck all over with little pins. We then ate and slept for maybe an hour. I was deep in a beautiful dream about the Lady Francesca when my master shook me awake. Doctor Agrippa, smiling benevolently, sat at the foot of the bed. Benjamin had apparently told him what had happened at the Tour de Nesle. The good doctor congratulated us on our escape before divulging the news he'd tried to give us earlier.

'Venner is dead.'

'Venner!' my master exclaimed. 'When?'

'Yesterday evening.'

'How?'

'By poison. Apparently Sir Robert and the Lady Francesca always partake of a glass of white wine before retiring. Venner poured it; the jug had been left in their chamber and someone had infused enough white arsenic to slay the entire château. Venner must have tasted the wine. He did not come down for the evening meal. Servants found him dead as a nail.' Agrippa made a face. 'Millet's been arrested for the crime.'

'Why Millet?' I asked.

'A phial of white arsenic has been found in his room.'

'It could have been placed there.'

'I thought that but other items were discovered in the secret compartment of one of his coffers; a ciphered message to the French court, a small, white, wax candle, the symbol of the Luciferi, and more gold than Millet would earn in ten lifetimes.'

'Where is he now?' my master asked.

'In the dungeons.'

'And what did the ciphered message say?'

'That he did not trust you, me or Sir Robert Clinton, and that we were on the verge of discovering his true identity.'

'And I suppose that's why,' I cried, 'he poisoned Clinton's wine?'

'Apparently, but Millet did not reckon on Venner taking a sip.'

We were interrupted by a loud knocking on the door and Sir John Dacourt waddled in.

'Everything is as you ordered it!' he bellowed angrily, glaring at Agrippa, this nondescript courtier who had usurped his powers.

Benjamin smiled falsely at him. 'Sir John, I thank you. But keep a close watch on Millet. Tonight I will produce the evidence to prove he is both traitor and assassin. He may try to take his own life. See that he is offered nothing but water and bread, and that's to be tasted before given to him.' He paused. 'Give Sir Robert Clinton and Lady Francesca our deep regrets on Master Venner's death but tell them to be most careful. Keep a close eye on the others for I will prove that Millet has an accomplice.'

Dacourt's face went as white as chalk. He mumbled a few words and left more quietly than he had entered. Agrippa looked curiously at Benjamin.

'So, the mask of Raphael covers two faces?'

'Yes, it does. But, Doctor, if you could leave us now?'

Agrippa smiled, winked at me and left the room.

My master spent the rest of the day poring over papers on his desk, muttering to himself, asking me abrupt questions about this or that, like a lawyer drawing up a bill of indictment, marshalling his arguments, ready to quote chapter and verse. In the late afternoon we slept for a while until a servant knocked, saying the evening meal was ready. We found the rest of the embassy staff tense with excitement and expectation, and, at Benjamin's and the Doctor's insistence, Raphael or Millet were not discussed.

The meal soon ended, Benjamin asked for the table to be cleared and the hall doors guarded. A crestfallen Dacourt agreed and we sat like the court of Star Chamber in that dark, candle-lit hall, seated round the table like a panel of judges. Benjamin, who had eaten and drunk sparingly during the meal, took Dacourt's chair in the centre of the table and brought out a small roll of parchment. He took a deep breath.

'We are here,' he began, 'to determine the identity of the blood-stained traitor Raphael, who has been responsible for the deaths of Giles Falconer, the Abbé Gerard, Richard Waldegrave, Thomas Throgmorton and Ambrose Venner.'

Benjamin paused and I stared round at the assembled company. Lady Francesca was wearing a dark blue dress of samite tied high at the neck, her thick, white veil of gauze, falling down to her shoulders, kept in place by a fine gold chain around her hair. She was haggard and pallid with dark shadows under her eyes. Beside her Sir

Robert was dressed like a parson in a black jacket with only a trace of a white lace collar peeping above it. I remembered his face as it was then, cold, impassive and inscrutable. Sir John Dacourt looked a beaten man, humiliated by the knowledge that his secretarius was a probable traitor. Peckle was tired and very nervous, his bony fingers moving continually, covered in blue-green ink stains. Agrippa sat silently watching us like some dark shadow, beside him my master, his long face as hard and white as marble – one of the few times I had seen him seethe in anger. He looked as cruel and as cold as any hanging judge at Westminster.

'We have the murderer, Master Daunbey,' Lady Francesca suddenly spoke up. 'I thought you agreed? Master Millet tried to kill us, as he did those other unfortunates you mentioned.'

Benjamin made a face. 'Ah, yes, Master Millet. Sir John, have your guards bring him up.'

Again we sat in silence. Dacourt went to the door and whispered instructions to the captain of the guard. A few minutes later the young secretarius was dragged in. He was no longer the fop. His hair was dirty and straggling, his face unshaven and there were large bruises under his dark eyes. His fine shirt was now grimy with dust and his breeches looked as if he hadn't changed them for weeks. His hands were tied securely before him and, when the guards let go of his arms, he sank in a moaning heap on the floor. Benjamin just sat watching this pathetic young man plead his innocence. Suddenly he rose, drew his dagger and, going down on his knees, slashed the prisoner's bonds with one stroke of his knife.

'What are you doing?' Dacourt demanded.

The young man crouched on the floor and stared tearfully up. Benjamin patted Millet on the back and returned to his chair.

'I am freeing Michael Millet,' he explained quietly, 'because he is guilty of nothing more than preferring young men to young ladies, as well as having the misfortune of being befriended by one of Monsieur Vauban's innumerable legions of spies.' Benjamin sipped from his cup. I tensed, for the drama was about to begin. 'Michael Millet is not the assassin,' Benjamin continued. 'He is not Raphael, is he, Sir John?'

Dacourt just shook his head.

'How do you know that, Sir John?'

'I don't!'

Benjamin looked down at Peckle. 'Do you, Walter? Do you believe Millet is an assassin and a spy?'

'I don't know!' was the snarled reply.

'Lady Francesca?'

She just stared blankly back.

'And what do you think, Sir Robert? You know Millet is not Raphael, don't you?'

'Why should I?'

'Because, Sir Robert, *you* are Raphael!'

The accusation, so quietly uttered, caused immediate outrage and consternation. Clinton sprang to his feet, his hand going to his dagger, but Agrippa banged on the table with his hand.

'You will sit, Sir Robert, as will you all. Anyone who leaves this chamber without my permission, whether he be the cardinal's nephew or the king's friend, will be killed immediately.'

'How can you say that?' Sir Robert's eyes blazed with

fury. 'I wasn't even in France when Abbé Gerard and Falconer died.' He blinked. 'Even if I was the spy, why should I kill Falconer and the Abbé Gerard? They were my friends!'

'So was the king!' Benjamin retorted.

'Let us examine things carefully,' Agrippa interrupted. 'Master Daunbey, please?'

My master leaned forward. 'Let us describe how things happened,' he began. 'And only later explain why. For eighteen months,' he continued, 'there has been a spy called Raphael at the heart of the English council. Master Falconer, through one of his most trustworthy agents, learned his name was Raphael. This was in Holy Week when, Sir Robert, you were here at Maubisson.' He waved a hand. 'Please don't give me your protestations that you were working with Falconer. Of course he told you about the spy. After all, you are the king's friend and head of the chancery which deals with French affairs. You passed this information back to your masters at the Louvre Palace and Monsieur Vauban arranged the death of Falconer's agent.

'Now Falconer became immediately suspicious about this and concentrated on the name Raphael. Before you left for England you probably noticed his change of attitude towards you and decided on a very clever way of removing this dangerous clerk. Remember, it was Holy Week when you left: Falconer, like everyone else, was observing the Church fast, abstaining from meat and wine. But once Lent was over, he would celebrate. He would use his liturgical cup, the Easter goblet, and you smeared that with a very special poison.'

Benjamin looked down at his own cup and swilled the

241

lees of wine round the bottom. 'It must have been a unique kind of poison, though quite an easy feat for you with your interest in chemicals and alchemy. I suspect the juice of Ergot or what the herbalists call "*Claviceps Purpurea*". You see, even Ergot or Mandrake will eventually kill, but rather slowly. Their primary effect is to cause the victim to hallucinate. They feel incredibly happy and believe they can do anything they wish.' Benjamin stared across at Dacourt. 'The wine you shared with Falconer, Sir John, was untainted, but Falconer's cup was not. After you left Falconer fell under the influence of the strong concoction smeared on his cup. He loved birds, loved to study them in flight. It was a warm, spring evening so he went to the top of the tower.' Benjamin shrugged. 'Did he slip or maybe even try to fly? Whatever, with the cup clenched in his hands, he fell to his death.' My master smiled. 'It's not too fanciful. Any man who has drunk too much wine knows how the mind plays tricks.'

'Nonsense!' Clinton, his face now white as a sheet, sprang to his feet and stared round. 'What nonsense is this? Even if I did that, how would I know Falconer would fall to his death?'

'Oh, that was an unexpected gain,' Benjamin replied. 'If he had not and had stayed in his room, the dream effect would have worn off. He would have fallen into a coma and died in his sleep without any visible sign of poison. His death could have been dismissed as due to natural causes. After all, the wine was untainted and who would think of examining the cup?' Benjamin stared at the top of the table for a while. 'Yes, you were very clever, Sir Robert. Oh, please do sit down, I haven't finished yet.'

Clinton slumped back in his chair. I kept my eyes on Lady Francesca. She now sat next to her husband, head bowed, clasping and unclasping her hands.

'Very clever,' Benjamin murmured, 'to poison someone by playing on their fantasies. And most subtle of you to arrange it from scores of miles away.'

'And the Abbé Gerard?' Dacourt barked, now recovering some of his bluster.

Benjamin held up a hand. 'I can say no more than that the abbé's death was easy to arrange. Once again it was Lent; the abbé, too, was fasting. He received gifts, one of them a flask of wine from Sir Robert sent just before he and Lady Clinton returned to London. Now the good abbé opened the wine after Easter Sunday, once Lent was over. It was only a small jar, perhaps two or three cups at the very most. Under the influence of the poison in the wine, the same poison Falconer drank, the good abbé turned to his constant absorption with the miracles of Christ, particularly the miracle of Jesus walking on water.' Benjamin stared at Clinton. 'As the abbé's friend you would know all about that, wouldn't you, Sir Robert?' Benjamin didn't wait for an answer. 'The good abbé, while hallucinating, went out to the carp pond and tried to walk on water. He was an old man and the shock of the cold water, not to mention the effects of the poison he had drunk, would have killed him in minutes. He struggled but was weak and so quietly drowned. Murder was not suspected, the body removed for burial. The cup he drank from fell into the water with him and was cleansed, whilst the wine jar was thrown out like any piece of rubbish. Once the abbé was dead, Vauban and the Luciferi began to search for the book.' Benjamin

243

paused and smiled to himself. 'But the old priest was astute. He really valued that book, so he hid it.' Benjamin looked straight at Clinton. 'Oh, yes, Sir Robert, I have the book in safe keeping.'

Do you know, I have confronted many murderers, men and women, who have dabbled in the blood of others. They have the arrogance of Cain, who could challenge God and proudly declare that he didn't know where his brother was. Nevertheless, there's a point when such arrogance will suddenly crumble as the murderers realise they have lost control of the game. So it was with Clinton. He stared at Benjamin, mouth half-open, like some weak, senile man devoid of wit and reason.

'I found the book,' Benjamin repeated. 'And I have seen what is written in it. Your first wife's surname was Harpale and, if you play with the letters of her name, as Falconer tried to, you can form the word Raphael.' Benjamin smiled coldly. 'I'm sure,' he continued, 'a scrutiny of papers and letters addressed to your wife would establish that you used such an anagram as a term of endearment towards her.' He coughed and drank some wine. 'Isn't that so, Roger?'

'Yes, yes,' I confirmed, though I still watched Clinton, especially his hands. 'Once Falconer had established that the spy used the term Raphael, you decided to silence the Abbé Gerard. You knew about his book. I suspect he had shown it to you with the name Harpale written in the back. Who knows? He may even have remembered that you called your first wife Raphael.'

Lady Francesca now began to cry quietly, her whole body shaking with sobs.

'Of course,' I continued remorselessly, 'others had to

244

be silenced. Drunken Waldegrave, who might have learnt more from Falconer than you thought. His was an easy death to arrange. You went across to see him one night when he was in a drunken stupor and smeared his robes with pig's blood. The sottish priest did not resist. Perhaps he was incapacitated by something more powerful, like a sleeping potion. Once his robes were stained with blood, you took him across to Vulcan's stable, opened the door, threw him in and bolted the stable shut. The war horse, fiery by nature and trained to kill, was alarmed by this sudden intrusion and the smell of blood, and pounded poor Waldegrave to death.'

'And Throgmorton?' Dacourt suddenly spoke up.

'In a while,' I continued. I stared where Millet was still crouching on the floor like some toper unable to move. 'I think, Sir John, you should remove Sir Robert's dagger and help Master Millet to his feet. Perhaps some wine might ease his discomfort?'

Dacourt obeyed with alacrity. Clinton gave up his dagger unresistingly. He just stared down the hall, lost in his own thoughts, as the old soldier helped a still-weeping Millet to an empty chair.

'Throgmorton,' I declared, 'was a busybody. A good doctor but he liked to spy on young girls and any woman who caught his fancy, including the Lady Francesca.'

Clinton's wife looked up sharply. Her face was ravaged by fear and tears; her skin had turned white and puffy like dough, her eyes red-rimmed. I glanced at Benjamin, for we had agreed not to reveal certain matters to all the company. 'At Fontainebleau,' I continued, 'Throgmorton saw something strange in Lady Francesca's chamber and, like the busybody he was, intended to declare it to all and sundry. On our journey back to Maubisson, Sir Robert asked Throgmorton to look at his horse's leg whilst Venner and he served the wine and food.'

'But we all drank that wine!' Peckle exclaimed.

'Of course we did,' Benjamin replied. 'Don't you remember, Sir Robert courteously filled each goblet and handed it out? Now,' Benjamin picked up his own goblet by the rim, 'Sir Robert handled each cup like this. If you look at his right hand, you will notice the heavy rings there. I suspect one of these has a miniature clasp which can be pulled back by the thumb, revealing a cavity where poison can be secreted. That is how he poisoned Throgmorton's cup. A few grains of some deadly poison and Throgmorton is dead within hours.'

Benjamin rose and went down the table. He pulled out his dagger and gently pricked the back of Sir Robert's neck.

'Sir Robert, your right hand, please?'

Helped by Dacourt, Benjamin grasped Clinton's unresisting hand, forcing it down on the table, palm up. The silver rings on the three fingers glinted in the candlelight. Benjamin touched the ring on the middle finger, telling Dacourt to push the candle closer.

'You see, Sir John, a small clasp! If you pull it back – there!'

Clinton struggled to drag his hand away but Dacourt held his wrist tightly and pulled the ring off. He passed it around for examination. It was a subtle design of hollow metal which, when the clasp was pulled back by the thumb of the same hand, would release a small sprinkle of deadly powder. Clinton would have released the poison just before he passed the cup down to Throgmorton.

246

'Of course!' Dacourt exclaimed. 'That's why he asked Throgmorton to see to the horse. Clinton wanted to make sure we all had our wine before the doctor was served!'

Clinton, ashen-faced, stared around.

'This is nonsense!' he mumbled. 'Complete nonsense!'

But his voice faltered and he sat slumped like a beaten man. Lady Francesca sobbed, then Clinton's demeanour suddenly changed. He glanced sideways and grinned as if he had remembered some secret joke.

'What about Venner?' Millet croaked. He flung his hand out towards Clinton. 'That bastard accused me of his death!'

'Oh, that was the clumsiest of Sir Robert's murders,' I remarked. 'You see, before we left for the Tour de Nesle, I came down to this hall and declared that I knew the names of both Sir John Dacourt's wife and Millet's dead sister. Clinton began to suspect that we had also found out about his first wife's surname, perhaps even about Raphael himself, so he launched a two-pronged attack: a secret message was sent to Vauban so that bastard could invite us to our deaths at the Tower, whilst Clinton carefully arranged for Millet to emerge as the guilty party. That wasn't difficult. Millet's nocturnal journeys to Paris, his pursuit of young dandies at the French court, the coincidence that both he and his sister had names of archangels . . .' I made a face. 'The rest was easy. Certain items were placed in Millet's coffer; Venner was given a poisoned drink; and Sir Robert's and Lady Francesca's wine was poisoned. But Venner would not drink from that. He had been poisoned earlier and his corpse left in Clinton's chamber.'

'How do you know?' Dacourt abruptly asked. 'That

Venner didn't drink the wine?'

'Because the poor fellow only ever drank watered wine. But Sir Robert didn't care about that. He hoped we would be torn to death at the Tour de Nesle, and Millet would get the blame, whilst he would continue to pose as the noble English envoy who had narrowly escaped death.'

Agrippa, who had hardly moved throughout the entire scene, suddenly leaned forward and tapped the pommel of his short dagger on the table.

'Now,' he said to the hushed group, 'we come to the question of why.' He rose to his feet. 'However, gentlemen, that is not for every ear. Sir John, Master Peckle, Master Millet, you must withdraw.'

'I will not!' Dacourt bristled back.

'Sir John, if you do not,' Agrippa replied quietly, 'you will never leave this château alive. I do not ask you to go. I beg you to, for your own safety!'

The old soldier sighed deeply, shrugged, and walked quietly down the hall, Peckle and Millet following. Agrippa made sure the door was closed behind them.

'Now, Sir Robert,' he announced, 'we shall tell you why you are a spy, a traitor and a murderer, as well as what made you smile a few minutes ago. Master Daunbey?'

Benjamin moved to sit beside Clinton like some priest ready to hear confession.

'I shall tell you a story, Sir Robert,' he began. 'About a young courtier, a soldier and a scholar, a friend of the king. Now this courtier loved his royal master and faithfully served him. He was sent on this errand and that and, when he returned, he and his beautiful wife were often together at the court of the king. What this diplomat did not know was that his royal master had an eye for a pretty face, no real feeling of friendship, and a raging lust which had to be slaked. The king seduced his friend's wife, treated her like a trollop, some courtesan from the city, and the courtier found out. All the loyalty, all the friendship, curdled and died. In the rottenness which was left, a black hatred and a deep desire for revenge were born.'

Clinton suddenly put his face in his hands. When he took them away, I felt a twinge of pity at the dreadful look in his eyes. There was no hatred, nothing except a silent, eerie deadness as if his very soul had shrivelled up inside him.

'This diplomat,' Benjamin continued, 'plotted a terrible revenge. He removed his wife to their family home, treated her most solicitously, yet all the time he was secretly poisoning her, so that she died a painful, lingering death, not from some abscess or tumour but due to the grains of poison he sprinkled in this dish or that cup. Once she was dead, or perhaps just before she died, this diplomat went to the French enemies of his king and offered to betray every secret he could. He would call himself Raphael, a mocking use of his wife's maiden name as well as the term he had once used about her, for Raphael is an angel of great beauty.' Benjamin looked down the hall, following Sir Robert's gaze, as if the murderer could see the ghosts of his victims moving through the shadowy darkness towards him.

'Now, Sir Robert, most men would have felt their revenge complete but this diplomat was a scholar with some knowledge of medicine and the ravages of disease. Whilst in the service of his French masters, this man met a young noblewoman at a convent. Ostensibly, she had been put there to complete her education but she, too, harboured a dreadful secret. The only daughter of aged parents, she had the misfortune to fall in love with a young French nobleman who fought in Italy. Like others he came back not knowing he carried the traces of a ravaging venereal disease, syphilis. So virulent an infection that hundreds died of it on their return, but not before they had transmitted it to their wives and loved ones. The young French nobleman died a lingering death and his betrothed too showed traces of this disease, so she was sent to the nunnery, not only for education but for the nuns' tender care and expertise with the sick.' Benjamin paused. 'Sir Robert?'

Clinton turned and stared like the man marked for death he was.

'Sir Robert, you are that diplomat, Henry of England is the king, and the Lady Francesca the young girl from the convent.'

'It's true!' she burst out. 'It's true! My betrothed returned from Italy ardent for me.' She looked up, tears brimming in her eyes though her lips curled in anger. 'He died but I'd already caught the disease. Sir Robert was kind. He chose to ignore it, married me, but said we would not live like man and wife.' She crumpled the dark fabric of her dress between her fingers. 'At first, my marriage to Sir Robert soothed my anger at the injustice of it all, but only for a while.' She wiped her eyes. 'You are quite right, Master Daunbey, about Sir Robert's final revenge. He took me to court and introduced me to the king who dallied with me. I was flattered.' She drew back her lips. 'We made love,' she snarled. 'And why not?

250

Gaston would not have died if it hadn't been for the ambition and greed of kings.' She caught her breath. 'I suspected Sir Robert was not what he claimed to be for he connived at his royal master's dalliance with me.' She fell back in her chair, laughing hysterically. 'Now Henry of England has what I have. May it rot his corpulent carcase!'

I stared in utter disbelief at the change in this beautiful young woman, her face white and haggard, her eyes filled with hatred and anger. I also realised what dreadful things we do to each other. I am a rogue, a villain born and bred, but I think Satan himself must weep at the cruelties we inflict on each other. Of course, it was Lady Francesca whom I had seen Henry cavorting with on the bed at Hampton Court. The woman's legs had appeared white whereas the Lady Francesca was golden-skinned. I smiled at my own innocence. She had been wearing her flesh-coloured stockings and our royal killer was no gentleman. (Anne Boleyn once told me he scarcely gave her time to undress!)

'How did you know?' Lady Francesca asked. She gestured maliciously at her husband. 'Did he tell you?'

Sir Robert just ignored her, lost in his own thoughts, his lips moving wordlessly.

'No,' Benjamin replied, turning to glance at Agrippa who had suddenly brought a roll of parchment from beneath the table. 'No, we gleaned it from scraps of information, little pieces of a puzzle which eventually fitted into place. First, the good nuns at the convent were so solicitous of your health and so appreciative of Sir Robert. Secondly, the attitude of King Francis. I thought he just disliked you but he knows of your disease. In his eyes, you simply don't exist. Thirdly, Shallot here saw you carrying a bottle marked with the letters SUL. This contained sulphur which, used with mercury, is one of the ways of halting that disease. I am sure this is what Throgmorton saw when he was snooping in your chamber. He baited you with it just as we left Fontainebleau. You told your husband and Throgmorton had to die.'

Lady Francesca glared at me and I shuddered at the darkness in her eyes.

'Dear Roger,' she murmured. 'I did consider seducing you, but you are too sharp. You even escaped the Luciferi plot to kill you in the boar-pit at Fontainebleau. One day, Master Shallot, you'll cut yourself.' She glanced back at Benjamin. 'I liked you, Master Daunbey. You are kind and sensitive. I told Sir Robert that you suspected I was ill.'

Benjamin looked away, embarrassed.

'I went back to your village,' I spoke up. 'They gave me further information about your betrothal to Gaston, and your sudden departure to the convent. My master became intrigued by the way messengers to the English envoys here in Paris always regularly stopped at the convent. Now, we knew you sent them gifts and wondered if Raphael could have used these gifts to send messages. Of course, we were wrong. It wasn't what the messengers took to the convent but what they brought back from it. Medicines for you.'

'That's why those two other messengers were killed,' Benjamin interrupted. 'I don't know how or why, Lady Francesca, but I suspect they stumbled upon your secret. I am sure the good nuns always kept the medicines well hidden in whatever gifts they sent. Those messengers,

252

however, pried too much, questions may have been asked before they left the convent. The nuns, under strict orders from Monsieur Vauban, passed this information on and the messengers had to die.' Benjamin gripped the table top with his hand. 'To test my hypothesis, I sent two messengers to the convent, pretending they took a gift from you. I instructed one of them to be talkative and say that you were not feeling well. The good nuns fell into a trap. They sent a present back: a quilted cushion. When I cut it open, I found a phial containing a mixture of mercury and sulphur.'

Doctor Agrippa leaned forward out of the shadows. 'Sir Robert, do you deny these charges?'

Clinton just sat stock-still, staring down the hall.

'Sir Robert,' Benjamin repeated, 'you are Raphael, you are the master murderer. You were trading the king's secrets to the French. You did not interfere with the despatches or the letters. You just passed the information on to Vauban's agents in London with strict instructions that the French were only to act on this information once the letters had arrived at the English embassy in Paris. That's why the saddle-bags and the despatches of the dead messengers were so readily handed over. You and Vauban wished to sustain the pretence that only after secret documents reached Dacourt were they leaked to the Luciferi.'

Clinton suddenly stirred, shaking himself. 'Yes, you are right,' he murmured. He glanced at Benjamin. 'Master Daunbey, you are brilliant. Vauban said that. He wanted you and your minion – ' Clinton stared at me – 'he wanted you killed immediately.' He patted his wife gently on the hand but this time she flinched as though in pain. 'She's

253

innocent, twisted but innocent. I used her. I loved Clare but the king abused me and now he will exist in the living hell I have created!'

Agrippa got up slowly. 'Sir Robert Clinton,' he intoned, 'you are a self-confessed spy, traitor and murderer of the king's good friends and liege subjects. You are,' he continued, 'guilty of the following deaths: the agent slain in the alleys of Paris, Giles Falconer, the Abbé Gerard and the two messengers killed on the road to Paris. Richard Waldegrave, priest, Thomas Throgmorton, physician, and Ambrose Venner, your own manservant. You have betrayed your king, placing both his body and his realm in great danger. You have been responsible for other deaths and misfortunes.'

'Stop!' I shouted.

Agrippa looked round in surprise. 'Master Shallot, you do not agree with this?'

I went round the table and leaned over to stare into Sir Robert Clinton's soulless eyes. It was a moment I relished and one I had been waiting for.

'Sir Robert, you are guilty of other deaths; for instance, that of Bertrand de Macon, captain of the ship which was intercepted by French privateers. But, above all,' I gripped his shoulder until he flinched, 'you are guilty of the deaths of Monsieur and Madame Ralemberg, their manservant and my beloved, Agnes Ralemberg!' I glanced up at Agrippa. 'Oh, yes, my good doctor.' I turned my back so that Clinton wouldn't see my tears. 'I was always puzzled,' I said, over my shoulder, 'as to how the assassins from the Luciferi entered Monsieur Ralemberg's house. He was a canny man and would have barred the doors against all strangers, but someone must have knocked, someone with authority, someone who could be trusted. And who better than one of the king's own ministers?' I turned and pointed my finger at Clinton. 'You let the assassin in, you bastard! Oh, you can sit there and your pretty wife can sob her eyes out but I'll see both of you bastards dance at Tyburn! Both cut down half-alive and your bodies hacked into steaming chunks!'

(Actually I wouldn't have done, I can't stand executions, but on that night at Maubisson I felt so enraged I could have done the dreadful act myself.)

'There will be no executions,' Agrippa replied, speaking above Lady Francesca's sobs.

'My wife is innocent,' Clinton repeated flatly.

'Sir Robert, you have a choice.' Agrippa got down from the dais and faced him squarely. 'We might not get you to Calais alive, Vauban may interfere, though there's a good chance we could. In which case, you would return to England, be tried as a traitor in Westminster Hall and suffer the most dreadful death. Or, we can arrange the same at Maubisson, at dawn tomorrow morning. Or . . .' Agrippa paused and stared at my master.

'Or,' Benjamin continued, 'we can leave matters to you yourself.'

'My wife,' Clinton repeated, 'is innocent of everything but her own anger and hurt.'

'The Lady Francesca may return to her convent,' Agrippa stated. 'But if she ever sets foot on English soil, she will be arrested, tried and executed!' Agrippa stared at the guttering candle flame. 'You are a poisoner, Sir Robert. I suspect you carry the weapons of your trade upon you. We will leave you for a while.' He pushed the jug of wine nearer. 'You may need further refreshment.'

Chapter 13

Agrippa snapped his fingers and we all, the Lady Francesca included, walked out of the hall. Agrippa ordered the weeping woman to be taken immediately to her chamber. She did not demur or resist or ask to spend one minute longer with her erstwhile husband but, helped by a sleepy-eyed maid and escorted by two soldiers, was led off to her own chamber. Dacourt and the rest, who had been standing outside, hurried to greet us. It was rather ludicrous to see how they had regained their usual composure. Dacourt, the bluff soldier, damning the French and Clinton as their spy; Peckle once more the industrious clerk; and Millet recovered enough to have cleaned the dirt from his foppish face.

'What will happen now?' Dacourt barked.

Agrippa smiled. 'Patience, Sir John, patience!'

We stood in a silent circle outside the door of the great hall, undisturbed by any sound except the calls of the sentries on the parapet wall and the yapping of a dog. We must have stayed a quarter of an hour before Agrippa, followed by the rest of us, re-entered the darkened hall. Clinton still sat in his chair behind the great table on the dais. At first I thought nothing had changed but, as we drew nearer, I saw his staring eyes were glassy and empty.

The lips were parted, the white face twisted in the rictus of death, and the cup which had contained some deadly draught still rolled eerily on the table top.

'A tragic end to a tragic life,' Benjamin observed.

'So may all traitors die,' Dacourt intoned firmly.

Agrippa pronounced, 'Amen,' issuing instructions for Clinton's corpse, chamber and possessions to be rigorously searched and for the Lady Francesca to be returned to her convent as soon as day broke. Agrippa then came between Benjamin and myself, linking his arms through ours.

'Master Benjamin, Master Shallot, you have my thanks and you will receive those of His Eminence the Cardinal and His Majesty the King.' He stopped and smiled at each of us. 'Hand me over the good Abbé Gerard's book and this matter will be finished.'

Benjamin gave Doctor Agrippa what he wanted but Wolsey's enigmatic clerk had scarcely closed the door behind him when my master announced: 'We aren't finished, Roger.'

'You mean the ring?'

He made a face. 'No, our noble king must accept that he wagered and lost. He will never get the ring back. I mean Vauban.'

'What about him, master?'

Benjamin caught my fearful look and tapped me on the shoulder. 'Clinton may have led the assassin to Agnes, but Vauban's the assassin. I am going to kill the bastard!'

I stared at my master's closed face. I have never seen such a change in someone so gentle. Despite the uncovering of Clinton's treason, the fury still seethed within him.

'Why, Benjamin?' I asked.

'Because he killed Agnes.'

'But she was my betrothed.'

'Yes, exactly, and you are my friend.' Benjamin turned away to hide his face. 'I have been through the same hell as you, Roger, only in my case Johanna's mind died, not her body. I killed the man responsible and I shall do the same on your behalf!'

'No, I'll do it, master,' I lied glibly, hoping he wouldn't hear my bowels churn in fright.

Benjamin turned round and, though he blinked, I saw the tears in his eyes. 'Roger, Roger, don't be silly. Vauban's a swordsman. He would kill you in a minute.'

'Oh, thank you,' I replied sarcastically. 'And how are you going to do it? Like Clinton would, poison in a cup or a dagger in the dark?'

Benjamin sat down on the edge of his bed. 'No,' he replied evenly. 'Today is Wednesday, tomorrow the Feast of Saints Peter and Paul. As in England, all our court officials will observe the holy day. No business will be transacted at the French court. Vauban will be with his family in the Rue des Moines.' Benjamin smiled bleakly. 'After all, Roger, he did invite us to call on him!'

My master would not be dissuaded. Next morning he drew a new sword belt, hanger, wrist guard and dagger from the château's stores and at my request obtained the same for me.

'You need not come, Roger,' he remarked.

'I would follow you to the ends of the earth, master,' I lied, and trusted the meagre breakfast I had eaten would stay in my stomach.

We left Maubisson at first light. The château was now strangely silent as if the servants knew about the terrible drama played out in the great hall the night before. In the courtyard grooms were preparing horses so we must have left before the Lady Francesca. All I can say is I never saw or heard of her again.

We reached Paris: being a holy day the city was strangely quiet, the great processions would not be held until the afternoon. We made our way by quiet side streets and narrow alleyways to the wealthy quarter on the right bank of the Seine and the Rue des Moines. The city was just about to stir: water-carriers and milk-sellers walked the streets crying for custom. The Provost's men were leading night-walkers and other malefactors towards the Chatelet prison. At last we found the sheltered, narrow street. On either side the great houses were protected from the general populace by high brick walls and iron-bound gates.

A sleepy-eyed fruit-seller showed us Vauban's house. We could see little except trees peeping over the walls, and the top casement windows which leaned out under a red-tiled roof. Apparently the household was not yet stirring so we went back and hid in the shadows of a small *auberge*, sipping watered wine and listening to the gathering noise from the street outside. Benjamin stayed quiet. Every time I tried to reason with him he just shook his head.

'We must kill Vauban,' he repeated. 'If we do not, he will be the cause of both our deaths. He needs to die. Justice demands it!'

After an hour we left the inn and returned to the Rue des Moines. We pulled our hoods well over our heads and walked down the street. The great gateway to the Vauban house was now open and Benjamin softly cursed when he saw a member of the *Garde Ecossais* lounging just inside the gate.

'How many more do you think there are?' I asked.

We crossed the street, as if pretending to look for our way, and passed the open gateway. Benjamin stared into the yard beyond.

'I think he's the only one,' he murmured. 'You walk on, Roger, only return when I signal.'

I protested but he pushed me gently away and entered the gateway. I stopped and waited. I heard the tinkle of coins falling on to the pebbles, the sound of a blow, and a few minutes later Benjamin reappeared and beckoned me forward.

'The oldest of tricks,' he whispered. 'It always works.' He pointed to the deep undergrowth just inside the gardens where the unconscious guard now lay bound and gagged.

'Oh, don't tell me,' I murmured. 'You dropped a few coins and he bent to pick them up?'

'Even worse.' Benjamin grinned. 'I used his own club to knock him unconscious!'

We continued up the pebbled pathway. There was a garden in front of the house. Benjamin stopped and we listened for the sound of voices.

'What about the servants?' I whispered.

'There will be few around.' Benjamin replied. 'Remember, it's a holy day.'

We walked around the house; a yellow-haired dog came running out barking but cringed away when I lashed out with my boot. At the back of the house was a small pleasaunce; green lawns, a few bushes, small pear trees in one corner and, in the other, a garden house. On the lawn a man in a white, open chemise and brown leggings pushed into soft leather boots was sitting playing with two small girls. He roared and they would run away, screaming with laughter. A woman sat on the stone bench watching this, clapping her hands and encouraging the game on. We just stood and watched, stupefied. Despite the lack of finery, we recognised Vauban but could hardly believe he was the centre of this pleasant family scene: a man, his wife and two children playing on the grass, enjoying the summer sun. Was this the chief archangel of the Luciferi? The French king's spy master, the spider who worked at the centre of a web? I glanced at Benjamin and saw pity replace the anger in his face.

'What shall we do, master?' I whispered.

Benjamin took a deep breath. 'We do what we came for.'

We walked soundlessly across the dew fresh grass and were almost on top of them before Vauban realised the danger. He was crouched on all fours, still pretending to be a dragon, when he heard the woman scream, saw our boots and looked up. His tawny skin was devoid of any make-up, his hair fell loose, and he had a look of such innocence. Once again I searched my memories for where I had seen his face before.

'I wondered,' he murmured. 'You escaped the maze but I thought you would flee.' He shrugged. 'Everyone makes mistakes.'

'Your last!' Benjamin replied.

'Louise!' Vauban shouted across to his wife. 'Louise, the children!'

His warning was unnecessary. The young girls, dressed in brown smocks and looking like two peas in a pod, ran quickly to their mother, clutching her skirt and hiding behind her as if they knew that we had come to end their game forever. Vauban rose slowly to his feet, ever the dandy, brushing the grass stalks from his leggings.

'What do you want?' the woman whispered in French. She was dark, petite, pleasant-faced, with a homely figure. I remembered the court beauties amongst whom Vauban worked and realised, with a pang of envy, that he at least had someone to love.

'What do you want?' she repeated.

'Louise!' Vauban ordered. 'Go into the house!'

Benjamin drew his sword, flinching as the little girls screamed even as their mother tried to hush them.

'Madame.' Benjamin bowed. 'My name is Benjamin Daunbey, my companion is my good friend, Roger Shallot. You will not go into the house.' He waved to the small garden bower. 'You may stay there. And your servants?'

'They have already left,' Vauban snapped, his face pale, no mockery in his eyes or lips now.

'All of them?' Benjamin asked.

'Just the old cook and her husband remain.'

'Call them out!'

Vauban obeyed and an aged, white-haired couple came doddering out; only when they reached us did they recognise the danger their master faced. They stood shaking with fear, their terror increasing at the sight of my master's grim face and naked sword.

'Monsieur.' Vauban's wife drew nearer, a protective arm round each of her children, 'what do you want?'

'Madame,' he replied, 'as I have said, I am Master Benjamin Daunbey, a gentleman of Ipswich in England. Your husband is my enemy. I am going to kill him!'

The woman bit back her screams. 'Why?' she gasped. 'Why now?'

'Louise!' Vauban snapped. 'Go to the garden house. Take the children and servants with you. If I am to be murdered, it's best if you do not see it!'

'Oh, I am not going to murder you, Vauban. I am going to challenge you to a duel.'

Hope flared in Vauban's face and those heavy-lidded eyes flickered.

'Louise,' he repeated softly, 'please go. I assure you it will not take long.'

The woman threw one tearful glance at Benjamin and, with the children huddled in her skirts and the servants doddering behind her, went into the garden house. I followed, making sure the door was closed behind them. There were windows high in the wooden wall; it was up to them if they looked or not. I returned feeling a little anxious: Vauban's sneer indicated he might be a good swordsman, perhaps even a skilful duellist. Benjamin might be sorely wounded, even killed, and Vauban would not let me walk away. The bastard watched me return.

'My dear Roger, I am sure Master Daunbey is a gentleman. You will find my sword belt hanging on a peg in the kitchen. If you would be so kind?'

I went and fetched both sword and dagger but, on a high shelf, I also glimpsed one of those huge horse pistols, a clumsy fire-arm stuffed in a holster. It was already primed so I took that for my own protection. Vauban saw it and grinned.

'Your servant seems to lack confidence,' he sneered.

'Only in you, Vauban!' I snapped. 'The duel is to be a fair one.'

He grasped the sword belt, pulling out sword and dagger, and stepped away.

'Of course,' he said. 'It will be *à l'outrance*. To the death!'

Benjamin doffed cloak and doublet and the two men, their white shirts gleaming in the sunlight, brought both sword and dagger up, edging away from each other, testing the ground for secure footholds and waiting for the signal to begin. They drew together, their swords high in the air. The tips clashed, both turned sideways, the hand holding the dagger going up. For a few seconds they looked like dancers waiting for the music to begin.

'Now!' Benjamin called.

The command was hardly uttered when Vauban suddenly dropped to one knee and thrust with his sword towards Benjamin's stomach. A clever move but Benjamin parried it with his own weapon and, as Vauban rose to lunge with his dagger, blocked it with his own. Vauban grinned, they drew away again, and the deadly dance began in earnest. The quiet garden air was shattered by the sound of scraping steel, the soft thump of their boots on the grass, gasps and muttered oaths. Vauban was a born swordsman and his mocking smile proved he thought Benjamin the weaker quarry. He put my master on the defensive, his sword whirling an arc of sharp steel whilst now and again his dagger would seek an opening. Vauban's confidence increased. He began to push my master back. Benjamin was impassive. His long, black hair became damp with sweat but his face betrayed neither fear nor concern.

He allowed Vauban to drive him back, then stopped. I can't really describe what happened next. Vauban repeated a parry. Benjamin blocked it from the inside whilst striking out with his dagger: there was a clash of steel and Vauban's knife shot from his hand, lost in the long grass which grew around the trees. The Frenchman backed away, his mouth open in surprise. Benjamin smiled.

'Monsieur Vauban, an Italian master swordsman taught me that. A clever ploy, isn't it?'

The smile faded from Vauban's face as he realised he had done his best. Benjamin, who had been schooled by the finest duelling-master Italy could provide, lifted his sword, whilst throwing down his own dagger.

'Let us be fair, Monsieur. Sword against sword. Now, let's finish this matter. Roger,' he called over his shoulder, 'the Ralembergs. How many did the Luciferi kill?'

'Four,' I answered. 'Monsieur, Madame, their servant and, of course,' I glared at Vauban, 'Agnes.'

'And the dog,' Benjamin murmured. 'Don't you remember that, Vauban? The little dog floating amongst the reeds?'

He shook his head. 'As God is my witness,' he replied hoarsely, 'I did not order that! Ralemberg, yes, but not his wife and child.' He half-smiled and shrugged. 'You don't believe me, do you? I told my master not to play with you.' He half-lowered his sword, glancing at both myself and Benjamin. 'We are the same,' he muttered. 'We live in the shadows of the great ones and thrive in the twilight world of our respective courts. I would kill you, Master Daunbey, and Ralemberg, but not the women!'

'Well, Monsieur,' Benjamin replied, 'your troubles are

over. Raphael is dead. Soon you'll join him and dance with the devil in hell for all eternity!'

The arrogance drained from Vauban's face. He looked over his shoulder to where his wife stood, framed in the window of the garden house. I glimpsed a gentleness in his eyes and knew where I had seen that face before.

'Ralemberg!' I shouted.

Vauban turned and looked at me. 'How did you guess?' he asked.

'You have the same look as he had,' I replied. 'Who are you?'

Vauban drove the point of his sword into the grass. 'Ralemberg was my brother.'

'He never mentioned you. He talked of one . . .'

'There were three of us. All Bretons. I was the youngest. My elder brothers believed in Breton independence but they came from the old world. France will be a great nation. One people, one heart, one head!'

'You killed your own brother?' I accused.

'Yes. He was a member of the Luciferi, he took the oath, but my elder brother won him over. He knew the rules of the game so I fought him. I tracked him down but I was not there when he died. They said it was quick. Only later did I learn about Madame and young Agnes. But come,' he raised his sword and stepped backwards, 'let us put an end to these matters.'

The swords clashed with renewed fury, Benjamin moving with consummate skill and expertise. He drove Vauban back.

'How many, Roger, did the Luciferi kill? Ah, yes, five with the dog. For number one!' Benjamin parried, thrust and nicked Vauban in the right shoulder. The Frenchman gasped, his face pallid and sweat-stained. His wife and children cried out in terror. Again the swords clashed. 'Number two!' Benjamin murmured. Again the cut. 'Number three and number four!' Fresh cuts appeared on both of Vauban's arms, the blood seeping out, turning the white sleeves crimson.

'Master!' I shouted.

(I can't stand the sight of blood, neither mine nor anyone else's.)

Benjamin drove Vauban back.

'And now the fifth!'

I closed my eyes as the swords clashed.

'Oh, Lord!' I prayed. 'Not dead, not here!'

I opened my eyes. Vauban still stood but his sword had been knocked clear from his hand whilst the point of Benjamin's was laid carefully against the pulse throbbing in his throat. The Frenchman didn't beg. He just stood for what he was, a beaten man. Behind him his wife wailed. 'Oh, no! No!' above the crying of her children. Benjamin's eyes were half-closed, his face marble white as he waved me over with his other hand.

'You have a choice, Roger. Shall I kill him or will you?'

(Do you know, I was fascinated by Benjamin. Here he was, a scholar and an academic, gentle and kind. Yet over the last few days I had sensed the dark side of him, and now I saw it in full flower. Something in Vauban had raised the demons in his soul and I wondered about the slippery line which runs through us all, separating what is sane from the dark world of madness. My chaplain, too, is surprised but he doesn't know the full story of my life; how Benjamin and I, years later, clashed sword against sword, dagger against dagger, fighting over a

268

woman whose dark beauty and cruel passions could sever any friendship. Ah, but that's another story.)

In that quiet Paris garden Vauban stared at me as he waited to die and, once again, I was reminded of Ralemberg for the duel had stripped him of his heavy-lidded arrogance.

'Well,' Benjamin repeated. 'What shall it be, Roger?'

Suddenly the door of the garden house was flung open and one of the little girls ran towards me, her baby face soaked in tears. She grasped my leg.

'*Soyez gentil, Monsieur, ne tuez pas notre papa!*'

I crouched down and gently wiped the tear drops from her soft cheeks. The door of the garden house opened and the others came out.

'*S'il vous plaît, Monsieur,*' the girl repeated.

I stared into her light blue eyes and wondered if she would be like Agnes when she grew up. What did it matter? I thought. Can death restore life? I got up and walked over to Benjamin. I pushed his sword down and stood facing him, my back to Vauban.

'Let him go, Benjamin! For God's sake, what would another death prove? And what will it make us?'

Benjamin tapped the edge of his sword against his boot. He looked past me, his eyes never leaving Vauban. 'You are sure, Roger?'

'As certain as there's a God in heaven!'

Benjamin re-sheathed both sword and dagger, put on his doublet and picked up his cloak. Vauban just stood staring disbelievingly at me. I still grasped the horse pistol for I didn't trust the bastard as far as I could spit.

'We will leave now.' Benjamin nodded at Vauban and

gave Madame Louise the most courtly bow. I grinned and raised the horse pistol.

'I will treat this as a present, Monsieur, for we intend to leave Paris alive. You will find your guard fast asleep, trussed and bound in the bushes near the gate.'

I followed Benjamin round to the front of the house when a voice called out.

'Shallot!'

I turned quickly, lifting the horse pistol, but Vauban just stood there holding the little girl who had clung to me. She now ran towards me, her long, dark hair flying out. I crouched to greet her.

'*Monsieur*,' she whispered breathlessly, '*un cadeau.*'

She opened her hand and showed me her present, a small, blood red stone. The sort of little geegaw or trinket we adults dismiss as cheap but a child regards as more sacred than life itself. I shook my head and gently clasped her fingers back over it.

'Thank you,' I smiled. 'But there's no need. *Comment vous appellez-vouz?*'

'*Je m'appelle Marie.*'

I rose. 'Then, *au revoir*, Marie.'

'*Au revoir, Monsieur.*'

I did not look back. Benjamin and I collected our horses, made our way safely out of Paris and thundered along the country lanes back to Maubisson. Only when we were sure of no pursuit did we rein in. Benjamin leaned over and wiped the white lather from the horse's neck.

'I should have killed him, Roger,' he announced tonelessly.

I leaned over and nudged him gently.

'And if I had said "yes", you would have done it?'

Benjamin stared back and his face broke into a boyish grin.

'I don't know.' His eyes narrowed. 'But you are a strange one, Roger. Any other man would have killed Vauban for what he'd done and then danced on his corpse.'

'Perhaps,' I muttered. 'Vauban said we were the same as him, yet he may be wrong. He may have killed. We wouldn't.'

Benjamin kicked his horse into a gentle canter.

'Come on, Roger!' he shouted. 'We are finished here. We are for Maubisson and then by fast horse to Calais.'

'What about that bloody ring?' I groaned, drawing close to him.

Benjamin made a face. 'The king will forget and forgive. Raphael is dead, the murders avenged. Let's pray he will be satisfied.'

I thought of the Great Killer's brooding eyes and prayed to God my master was right.

We left Maubisson two days later, accompanied by Doctor Agrippa, still elated by our success and eager to bring the good news to Wolsey and the king. He was as sanguine as Benjamin about our failure over the ring.

'His Majesty will have to be satisfied with what we have achieved,' he muttered. 'There'll be another day.'

Both he and Benjamin were in high spirits and chose to ignore my gloomy forebodings, my master chattering about his school at Ipswich and wondering if the good doctor could recommend a tutor of Classics. Talking like two magpies, they rode briskly along the lanes whilst I trailed behind, uncomfortably aware that the king had

271

made me personally responsible for returning his ring. Now, we expected little trouble on our journey. Agrippa carried warrants and safe conducts. We were well armed and Dacourt had informed us before we left Maubisson that horsemen would be at the Pale of Calais to meet us.

We were within an hour's ride of that, threading our way through a clump of woodland, when a troop of horsemen suddenly burst out of the trees, blocking our passage and circling us in a ring of steel. I moaned with fright; they were all dressed in helmets and brigandines and wore the personal emblem of the King of France alongside the Red Lion Rampant of Scotland. The *Garde Ecossais*. Each bore a small crossbow, loaded and pointed threateningly at us. Agrippa pushed his horse forward and stared angrily around. My terror only increased when I noticed his agitation.

'What is this?' he yelled, standing high in the stirrups. 'We are the personal envoys of His Majesty, King Henry of England, you have no right to block our passage!'

The ring of horsemen parted and Vauban walked quietly toward us. He had dropped the pretence of being the courtly fop or dandy. His hair was pulled back and tied with a gold ribbon. His face was grave and stern and the dark eyes watched us broodingly for a while. He was dressed for battle in a light mailed shirt and cradled a steel conical helmet in his gauntleted hands.

'If you are envoys,' he declared, 'let me see your warrants!'

Agrippa handed them over. Vauban spent a few minutes carefully reading them. Never once did he look up at me.

'You are correct, Doctor Agrippa. You are the English

king's envoy but one of you is a thief!'

'What nonsense is this?' Benjamin snarled. He leaned over his horse and glared down at Vauban. 'I should have killed you!'

Vauban grinned and shrugged. 'I am not here, Monsieur Daunbey, about that. One of you is a thief. A horse pistol was stolen from my house!'

I gasped in terror and my hand went to cover the great leather holster which now swung from my saddle horn. Vauban saw the movement and his smile widened. He came over, tapped the holster gently and held out his hand.

'You are the thief, Monsieur. I want my property back.' He tapped the saddle-bags behind me. 'And a look at these, as well.'

Despite Agrippa's and Benjamin's protests three of the guards, smirking from ear to ear, grabbed my leather holster and emptied the contents of both my saddle-bags on to the dirty country track. Vauban knelt and sifted amongst them.

'Nothing else,' he murmured. He picked up the saddle-bag and grinned at me. 'You may have your property back.'

'You emptied them!' Agrippa shouted.

Vauban shrugged, reached up, and with surprising strength plucked me from the saddle. I crashed to the ground in an untidy heap, my discomfiture increased by the soldiers' obvious enjoyment of an English envoy's humiliation. Benjamin's hand went to his dagger, one of the crossbows clicked and a bolt whirred through the air, just missing my master's head by inches.

'Leave it, master!' I shouted. 'I shall do what he says.'

Vauban mimicked me so cleverly the laughter grew. I hastily re-packed the saddle-bags and remounted my horse. Vauban came to stand in front of me, shaking his head and clicking his tongue.

'Such dishonesty,' he murmured. He waved his hand airily. 'Let the thief proceed!'

His men pulled back into the trees and we rode forward with Vauban's laughter ringing in our ears. An hour later, just outside Calais, we were met by lancers wearing the royal livery, who escorted us into the fortress town. Benjamin was still muttering furiously about Vauban's conduct, whilst Agrippa swore that on our return to England every French envoy would suffer the same humiliation. I couldn't have cared a whit. All I wanted was to be out of the damned country. Yes, I was frightened, humiliated and, if the truth be known, secretly hurt by Vauban's ingratitude.

We had a wretched journey across to Dover, drenched to the skin and made as miserable as lepers by one of those sudden summer storms which sweep the Narrow Seas. We stumbled ashore, grateful to be on dry land. We decided not to continue our journey to London but to stay a day in Dover, in a small tavern overlooking the sea, where we could dry out and calm our queasy stomachs with what Agrippa called good English food.

I remember stumbling up the stairs to the garret we had rented. I stripped myself of every article of clothing and emptied the contents of my soaked saddle-bag on to the pallet bed in search of something not drenched with salt water. I saw a small, brown leather pouch lying at the bottom of one of the bags. I pulled it out, undid the cord around the neck and emptied the contents into my hand. Two objects: the small, blood red, polished stone Vauban's daughter had offered me, and a ring I had last seen on the finger of His Most Christian Majesty, Francis I of France. I went and stood by the window watching the breakers turn to a boiling, frothing white. Now I understood why Vauban had staged that mummery in the forest outside Calais.

Of course, both my master and Doctor Agrippa were delighted. When we met the king in his palace at Greenwich, the Great Killer threw his arm around me, calling me his brother, pinching my cheek and declaring that I was the boldest knave in all his kingdom. I was praised, feasted and rewarded, hugged and kissed, lavished with gifts of many kinds, but old Shallot was beginning to learn that the pleasure and favour of princes is indeed a fickle thing. I saw the king burn the book my master had discovered in Abbé Gerard's church and watched the parchment turn to ashes. Abbé Gerard was your friend, I thought, and he was killed because of this book. Clinton was your friend and you drove him into his homicidal madness. Catherine, your wife, a Spanish princess, is your friend, your lover and wife. Now you plan to set her aside like some public whore or common courtesan. Wolsey in his purple silks laughed when the king did and looked favourably upon both myself and his 'beloved nephew', but I had had enough of princes.

(Oh, by the way, no one told the bastard about Lady Francesca's infection. We concluded there were certain things our bluff Hal should find out for himself. We simply told him Clinton had been seduced by French gold and left it at that.) Benjamin and I travelled on to London. I visited the graves of the Ralembergs under a cypress tree just inside Greyfriars graveyard. I left a red rose on Agnes's tomb, said a prayer, shed some tears and rejoined my master in a nearby tavern. We drank our fill and took the road north to Ipswich.

Epilogue

Well, I have told my story. My old friend Will Shakespeare recently staged one of his plays here in the great hall, *The Winter's Tale* I think it was called. A subtle conceit of jealousy and intrigue. The king in the play reminded me of the Great Killer whilst another character, Autolycus, was definitely me: 'A teller of tales, a snapper up of mere trifles'. My chaplain giggles and thinks that another of Will Shakespeare's quotes is more apt for me, being 'full of sound and fury, signifying nothing'. Ah, hell, but what does he know? Wolsey's gone, the Great Killer's gone, they are all shadows, yesterday's dust. But in their time they controlled the stage and dominated the play. Wolsey turned the tables on the French whilst the royal beast began to surround his wife Catherine with a web of lies. Nevertheless, the Lady Francesca had done her damage: the syphilis lay dormant in Henry's fat carcase for years before raging forth like the fires of hell, blackening the open ulcer on his leg and tipping the royal beast's mind deeper into madness.

Yes, they have all gone, even Benjamin. And what am I? An old man who sits in the centre of his maze, telling his tale and drinking himself stupid on sack. Nonetheless, if I half-close my eyes and grasp in one hand the dark, faded petals of a rose, and in the other a young girl's small, blood red stone . . . well, then I can dream. If I forget my crumbling body and just sit listening to the wood pigeon sing its heart out, and half-open my eyes, the rose in my hand is in full bloom and across the grass Benjamin walks, shouting cheerily at me to join him. If I catch the smell of roses, I am young again, standing in the springtime of my life in a London garden, the scent of flowers heavy on the air and young Agnes standing demurely before me. But when I open my eyes the dreams fade and I know that even the flames of the hottest fire will end in nothing but smoke.

My chaplain says I am a rogue and a villain, that I am to enjoy the things of earth for I will find no heaven in the next world. But what the sod does he know? I put my trust in Christ and his holy Mother for I hope they judge us not for what we are but for what we wanted to be. Oh, yes, I am a rogue. I call for fat Margot and bury my face in a deep-bowled cup of sack. Perhaps that's the way I want it, for when you are gulping sack and crying for a wench no one can see the tears in your eyes. Oh, and the good Lord knows, I could murder a cup of sack.

Author's Note

Shallot is more than 'a snapper-up of mere trifles', he is a rogue, born and bred, who may be telling the truth. We do know that the French secret service was very active in England in the 1520s and there are rumours that they had a spy amongst the high-ranking councillors of Henry VIII. The Great Killer himself was as Shallot describes him: vain, lecherous, treacherous, a man who hated to be beaten. Henry VIII's rivalry with Francis I was legendary and there is evidence to suggest that each king tried to assassinate the other. Henry's love of masques, mummery and other foolishness is well documented, as is the clash of humanism and barbarism which occurred at the court of Francis I. Shallot cannot be accused of exaggerating any of this.

The use of drugs, especially in France, whether poisonous or hallucinogenic, is also well attested. Some historians now claim that many of the visions experienced by monks and recluses were the result of the unwitting absorption of toxins such as the mould which grew on rye bread. Indeed, some of the subtle poisons used at this time are now lost to modern science. Catherine de Medici was well known for her expertise in the field, and the employment of expert poisoners at the French court climaxed in one of the greatest scandals in French royal history within seventy years of Shallot's second journal being written.

Of course venereal disease was common in medieval Europe but, during the French invasions of Italy in the early 1500s, syphilis, a virulent and deadly form of VD, made its presence felt amongst French troops outside Naples to such devastating effect that Francis I had to withdraw his troops across the Alps. It is not impossible that Henry VIII was deliberately infected with the disease as described by Shallot. Such a ruse was definitely used by outraged husbands in the seventeenth century at the courts of Louis XIV and Charles II. When Francis I himself caught the infection, his body became so rotten and putrid that, as Shallot describes, many of his courtiers refused to attend the funeral. Shallot maintains that Francis caught it after seducing *La Belle Fertonière*, and that this seduction was permitted by her outraged husband who wished to avenge himself on the French king. Shallot may be telling the truth, even though his journals are full of mysterious murders, subtle assassinations, dark intrigue. I have looked at the third journal and really do wonder if it should be launched upon an unsuspecting public, so dreadful are its revelations.